DEATHLY REMINDERS

T. PATRICK PHELPS

BLACK ROSE writing™

ISBN: 978-1-61296-929-9
PUBLISHED BY BLACK ROSE WRITING
www.blackrosewriting.com

Printed in the United States of America
Suggested Retail Price (SRP) $19.95

Deathly Reminders is printed in Adobe Garamond Pro

For my wife, Michelle.

DEATHLY
REMINDERS

Chapter 1

Today
12:17 AM

His eyes felt like burning stones in their sockets. There were no tears. Not yet, anyway. Just like before.

She was dying. Of that, he was certain. At best her life was dangling over the great edge, held only by the strength of a single strand of hair, and that strand was frayed and splitting quickly. He held her head, wrapped in his arms, tightly against his chest, rocking her with gentle movements. He didn't need to inspect the crimson colored bullet wounds on her chest again, for he knew their locations were as close to having been as fatally placed as possible. Practically placed in specific locations by hands as skilled as those of a surgeon. Close enough to deliver the shooter's intentions. Maybe not as quickly as desired, but just as certainly. Or perhaps the time drag between the act and the final act was a bonus for the shooter.

The bullet's entry afforded her just enough time to scribble out two letters, written in her own spilled blood, onto the cold tile floor on which her life would soon end. The growing pool of her blood was now swallowing those two letters as it was pumped to the foreign destination, out through the impossible-to-close-up holes and onto the cold floor.

As he rocked her gently back and forth, he began whispering a song his mother would sing to him when he was a child.

"To bed, to bed, cried Sleepy Head.
Tarry awhile, said Slow.
The moon is high, my love is nigh
It's time for dreams to go."

He glanced down at the scrawled-in-blood letters, burning the frantically drawn letters into his mind. He knew he didn't need to see them again; they would forever be available for immediate recall. They were both familiar and expected.

He turned his attention away from the letters and onto the thinness of her breathing. Each struggling breath seeming to grow weaker than the one before, as if her very act of breathing was draining what few reserves she had remaining.

"In and out," he whispered. "Just keep doing what you're doing. In and out."

He was tempted to feel her neck again; to fumble his fingers in the vain hope of finding her pulse strengthening. To discover her heart was building strength and momentum instead of simply following the now distorted commands of her blood-starved brain. But he knew a check would reveal nothing glinting towards hope. He knew, despite his call to 911 the moment after he found her lying on the floor in a pool of her blood, that there was no medicine to save her. No hands, no matter how skilled, could stem the receding tide of her life's force. For he had held another in nearly the same position, the same situation, only six years earlier.

Then, it was his wife, Lucy. Her brain invaded and turned to instant mush by a mad man with a gun. Then, he had arrived too late to hold her before the other side took her. Though he rocked her body then as he was doing to this one now, his gentle touch didn't offer any comfort. It was too late, even though he was by her side only moments after the stinging sound of the pistol had stopped bouncing its terrible rings off the walls of the bank's lobby. He sang the same song then as well, for it was all he could drag up from a mind so occluded with the certainly approaching sorrow, pain and anger.

He loved his wife more than he thought possible. And when his fellow police officers finally convinced him to let her body go, he knew he would never be able to let her go. He knew he would always hold on to his anger, to his pain and to the final images of her beauty-erased eyes. He thought, no, knew, as he walked away, braced on either side by two police officers, that he would never love again. He would never allow himself to. Even if someone entered his life and somehow commanded the soon-to-be-forgotten emotion of love to rear its head, no one would ever command each drop of his love the way Lucy had.

And then Nikkie showed up. With her dark skin, radiantly green eyes, her body a near perfect expression of beauty and her soul an intoxicating elixir against which he had no defense.

And now he held her and was about to witness her death.

It was slow, painfully so perhaps, but also infuriatingly quick. She had just turned thirty years old. Had just told him how she felt about him and had smiled when he told her of his feelings. Of his fears and of his reluctance.

"We'll just take things one step at a time," he whispered into her ear, repeating what she had told him just a few weeks before. "Step by step till we see where we end up. Okay?"

But now he knew there would be no destination their steps would bring them to. They would never be together outside of the darkened office where Nikkie was about to die. There would be no more steps, taken one at a time or grouped in a passion driven dash.

He recognized the change in her breathing. Short, raspy draws were being replaced by struggled gasps and painfully long delays between each breath. He knew there was a medical term for the type of breathing Nikkie was engaged in, but the term escaped him.

"Doesn't matter," he thought. Knowing the markers of an approaching death did nothing to prevent or delay death's silent march.

In the distance, he heard the growing wobble of an ambulance siren. There would be at least three cop cars as well, he figured, and then grew angry with himself as he caught himself assuming what questions the assigned detective would soon be asking him.

Questions were part of the protocol. They would be asked and answered because they had to be. Following the rules and procedures was important. And as he felt Nikkie draw a breath thinner than those she drew before, Derek Cole, the ex-military cop turned ex-Columbus Police Department officer turned freelance detective understood the few rules, protocols and procedures he did follow were seconds from being abandoned.

Nikkie Armani, his partner in his Private Investigator business for the better part of the last year, died in his arms as the telltale emergency vehicle wobble and angry, red flashing lights were joined by indecipherable voices squawking over treble-heavy radios on the street outside the office. Derek cradled her face in his hands, leaned down and kissed her cheek.

Then his eyes and mind focused on what he needed to do.

He knew there would be a series of questions, perhaps taking him as long as an hour or two. He would be as helpful as he possibly could while maintaining his true intentions going forward.

Secret and silent intentions, made clear and granite-hard. Cast the day his wife was killed and fired in a blistering hot furnace for six years. It was time for the fired fury to be released.

He may even offer the investigators, detectives and plainclothes cops a smile, a handshake and agree to their proposed understanding and recounting of the main objectives. He would walk away, after receiving and acknowledging their altruistic condolences and promises to "make the son of a bitch" pay for what "that bastard" did to Nikkie.

But Derek Cole would walk into his own future. He would stride forward utterly free from any of the remaining burdens of rules, of protocols, of established justice.

The sirens continued to grow louder as more responders screeched their vehicles to stops on the street and the angry, flashing lights of red and blue began painting the office's walls and ceiling with their warning colors. The squeal of radio transmissions, the words devoid of meaning in the rapid flurry of controlled panic, occluded every other sound.

Including the sound of rage building to a necessary crescendo inside Derek Cole's mind.

He thrust his foot out and scraped it through the pool of Nikkei's blood, smearing the two letters she had written.

Two letters, intended to be accusations, were lost to all eyes save those of Derek Cole.

This was his battle now.

Chapter 2

August 19

She had never been accused of any crime before, let alone of murder. But there she sat, dressed in a county-issued, olive drab jumpsuit, in a damp room, dripping with humidity and despair. The jumpsuit scratched at her back and shoulders, preventing her from finding even the smallest amount of comfort. She rested her arms on the stainless steel table in front of her, and then pulled them back when Derek and Nikkie were buzzed in through the locked door, which separated her from the corridor beyond. Her first thought was how sturdy Derek looked; broad in the shoulders, tapered waist, arms defined and vascular. She noticed his eyes next. They were a piercing blue. She thought they were the type of eyes which had melted a thousand hearts. She felt her own flutter a bit. The feeling, if only for the briefest of moments, pulling her away from her current surroundings and into a desirous world where even those facing a life behind bars, wearing nothing more appealing than a simple iteration of what the intake guard had issued her the day before, might risk a fleeting dream.

She shot Nikkie only a glance. One intended only to acknowledge her presence but not to suggest importance.

She waited—as the manners she had been taught instructed her to do so— till both recently arrived guests had been seated before she spoke.

"I didn't know where else to turn. I…I've never been…I have no idea what to do." Her voice was a flood of emotions, as if she had been thinking of what to say to Derek when he finally arrived. She probably had rehearsed a thousand different opening lines but all took flight when the scene was complete, leaving her only with a staggered expression of desperation.

Derek Cole sat in the visitor's room inside the steel reinforced concrete walls of the Pinellas County Sheriff's department. His associate, Nikkie Armani sat to his right, directly across from Maryanne Jenkins, Jessica Gracers' attorney. He sighed, recognizing both the desperate words his potential client had said and the suspicious look etched across Maryanne Jenkins' face.

"You'd be surprised how many times a client has told me the same thing," Derek said. "So, despite the obvious doubts your counselor at law has about our services, why don't we start with how you heard about us?"

"I heard about you," Jessica said, her voice struggling for a solid purchase onto composure. "My cousin in Maine told me about you. She said she and her husband hired you to solve a challenge they were having with their son."

A distant memory of pain flashed across Derek's eyes. "Maggie Bryant is your cousin?" he asked.

"Yes. And she told me about how good an investigator you are when I spoke with her last year." Jessica turned and glanced at Maryanne, as if the two had had more than one conversation about hiring Cole and Associates. From that one look, brief as it was, Derek understood Maryanne, like many lawyers with whom Derek shared a mutual client, was not in favor of him being hired. That look Jessica shot at her lawyer also told him Jessica, though the obvious victor in whatever battle she had with her lawyer, was filled with doubts over her own insistence about hiring him.

"I need your help," Jessica said as she surrendered all hopes at remaining composed. "Please. I need your help."

Derek looked directly at Maryanne, studying her face, reading the thoughts crowding her mind. She wasn't going to be easy to work with, that was for damn sure, but he was used to working with lawyers whose noses got bent out of shape when their clients called in their own reinforcements. Maryanne Jenkins may try to get in his way if and when he started his investigation, but she wouldn't stay in his way for long.

Hearing Maggie Bryant's name sparked a glint of pain in Derek. It was Maggie Bryant who had hired him when she and her husband believed someone had convinced their son that a ghost was visiting him. It was Maggie Bryant for whom Derek had violated his cardinal rule and had allowed himself to have growing feelings for. It was Maggie Bryant who stood beside Derek when he had seen what could only be described as an entity turn to mist as he stood on the Marginal Way on Maine's coast. And it was Maggie Bryant who, once the case was closed and the mystery solved, had told Derek she needed to mend her relationship with her husband. Doing so was the right thing. Derek knew that, as did Maggie. But doing the right thing doesn't mean emotional pain is not delivered. And sometimes, the pain is delivered with a hell of a punch.

Derek wasn't emotionally ready for what may have happened if, instead of choosing to work on her fractured marriage, she had given herself to Derek. But

Maggie was someone with whom his fears seemed to have grown shallower when he thought of her.

"You understand how we work?" Derek asked as his thoughts raced back to the present. "You already paid our retainer, which we keep if we decide we aren't going to accept your case. If we do accept it, we require…"

"My client understands your terms quite well, Mr. Cole." Maryanne Jenkins said. She looked like a hard woman. To Derek, she looked competent, intelligent and like someone who would rather take a bullet than someone's shit. Derek glared at her, measuring her character with the distance of his gaze. He estimated her age to be late forties. Probably stood five-seven, though since she hadn't stood the entire time he and Nikkie joined her and her client in the interview room at the jail, Maryanne could stand five-flat or six-one. Didn't matter.

She was fleshed out, like someone who conducted most of her professional meetings over four-course meals and heavy lunches. Maybe one ninety to two fifteen but two hundred and twenty wasn't too many business dinners away. She was a black woman, though Derek felt she was more Caribbean sounding than African-American. Dark hair, almost pitch black with several rivers of gray and white marking lines in the tight pull of her hairstyle.

"If you're trying to intimidate me with your stares," Maryanne continued, "you might as well give up that ghost."

There was a bit of a Caribbean accent in her voice. Distant, like Maryanne had done a damn good job of losing most of the telltale drawl. But to someone like Derek Cole who made a living out of noticing what people were openly showing, he also noticed what people were trying to hide. To Derek, the accent was clear.

"Not trying to do anything," Derek said. "Just making sure we're on the same page, is all."

"Here's how my client understands the situation: She paid you five grand just to get you and your associate, whose name I do not know, to travel down in short order from Ohio to Florida. You two will sit here, listen to what she says, spend a day doing some prelim investigation, which will probably include you doing no more than speaking with the DA and a few cops. Then, you and your associate will arrange to meet with my client and me and tell us either, 'Thanks for the five large, but there ain't too much we can do for you,' or—and this is what I feel is the more likely outcome—you'll sit down across from us and tell us 'Good news, we think we can help you out.' You'll toss a few papers in front of my client to sign; releases, non-disclosure agreements and some agreement drawn up by some two-bit law student. My client will sign them, since her back is against the wall and puts more trust in something her relative told her about last year than she has in my recommendation." Maryanne shot a sideways glance towards Jessica, who held her gaze directly on Derek's face. "Then, you'll tell us you two can't start, or *rather,* won't start your investigation until my client pays you for at least five days of your time. And, based on what I read on your webpage, which also seems to have been designed by a two-bit nobody, that will run my client another seven thousand, five hundred. How 'm I doing?"

"My name is Nikkie," Nikkie said without pausing a beat.

"Good for you," Maryanne replied.

"What you said so far sounds about right," Derek said. "Except for a few minor things."

Maryanne breathed deeply, crossed her arms over her ample breasts and sat back against the chair. "Those being?"

"Our fees go *up* when there's a pain in the ass lawyer involved. Call it 'hazard pay' if you'd like. So, if you want to do what's right for your client, whose name is Jessica in case you've forgotten, I'd suggest you drop the attitude and let us do what we're damn good at doing."

Maryanne didn't flinch. She just sat, still as a stone. Eyes fixed and locked.

"You said 'a few minor things.' That's only one," she said.

"Second, Jessica, I'm going to ask you three questions to start. If I think you're lying to me, we'll stop our investigation before we even begin."

Jessica nodded her head.

"I'll answer anything you ask. Anything."

"Third, if you answer our questions and we start the investigation, understand if at any point, we feel you are guilty of the crime you are accused of, we're off the case. We're not interested in helping guilty people go back to their lives."

"I didn't kill my husband."

"Fourth, we will speak with the DA, if he chooses to give us an appointment."

"She," Maryanne shot back. "The DA is a woman. Imagine that! A female DA. Ever heard such a thing, Mr. Cole?" The sarcasm was practically dripping off her words.

"If *she* will give us an appointment. I'm sure your lawyer has already asked for full disclosure which we expect to be shared with us, so meeting Mrs. or Miss DA won't be to ask any favors, but rather to get a feel of how she'll prosecute if your case goes to trial. And," Derek continued as he raised his hand, stopping Maryanne who seemed about ready to say something, "we will also speak with as many of the cops and investigators as will give us their time."

"Detectives," Maryanne said. "They call them 'detectives' down here."

"Whatever. Again, we won't try to get any inside info from them, so don't expect us to come back with any case-blowing information. I'm an ex-cop and ex-cops and cops know how to talk with each other. They'll be much more relaxed speaking with me than with your charming lawyer."

Still no reaction from Maryanne Jenkins.

Derek leaned back against his chair, glanced to Nikkie who was scribbling on the yellow legal pad sitting on the table in front of her. Without needing any additional cue, Nikkie took over the conversation.

"Fees are as you expected, Mrs. Jenkins."

"Miss Jenkins," Maryanne said.

"Good for you. Most of our cases are tied up within a week, so we don't expect to be here longer than seven days. If our investigation warrants, we've already made arrangements to have other pending cases worked by our Ohio-based team."

The truth was, there was no Ohio-based team. Not anymore. The last case Derek and Nikkie worked put Crown, their office manager, in the hospital with a traumatic brain injury. One of their associate investigators, Alex, turned out to be a drug-selling psychopath, currently on the run from the law and from Derek. Alex was responsible for Crown's condition and occupied the "Most Wanted" position on Derek's list. When their team of five was cut to three, Derek decided he and Nikkie would comprise the entirety of "Derek Cole and Associates" and would handle all cases, front to back, start to finish. He let their other associate investigator go find another job, giving him a more than generous severance package and a glowing letter of reference.

"I understand," Jessica said, cutting off whatever else Nikkie had to say. "Can we please just get started? Please? I'm not made to stay in jail. I can't take it much longer."

"Bail?" Derek asked.

"My client, Jessica, is a woman of significant resources. However, the vast majority of those resources are tied up with her recently departed husband's untimely passing. Judge set bail at two million. Two hundred large in bond. While that amount would normally not be an issue...well, under the circumstances, I'm sure you can deduce my client is having a challenge accessing the funds."

"Time frame?" Derek asked.

"Another day or two. Three at the outside."

"Jessica hiring a private investigative firm may help her case in a bail reduction hearing. Wouldn't you think?"

"Might. But you haven't agreed to take her case yet, so I can't rightly go to the judge, request another bail hearing just yet."

Derek smiled, nodded his head.

"Question number one: What happened the day your husband was killed?"

Jessica detailed how she had found her husband Sam. She went over how she had just returned from a weekend away.

"The detective told me Sam had been killed around two hours before I found him. They wouldn't believe me when I told them I found him the way I did. That there was no way in the world I could have murdered him since I wasn't even home at the time he died. I don't know how they could tell what time he died, but I was still two hours away from home when he was murdered."

"Liver temperature," Derek said. "They know time of death by liver temperature. Condition of any spilled blood. Skin temp compared to the ambient temp of the room he was found in. Pretty accurate measurements. If the detective told you thirty-minutes, then the medical examiner told him thirty-minutes." Derek paused a beat, looked at Maryanne then back to Jessica. "I'm assuming the detective was a man. At least, the one who told you your husband's time of death."

"Yes," Jessica said.

"And I bet he had a partner with him. A female detective. At least she presented herself as being his partner."

"Yes. His name is Detective Mathers. The woman detective was Rachel. I don't remember her last name."

"That's because she didn't tell you her last name. Oldest trick in the book. Male detective goes over the charges, gives some details of the crime, some of them pretty descriptive I'd imagine. The female detective—who probably isn't Mathers' partner at all—probably sat in on the interview, offering you a box of tissues and cold drinks while Mathers kept on with the questions. I bet at one point, Mathers got up and left the room. Maybe grabbed his cell phone from his pocket and acted like he had to answer a call."

"Exactly. That's exactly what happened. How do you know that?"

"Because I was a cop. A cop in the army and a cop with Columbus PD. I wasn't a detective with either but I know how they operate. Second question: What did you say to the female detective, to Rachel, that you didn't say to

Mathers?"

"Nothing," Jessica said. "I mean, we just sat in that awful room alone for ten minutes talking about Sam. She asked if our marriage was a happy one, asked if we had any kids. She asked if I suspected he was having an affair or was having difficulties at work. She was nice. She didn't press me on anything. She just…she was just nice."

"Third question: You say you didn't kill your husband but you haven't said where you were when he was killed. Where were you and who were you with?"

"I can't tell you that. Not yet. I can't until I speak with someone."

"You looking forward to spending more time in your jail cell?"

"No," Jessica said, her voice louder, more determined. "I hate this place. I'm not made to be in a place like this."

"Without an alibi that can be corroborated, you're not likely to get bail reduced. You may get another bail hearing, but, without an alibi, no judge will lower your bail."

"You're stepping on my turf now, Cole. I already discussed the importance of sharing her whereabouts with my client. I don't need you to tell her or me how my part of this game is played."

"And yet," Derek said, staring directly into Maryanne's eyes, "here we sit. An unknown alibi. Unknown potential witness to her alibi. Maybe potential witnesses. You may not need me to tell you how to play your part of this game, but you may need my help in getting you on the field."

Maryanne screwed up her face.

Finally, Derek thought. *A reaction. I can work with this lady.*

CHAPTER 3

It came down to a choice. Not a simple choice, but a choice nonetheless. A or B. Left or right.

Either tell them it was Brian Hilton she had been with or keep her promise, and with its keeping also came keeping the view from her cell. Jessica knew that. Knew she would have to talk about who she was with and the relationship she had with her alibi soon. But there were other circumstances. Other factors and she needed to meet with the person she would soon claim to have been with while her husband was murdered first and let him know what she needed to do.

"It's not that simple," Jessica said to Derek. "The person I was with when Sam was murdered will lose everything if I say anything. Everything."

"His life?" Nikkie asked. "Will he lose his life? Because, in case you didn't know, Florida still has the death penalty. I'm not sure that the DA's office will pursue the death penalty, but I'd be willing to bet they're having conversations about it. Regardless, without an alibi that puts you anywhere but at the scene of your husband's murder, you're looking at a very long stretch of your life behind bars."

"You need to tell us who you were with, Jessica. And where. Like I told you and as these two are telling you now, there's just too much evidence against you for you to be protecting whomever it is you are protecting." Maryanne's face, still set in an angry twist, seemed to soften at the edges with the prospect of Derek and Nikkie helping persuade Jessica to share her alibi. She knew without an alibi, Jessica's case would be difficult, if not impossible to defend. She also knew requesting Jessica's bail be lowered or granting her access to the bank accounts would be shot down three seconds after the judge heard Jessica say she wouldn't say whom she was with while Sam Gracers was being shot.

There wasn't an avalanche of evidence, but what evidence there was would be damn near impossible to overcome without a rock-solid alibi that put Jessica Gracers someplace besides standing over her husband's dead body, holding a gun and firing three shots into his torso, just in case the shot to his forehead hadn't been enough. The four bullet casings found at the scene each had Jessica's prints on them. The bullets found inside Samuel Gracers' body all came from a .380 caliber pistol, each fired from the same gun. Those bullets were fired by the gun registered to Jessica Gracers, confirmed in the ballistics lab in Tampa. Jessica was seen leaving her residence, gun in hand. When tested, the Glock .380 revealed it had been fired recently. Though no gun shot residue was found on Jessica's hands, the small caliber .380 used in the murder was known to not leave gun shot residue, or GSR, on a shooter's hands.

When questioned by Detectives Gary Mathers and Rachel Gonzales, Jessica's story about being away for the weekend was as thin as tissue paper. Without anyone to corroborate her alibi, the gun in her hand and the evidence that her gun was the murder weapon was the sheriff's entire department needed to formally charge Jessica Gracers with murder.

"We've put people away on less evidence than what we have on your client," the DA, Julia Steinberg, told Maryanne when the two met over a late breakfast earlier that day. "We have her at the scene, holding the murder weapon in her hand. Ballistics tests confirm it was the murder weapon and her prints on the casings add to the proof. I'm not telling you how you should run your case, Maryanne, but murder in the second with twenty-five minimum would save us both a lot of time and the tax payers of the county plenty of money."

"Little early to be offering my client a plea offer, doncha think? Hell, I just met with her for fifteen minutes this morning and you're already offering..."

"I'm not making an official plea offer, Maryanne. Just suggesting if that plea offer crosses your desk, you may want to give it some serious consideration. No alibi coupled with forensic evidence? Damn, I might be a fool to even suggest a possible plea."

"Not nearly the fool you'd be to try for murder one with no motive. And if you're thinking ahead about the penalty phase, there ain't no way no jury will send a woman—especially one as wealthy and as attractive as my client—to any death chamber."

Julia drained the remains of her coffee, proffered her hand to Maryanne. "Open and shut, Maryanne, and I think you know that. I have to run. We'll be talking soon." Julia dropped a fifty dollar bill on the table. "Tell the waitress to keep the change," She left the small diner without another word.

She didn't need any other words. Julia was right. Maryanne's client was going to spend a very long time behind bars unless she had an alibi.

Despite numerous attempts, Jessica refused to tell Maryanne anything except, *"I wasn't even home. I was away."* But the look of fear dancing across her client's face now that Derek and Nikkie were driving the point home, gave Maryanne a flash of hope.

And hope was something Maryanne had been in short supply of for the last fourteen months of her life.

After nearly forty-nine years being "blessed with kind folks outside and strong health inside," her doctor delivered the news as only a doctor who had decades of delivering an equal mix of good and bad news could have.

"It's what we expected, Maryanne," the old doctor began as he dropped into the hard-wooden chair behind his incredibly cluttered desk in his office. "ALS. Lou Gehrig's disease, but I do not like to call something as awful as this disease after a man of such high character as old Iron Lou. But, that's who made this damn disease famous, I suppose. So, Lou Gehrig's it is."

"And now it's mine, too."

"You'll want to do what you can, while you can, to keep your strength up. Eat more than you're normally accustomed to, cut back on alcohol and get used to spending time in the water. I hear the YWCA over in Tampa teaches water aerobics. Might be a good way for you to build up some muscle before…well, before Gehrig takes back from you what was taken from him."

"How long do I have?" Maryanne asked as if she was questioning a witness and not asking about a disease she knew would take her life after stealing every ounce of pride and independence from her first.

"Most pass after three years from diagnosis, but, there's a pretty decent number who reach five years. Maybe more, depending on their condition before and what they do after. Like I said, eat more and try out the pool over at the YW."

"Three years, most likely, then. Five if… what? If I'm lucky?"

"Hard to call what you're most apt to experience as 'luck,' if I'm going to be fully honest with you. First year or two should be okay, for the most part. You'll have spells, some lasting a few hours, some a few days, when your muscles just won't want to cooperate. Numb feeling, weakness, but not pain. A bit slowing down, getting tired easier and easier as days pass. Don't let your pride keep you from a wheelchair once your legs tell you they're about done. No use in you falling, banging your head and messing with that keen mind of yours. From what I've read and seen, two years and on is when things usually start to get more complicated. Less moving, less control of your body when you can move.

Difficulty swallowing will creep up on ya, so, again, get to eating when the food still goes south like it should."

"Treatment options? Medicine?"

"I'll write you up some scripts," the elderly doc said. "Truth is, Maryanne, I'm an old country family doctor. Probably fifteen years past my expiration date. You ought to consider seeing a specialist after our sit down today. There are docs in Tampa and St. Pete who know this disease like I know the chicken pox. Inside, outside, backwards and forwards."

"Can they give me more time?" Maryanne asked, her face, as her emotions, set in stone.

The doctor shook his head. "Probably not much more than I could. But, there's new advancements everyday, I'm sure. Go see one of them specialists. I hate to say this, but there's nothing more I can do than to follow what I read in the journals at this point."

Maryanne went to an ALS specialist in Tampa two weeks after being told of her diagnosis. The specialist—who had turned out to be a team instead of a single physician—started her on a gluttony of medications, a special diet, prescribed a regimen of muscle building exercises and made an appointment to see a psychologist who specialized in working with clients recently diagnosed with terminal illnesses. Maryanne filled the prescriptions, joined the YWCA in Tampa instead of seeing a physical therapist and tossed the appointment card for the shrink in the wastebasket outside the ALS specialists' office.

For the fourteen months since she sat in her doctor's office, Maryanne Jenkins felt small bits of her wasting away. The first six months revealed small, almost imperceptible declines in her gait, the steadiness and strength of her hands and her ability to remain seated or standing for any period of time. Months seven through fourteen were filled with days of more appreciable decline. She could still walk without people taking notice of her unsteadiness, but it wouldn't be long before others would not only notice, but also begin to ask questions. She had already heard a couple of whispers from people she had passed on the street.

"Looks like Miss Jenkins started a little early on the bottle today," one person had said last week when her legs felt more like buzzing sticks of Jell-O than the legs she had known for nearly five decades.

During court last week, while defending a triple-repeat offender of Florida's DUI law, the presiding judge actually stopped the proceedings, called the counselors to her bench and asked Maryanne if she needed a recess.

"I'm having a challenging time understanding you, counselor," the judge had said. "If I didn't know you, I might be prone to wonder if you've been drinking before court."

"Not drinking, your honor," Maryanne replied, summoning all of her control to pronounce each word, each goddamn syllable with pristine accuracy. "Just not feeling a hundred percent."

That case was adjourned for three days, giving Maryanne enough time to persuade a fellow attorney—the one and only person in Pinellas County she had told about her disease—to take over the case.

"I feel terrible even suggesting this," her attorney friend had told her, "but you may want to consider…"

"I'll pull down my shingle when it's time," Maryanne shot back. "I can still whoop most of our county's ADA's asses in court, which I plan on doing till…well, I'll know when it's time to call it a day. I won't put any of my clients in a compromised situation. If they trust me enough to pay my fees, they deserve my best. And when I can't deliver my best, I'll retire. Probably roll myself off a cliff somewhere if I can find one high enough in this damn flat-assed state of ours."

Her decision to take on Jessica Gracers' case was not easily reached. Jessica had called her the day her husband was murdered and she had been officially charged with the crime. But Maryanne wasn't sure she'd take the case until yesterday morning, one day after receiving Jessica's frantic call. She woke up feeling like her arms and legs were vibrating but was shocked — and more than a little pleased — when she felt strength in her limbs, as if they hadn't lost an ounce of strength to the advancing disease which was wasting her body away in silence.

After meeting with Jessica yesterday morning, and attending her early morning court appearance, she felt her returned strength being sucked out of her body. Slowly, marking its departure not with pain, but with promises of things yet to come. Maryanne Jenkins, for the first time in her nearly thirty years of being a lawyer, questioned her ability to provide her client proper representation. When Jessica insisted on her desire to call in an outside private investigator, Maryanne put up a weak resistance. She usually preferred to handpick a private investigator from a group she occasionally worked with when cases demanded outside assistance, but, despite her vocalized objections to her client, she didn't have the energy to choose, and then direct, a private investigator for this case. She acquiesced to Jessica's request; something she would have never done if old Iron Lou hadn't come calling.

She sat at the diner's table for several long minutes after District Attorney Steinberg dropped the Grant on the table and walked away, flashing a smug grin Maryanne wanted to wipe off her face with an iron skillet filled with boiling hot bacon grease. She sat, worrying if her legs would obey her command to stand, to walk and to keep walking until she didn't need them to walk anymore.

"You just stay your hand, Iron Lou. Let me see this Gracers' case through, then you and I will discuss terms for payment due."

CHAPTER 4

Derek and Nikkie left the county jail around three in the afternoon, drove their rental car to their hotel, where, after checking in, they decided to start their preliminary investigation by splitting up.

"You head down to the DA's office," Derek said to Nikkie, "and I'll make some calls to the sheriff's department. Don't know much about the DA or the detectives, so not sure how willing they will be to meet with us."

"Only one way to find out," Nikkie said. She paused, leaned back and braced her body with her arms. She crossed her legs as they dangled off the end of the king-sized bed in Derek's hotel room. "Initial thoughts?"

Derek held a long gaze at Nikkie. Let his eyes wander about her body. Her dark skin seemed to shine as if it had absorbed the Florida sun and was now reminding him of its radiance. As beautiful as she was, it was her eyes which held the greatest magnet for him. Every inch of her body charged him with an energy he hadn't felt since his wife was murdered in a Columbus-based bank's lobby. The feeling, at first, was unsettling. He felt committed to his wife, despite her being dead six years. Though the wedding ring Lucy put on his finger as the couple stood in front of the priest who married them was tucked into a plain, white envelope, stacked neatly inside Derek's home safe, and even though the telltale markers of its position had long since been erased by the sun, the invisible ring which bound him to his wife remained. And like Lucy's, Nikkie's eyes held power over him.

He traced the fading scar—now a thin, whitish line crossing three inches of his left cheek—with his index finger, then took a small step away from Nikkie's warm and inviting body.

"It's all about her alibi, isn't it? I mean, if she doesn't share it with us, our time here is wasted."

Nikkie bounced her crossed leg slightly. "What about her lawyer? Maryanne Jenkins? Notice anything about her?"

"I noticed she hated me. Probably hates you, too. Also noticed she flinched a bit there at the end, when we were talking about what will happen if her client doesn't give up her alibi."

"What did that tell you?"

"Two things, actually. One, she knows we were right about what will happen without an alibi and, two, that twitch told me we had gotten through to her client, more so than she was able to. Probably relief more than anything else. No lawyer wants a client who holds back a crucial piece of their defense. I think Maryanne's flinch, as slight as it was, said she was happy as shit we were called in."

"Anything else?" Nikkie pressed.

"Probably a smart woman. Capable. Hell, more than capable. Has seen her fair share of the inside of a courtroom. Won more cases than she's lost. Pride filled." Derek searched his memory, looking for any other clues to Maryanne Jenkins's personality he might have overlooked. Nikkie was better at picking up subtle things in the way other people carried themselves than he was. He looked past what words people used and into what was driving those words. Nikkie had an entirely different insight into people. She noticed things that were far beyond words, body language and facial expressions. These other "things" gave her almost a psychic ability. She'd never call it that, but, to Derek, that's how it felt.

"Don't know what else I should have noticed, but I have a feeling you did."

"She never stood, never moved her legs at all, for that matter. And her arms seemed too thin for the rest of her body. Did you notice that?"

"I'm not the type of guy who looks too closely at a woman's arms." He flashed a small grin as he raised his eyebrows and dropped his sights a foot or two below Nikkie's eyes. "As for her not standing, I took it as her attempt at insult. You know, you stand up to meet people you have some respect for. Keep your ass planted when you couldn't give two shits about the person or people who just walked up to you. Plus, I thought a man stands to shake hands and a woman, if she's already seated, stays seated. Miss Manners, right?"

"Old school," Nikkie said. "Everyone who can stand does so when meeting someone. But Maryanne didn't move an inch when we walked in, and she didn't stand when we left, either."

"So?"

"Notice the little wobble in her voice?"

"I took that for a Caribbean accent," Derek said. "Sounded Caribbean to me. Not you?"

"I have no idea how you got Caribbean out of her voice. Honestly, Derek, sometimes I think you get stuck on a train of thought and look for any proof, no matter how insignificant, to prove your thought was correct."

"Okay, so, thin arms, didn't stand and has either a Caribbean accent or a wobble in her voice. What's that all point to?

"Don't know." Nikkie looked off into the distance, as if the answer to Derek's question was hiding in a faraway land. Maybe a land from her past. "Maybe nothing, but I think I'd like to stop by the law offices of 'Jenkins and Whoever Else' for a little 'girl to girl' chat after I meet with the DA."

· · · · ·

Coffee has a certain draw to it. Offer a cup to someone early in their day, and their reaction is usually immediate. Call someone up in the middle of the afternoon, tell them you're paying for a quick coffee, and, more than likely, you won't be drinking alone.

For cops, coffee takes on a different meaning entirely. It's not only an excellent way to deliver stimulating caffeine into a blood system, but it's also a moment or two of pause. A break from either the hours stacked upon hours of a boring shift or a reminder that there is respite from a world gone crazy when the hours of boredom are interrupted by the madness of human beings and what they are capable of doing to each other.

Derek waited till close to three in the afternoon before calling the Pinellas County Sheriff's Department and asking to speak with either Detective Gary Mathers or Rachel Gonzales. Gonzales was in the detective's bullpen, took the call and agreed to meet Derek for a quick cup of coffee.

"You know I can't talk about the Gracers' case, right?" she admonished before agreeing to meet.

"Believe me, I know. Just one cop drinking a couple of cups of coffee with one ex-cop. Trying to get a lay of the land."

They met at a Denny's on the outskirts of Belleair; a twenty minute drive for Derek from the hotel and a short walk for Gonzales from the sheriff's office. They sat in a booth in the far corner of the restaurant. Blue vinyl seats, paper placemats with a map of the area printed in blue ink, displaying the local businesses who decided advertising on Denny's paper placemats was a good way to drive revenue.

"Hell of a case I picked up," Derek said, after he and Rachel Gonzales introduced themselves and after Derek gave a quick rundown of his military and Columbus PD resume. "Without an alibi, not sure why the hell I'm down here."

"She'll talk," Rachel said as she held her mug of coffee in both hands. "They always do. Either it takes them time to come up with a whopper of a story, or they need to check with someone to make sure their stories line up." Rachel Gonzales was no older than thirty. Deep, brown eyes and even darker hair, pulled back into a tight bun.

"*Typical hairstyle for female detectives,*" Derek thought. The ones he knew always seemed to believe they needed to hide their femininity from the male officers and detectives. No matter what police department you walked into in the world, they were still dominated by men. A woman rising the ranks to an officer's position or a detective's wasn't all that uncommon, but the women were still outnumbered five or ten to one when compared to men holding the same positions.

Gonzales was attractive. No doubt about that. Derek could tell that behind the white shirt, which was at least a size and a half too big for her thin, well conditioned frame, and dark blue pants that were about as flattering to her figure as olive drab paint was to an ocean side villa, Gonzales was all woman. Her choice in clothing and in the fit of those clothes was too intentional. She wanted to hide her body from people who may be too distracted by her looks to give her a chance to impress them with her skills. The glide in her step and the confidence behind her brilliant white smile also told him she was damn good at her job.

"Jessica said she needs to speak with someone first before she's willing to give her alibi. Said telling us who she was with could cause a world of problems for this mystery person."

"Probably wants to meet to get stories straight, is all. Or, she could be having an affair with some married dude or some high-ranking political asshole. She may not want to ruin his career. May also be testing to see what he's willing to do for her if she keeps her mouth shut."

"Would have to be someone with a lot of pull. If she doesn't talk, she's facing, what? Twenty-five to life?"

"Pretty, rich woman like that? And white, to boot? Hell, she'd get ten and probation at most."

"Still," Derek said, trying to find some angle to turn the conversation into one of actual value. He wanted Gonzales to share the one thing the DA and the sheriff's were concerned about. One missing element in the case. There was always one "something" no matter how simple the case appeared. "Any time behind bars for a woman like Jessica Gracers would be hard time. Damn hard time."

"Like I already said, she'll talk," Rachel said as her brown eyes drifted away from Derek and outside the window. "They always do."

The way she said it was all Derek needed. Maybe she was alone in her thinking, but he could tell Rachel didn't think Jessica Gracers killed her husband. Sure, the evidence was all pointing directly at Jessica, but there was something, some question driving the falling off of her voice and the obvious drifting of Rachel's gaze, that suggested she wasn't as sure as the others in the department may be.

"Gotta say," Derek said after giving Rachel a few moments to let her mind wander to wherever she needed it to, "I am pretty curious about what she's going to tell us. And by us, I mean me, my associate, her lawyer and you all. I get what you said about her maybe waiting to get her story straight, but…I don't know. I've seen my fair share of guilty people and she doesn't fit the mold. You know what I mean?"

Rachel returned her sight to Derek. She smiled and let out a brief puff of air disguised as a laugh. "Murderers come in all shapes and sizes," she said, and then took a long pull from her coffee. "They come rich, they come poor, they come pretty and out right ugly as sin, some do. They all say they're innocent at first, just like Gracers did. She may not fit the mold but, in my book, there's no such thing as a mold for killers." She paused, danced her eyes between her mug and the view out the window a few times. "Still, I'm pretty curious about what story she comes out with, too. Not quite sure I see the balance between the whole 'risk versus reward' thing with this case."

"Running out of the crime scene, holding the gun and screaming for help doesn't make a ton of sense, does it?"

"Said she was holding the gun because a little voice inside her head was telling her someone may be in the house still. As soon as someone stopped to help her, she dropped the gun and ran into the street. Some neighbor was driving past the house, saw her running out screaming her head off. He said she was shaking like a leaf and was babbling on about her husband lying dead on their kitchen floor. Uncontrollable, the neighbor described her as being. Uncontrollable and inconsolable."

"Doesn't fit the mold of how someone who just killed their husband would behave, does it?" Derek pressed.

Rachel fixed her gaze deeply into Derek's sky blue eyes. Her face went emotionless. Flat. Unreadable.

"It fits a mold. The mold of a victim."

"Glad to hear you say that," Derek said, leaning back, causing the vinyl bench seat to call out with its scratchy voice. At six foot one and tipping the scales at a few ounces over two hundred, Derek's size had made plenty of diner seats moan. "Wonder if Detective Mathers felt the same?"

If a laugh could sound sarcastic, Rachel's quick one was as sarcastic as they come.

"Mathers is a good guy, no doubt. A little too set in his ways and being less than a year from retirement isn't motivating him to change things up at all. He'll see what he wants and think along the easier tack. Truth is, the DA in the county, Julia Steinberg, barks out orders like a short-order cook barks out readied meals. Rumor is she's interested in running for a congressional seat that's about to be vacated."

"Then putting a rich, white woman in jail probably won't help her much," Derek said. "Not sure of the area's demographics but I see a whole lot of rich, white people around here."

"Congressional district is Tampa. Good mixture of the population. Her being Jewish means she probably needs to do a little more than whomever she runs against to prove she's fair and balanced." Rachel paused, looked around the restaurant in staggered glances, then turned back to Derek. She leaned in close, pressing her chest against the table. "I wasn't invited in on the meeting since I'm not Mather's normal partner, but I heard Steinberg met with the sheriff, Mathers and his normal partner, Detective Jose Posada, after hours last night. Posada is a good guy. Probably consider him my closest friend in the department. He didn't tell me much about what was said in the meeting except that Steinberg wants the department's part of the investigation tidied up and tied up as quick as possible."

"You see a problem with that?" Derek asked. He, too, had leaned in closer to match Rachel's move. He was close enough to get a close-up look at her eyes. Could smell the perfume she was wearing. He liked being close to Rachel. Felt a little charge of energy pulsing through his body, like being close to her was infusing him with a magnetic pull towards her. He pushed himself back a few inches. Though he and Nikkie had shared their growing feelings for each other a few months back, they hadn't moved their relationship into any physical territory.

Yet.

Still, Derek had always been completely faithful to his wife and, though their relationship was utterly lacking in any hint of commitment, he felt he owed a degree of fidelity to Nikkie.

She smiled, almost sensing Derek's reason for moving back away from her. She held the smile and the lock her eyes held for a few beats, then said,

"Election is coming up in November. Just a couple months from today. From what I'm hearing, Congressman Walter Wiggins hasn't announced his retirement yet, but plans on doing so first week of September."

"Doesn't give much time for Steinberg or anyone else to start a campaign," Derek said.

"Exactly the point, I think."

"You think this Congressman Wiggins has arranged some agreement with Steinberg?"

She inched a bit closer. Lowered her voice to just above a whisper. Derek moved back in.

"Think about it. Wiggins holds off announcing his retirement just long enough for the board of elections to throw together a primary in September. She knows what's happening, probably has her campaign team all set, ready to go. All of a sudden, a fairly high profile murder happens under her watch, one she now wants to make go away as soon as possible."

"Having a murder case hanging out there with the potential of making her look bad might jeopardize her public opinion."

"Exactly. So, whatever agreement she has with Wiggins probably doesn't matter, but what does matter is getting the Gracers' case taken care of as quickly as possible."

"Meaning she probably told Mathers and his partner to make damn sure every last drop of evidence points in only one direction," Derek said.

"Directly at your new client."

"Damn."

"Damn is right."

Chapter 5

Nikkie waited in the front hallway outside of DA Julia Steinberg's office for well over thirty minutes. Closer to forty-five if anyone was counting. No one but Nikkie was.

She passed the time searching Google for information on Samuel Gracers but beyond a few mentions about his contributions to local charities, she found precious little. More of the same when she turned her focus to learning what was being said online concerning Jessica Gracers. Nikkie skipped over the numerous news and social media mentions about how Jessica was sitting in a jail cell and focused her attention on the pre-jail-cell-sitting Jessica Gracers. Again, beyond a few mentions in the "Happenings Around The Area" sections of local newspapers, Nikkie didn't find much at all.

"Private citizens leading private lives," she thought.

She dropped her Android cell phone to her lap, checked her watch for the eighth time, and thought about asking Steinberg's office assistant if the DA would be much longer when the door leading to the DA's office swung open.

"I don't usually meet with private investigators," said the woman, who was standing with one hand gripping the door handle and the other waving Nikkie to come inside. "I'll give you five minutes but, I'm telling you upfront, this is an active investigation so I won't accept or answer any questions pertaining to our activities. Understood?"

Nikkie put Julia Steinberg in her mid-forties. Tall, thin, with shoulder length blond hair that had certainly seen its share of a hairdresser's coloring bottles. Julia held her sharp-featured face in a manufactured smile that didn't reach her bright blue eyes. As Nikkie drew closer, she noticed Julia's forehead looked flat as a pancake. No wrinkles at all. Not even a hint of worry in that forehead.

"Botox, and a recently administered healthy dose of it," she thought as she extended her hand for an introduction.

"I really appreciate you taking time out of your day to meet with me," Nikkie said as she followed behind the swift walking DA.

"Like I said, five minutes and no questions about the department's ongoing investigation nor this department's thoughts on possible charges." Julia didn't bother shutting the door behind her. Didn't bother sitting down, either. She just leaned her backside against the front of her desk, crossed her legs in front of her, and braced herself with her long, lean arms on the top of the desk. "And what can I do for you, Miss…?"

"Nikkie Armani. I'm with Derek Cole and Associates. We've been hired to investigate…"

"I know what Mrs. Gracers hired you for, Miss Armani. But that's not what I asked. What I asked was what I can do for you." It was a statement, not a repeated question.

"Mr. Cole and I work an awful lot of cases, some as serious as Mrs. Gracers', some not so critical. When providing our services to a client in a situation as precarious as is Mrs. Gracers', Mr. Cole and I find it important to view the case from all possible angles. Unlike an attorney, we are not interested in assisting our clients to beat the system. I thought it might be a good way for me to better understand your department's position on this case while Mr. Cole explores other avenues."

Steinberg, her face still set in what Nikkie was beginning to believe a permanent smile, slowly began shaking her head. Small, rapid shakes growing longer and slower.

"Let's dispense of the bullshit, shall we, Miss Armani? That's a wonderful line you just tossed out, but I'm not taking the bait. The DA's office has already presented its initial findings and will soon be presenting more details of the case against Jessica Gracers before a grand jury. I'd expect that presentation to be scheduled in no more than a few days."

"You must have plenty of evidence to go before the grand jury so quickly," Nikkie said, unfazed by Steinberg's harsh refutation.

Julia Steinberg glanced at her wrist. And while she wasn't wearing a watch, she began tapping where a watch would have been. "Time's about up, Miss Armani. Is there anything I can do for you that has nothing to do with the Gracers case? If not, then I should be getting back to my duties. I am, after all, paid by the hardworking tax payers of this county and fully believe they deserve nothing short of my best efforts." She stood, extended her right hand to Nikkie. "Will that be all?" she asked in a voice at least a full octave higher than her normal voice.

Nikkie shook her head then shook Steinberg's hand.

"I don't want to take up any more of your time, Miss Steinberg. Thank you. You've been a gracious host."

.   .   .   .   .

Nikkie wasn't one to get flustered easily and nothing District Attorney Steinberg did was all that unsettling. But still, as Nikkie walked briskly out of the DA's office building, out into the oppressively hot Florida heat, she felt herself shaking.

"Get a grip, girl," she said to herself.

She walked several blocks before realizing she was moving fast enough to have worked up a decent sweat. Turning herself around, she was about to head back to the DA's office where she had parked her car, when she saw a brass plaque adorning the front of a small office, situated in the middle of a line of similarly sized, one story offices.

"Law Offices of Maryanne Jenkins, Esq.
Est. 1992"

The blinds in the office's two front windows were drawn, probably to prevent the glaring sun from causing even more of a challenging workout for the office's air conditioning system. Nikkie pressed her face against the sun-heated windowpane, cupping her hand around her eyes to block out the sun, but couldn't tell if the office lights were on or off. She thought she saw movement but, considering her view was through the quarter inch where one slat of the blinds hadn't fallen all the way into place, she couldn't be sure she saw anything.

The door to "The Law Offices of Maryanne Jenkins, Esq." was a solid pane of glass, framed in some type of brushed metal, and, like the front office windows, had its view of the interior of the office blocked by drawn blinds. Nikkie pulled the door, finding it locked. The small play in the gap between the dead bolt and the strike plate caused a bit of a rattle when pulled. Nikkie gave the door a few more pulls, hoping that if someone, supposedly Maryanne Jenkins, Esq., was inside; the obvious sound of someone persistently attempting to open a locked door would grab their attention.

Nothing.

She rapped her knuckles on the glass pane, hard, producing a sound louder and more determined than a rattling door.

Nothing.

Unless…Nikkie thought she heard something from inside the office. A shuffle of paper? A roll of a desk chair? Something made some type of noise. Of that she was certain, but what the noise was and what had made the noise was unclear.

She knocked again, this time letting her knuckles bounce off the door so many times she needed to stop at one point to make sure she hadn't split a knuckle open.

And that's when she heard it. A voice from inside the office.

"I'm closed. Weren't the locked door and closed blinds clues enough for you?"

Both the street noises and the closed door muffled the voice, but Nikkie was sure she recognized the voice.

"Miss Jenkins?" she called. "It's Nikkie Armani. We met…"

"I know where we met, for Christ's sake. What do you want?"

The voice was weaker, had more of the wobble Derek had mistaken for a Caribbean accent.

"Are you okay? Everything all right in there?" Nikkie called, her mouth set at an angle to the door to avoid a more direct and sound-altering reflection.

"Why wouldn't things be all right? I'm busy. If you need to speak to me, call me. I gave you my business card. Use it."

"Ten minutes is all I'm looking for, Miss Jenkins. Ten minutes and I'll be out of your hair."

There was a long pause. Terminally long for Nikkie but not long enough for Maryanne.

Nikkie wasn't going to just walk away. Leave her alone. No. This one, the woman with the perfect body, dazzling green eyes, flawless dark skin and legs and arms that weren't slowly slipping away from her command, knew something was wrong. Maryanne didn't know how Nikkie knew. Maybe it was woman's intuition or maybe she had a family member who was visited by Iron Lou.

As she sat behind her desk, rubbing her thighs in an attempt to vacate the "pins and needles" feeling which had taken up residence in both legs, Maryanne felt desperately afraid she'd never be able to stand again. What she read about ALS, suggested it advanced slowly. Inch by inch. Muscle cell by muscle cell, and not in a sudden barrage of painless immobility. But after returning from her visit with Jessica, Derek and Nikkie, Maryanne sat herself down in the chair behind the desk and hadn't been able to stand up again since.

"I shouldn't have walked to and back from the jail. Damn, woman. It's too damn hot and I'm too damn far along to be strolling down the streets like nothings wrong with me," Maryanne thought.

"Miss Jenkins?" Nikkie was calling from outside the door again. "Ten minutes, I promise."

"I'll give you ten if you just leave me to my business and call me," Maryanne shot back. Her voice was slurred, even she noticed it.

"I met with the DA," Nikkie said, her voice loud but laced with less emotion. "Tried to, anyway. She's a tough woman. I figured she'd at least be pleasant with me. Wasn't expecting her and me to become best friends, but I thought she'd at least have a conversation with me."

"Why the hell did you try and meet with her?" Maryanne's voice was sharper. Stronger. The wobble was gone, perhaps evicted by her anger.

"I had a feeling I could help if I built some type of professional relationship with her."

"Well all you did is piss her off! That's what your visit did." Maryanne paused a beat. "She called me, you know. Not two minutes after your tight little ass was walking its way out from her office, DA Steinberg called me. Told me I'd better keep my investigators in line. Said she hasn't the time for social calls."

"It wasn't a social call."

"You just said you were trying to build a relationship," Maryanne said. "That sounds social to me."

The Florida heat was growing more stifling as Nikkie stood inside the enclosed alcove. No breeze was finding its way to the doorway, not that there was much of a breeze, anyway.

"Miss Jenkins, please. It's hot and all I want to do is sit and talk about the case with you for a few minutes." She paused. "I understand you're not happy about Derek and me being part of this case, but we are. We are *all* on this case together. Same team, same objectives."

Maryanne sat in silence. She didn't know Nikkie but could sense from the tone in her voice she wasn't the type to just give up, walk away and leave her alone. She looked down at her legs, noticed the darkness between her legs was still much too visible. The smell of urine had, thankfully, passed but in the Florida humidity, her pants wouldn't dry for a long time.

She wasn't sure what angered her more: Not feeling she could stand and walk to her bathroom only twenty steps from her desk, or the fact she didn't even know she had pissed her pants till she felt the warmth between her legs. Both things pissed her off, she guessed. Both damn things.

"My car is parked around back," she called out. "In the lot. Green Buick. I keep an extra set of keys in the glove box. In the wheel well of the rear, driver's side, there's a door key hidden. Use it to unlock the car door, grab the set of keys from the glove box. You can come through the back door if you want. Saves you from walking all the way around to the front."

Nikkie screwed her face with concern. "Maryanne, are you okay in there? Can I get you something? Call someone?"

"You asked for ten minutes with me," Maryanne shot back. "If you want those minutes, this is the only way you're going to get them. Take it or leave it. And don't go calling no one on my account. Ten minutes. Take it or leave it."

Nikkie was already walking around the row of offices towards the back parking lot.

Chapter 6

"Are you okay?"

It was the first thing Nikkie asked once she entered the Law Offices of Maryanne Jenkins, Esq. and was almost the last.

"I have zero, I repeat, zero interest in discussing personal things with you. I told you I'd allow ten minutes, which I assumed you wanted to spend discussing our mutual client. Unless I was wrong, I suggest you alter your course of questioning."

"You're a real bitch, aren't you?"

"Excuse me?" Maryanne's face was a bit too slack to display her shock and anger and the weakness of her voice also failed to deliver her intended response.

"You look like shit and smell like piss. Not a great combination, if you ask me. I just asked you if you're okay, if you need anything, and you snapped at me like I asked if you if you're as stupid as you smell. I didn't ask you to tell me your deepest, darkest secrets."

Maryanne stared at Nikkie. Their locked gaze was like a game of chicken: She, who flinches first, loses.

"I am one of the finest lawyers in the area," Maryanne said, breaking the shared gaze and, perhaps, losing the game. "I've taken on and won some cases most of the other so-called lawyers in the area wouldn't touch with a twenty-foot pole. But I take them on. I don't back down from any challenge. So if you're thinking I'm not capable or not up to providing superior defense services for Mrs. Gracers, you better change your thoughts, and right quick."

"Then we have something in common. We don't run from challenges. But we also have some serious differences, which, if we are going to work together on this case, we need to resolve. Now," Nikkie said as she sat in a chair opposite Maryanne, "I can tell something is not right with you. Noticed it the minute I met you in the jail. You don't have to tell me what it is or even that there is something, but…"

"I have ALS. Lou Gehrig's disease." Telling someone, even though that someone was practically a complete stranger, sent a wave of relief over

Maryanne. "A tick less than a year and a half into it. Based on what I've read, I'm halfway through the disease's run rate. That means I've been traveling with Lou Gehrig for fourteen months and will probably travel another fourteen or so before I stop all travel completely."

"I'm very sorry, Maryanne," Nikkie offered.

"I didn't tell you to get your sympathy or your pity. I told you because there may be certain things on certain days I won't be able to accomplish." Maryanne paused to consider Nikkie's reaction. "I know what you're thinking, that I should be in some goddamn nursing care facility instead of handling cases for clients. But, let me tell you something, Miss Tight Ass, my mind is as sharp as ever. Maybe even sharper since I am relying on it to be so even more now. I can not only handle the Gracers case, but will see it through to the end."

"You're wrong. I wasn't thinking about that at all. What I was thinking is whether or not you told Jessica about your illness."

"I have not and demand that you keep your mouth closed on the subject."

"You have an obligation to reveal any and all physical or mental disabilities to your client which may negatively effect your ability to provide capable legal counsel."

"You gonna sit across my desk and tell me how I should run my law practice? I suppose that if I choose not to reveal my little disease, that you're gonna feel compelled to reveal it for me?"

"I'll do no such thing," Nikkie said. "The way I see it, without an alibi, your client is going to prison. Sooner or later, your disease will be impossible to hide. Meaning people will know. Jessica may be in prison by then and will have a very strong case when she appears with her new lawyer in front of the appellate court. She'll have a rock solid case that she didn't have proper representation since her lawyer, *you,* was suffering from ALS and never revealed her condition. She'll get a new trial and Derek and I will be hired again. We'll be back down here, hopefully when it's not so damn hot, working with a different lawyer who won't be hiding anything from Jessica or us. I'll make sure we stop in and visit you in whatever nursing care facility you end up in. That is, of course, if you're still alive."

"And you call *me* a bitch? Honey, you take bitchiness to a whole new level."

The two sat in tense silence; both knowing their conversation was at a crossroads. To Maryanne, who was quickly regretting her decision to tell Nikkie about her illness, the conversation was now threatening her ability to continue practicing law. Should Nikkie raise her concerns, Maryanne could be removed from the case. She'd need to be "checked off" by a doctor — more like a team of doctors — before she'd be allowed by the Bar Association of Florida to serve as lead counsel for the Gracers case, or any other case which might happen to come her way before Iron Lou made her decision to retire for her.

For Nikkie, the thought of telling Jessica, or anyone else, about Maryanne's condition was already resolved: She would say nothing. It was none of her business and if someone as wealthy and as influential as Jessica Gracers is had chosen Maryanne Jenkins over countless others, Maryanne must be one hell of a lawyer. What was occupying Nikkie's mind was why Jessica chose Maryanne in the first place.

Jessica was a millionaire, probably several times over, and had the means to afford any law firm in the country. In the world, possibly. Sure, Jessica's access to the shared financial accounts was constricted, but it wouldn't be for much longer. There wasn't a judge in the country that could justify locking her away from her deceased husband's accounts, creating a hardship for her ability to secure legal counsel. Yet despite the options her wealth afforded her, Jessica had chosen a law firm consisting of exactly one person. The office she was sitting in had only one desk, meaning Maryanne either did her own paralegal work or employed a home-based paralegal on a contract basis.

A single employee law firm, with an office close enough to the jail to make for an easy commute to find new clients? It didn't make sense.

Nikkie wasn't questioning Maryanne Jenkins' skills, but only why she was chosen. As her thoughts followed their present pattern, she wondered how Jessica was able to secure funds to pay for the $5,000 retainer fee for her and Derek's fee. In her experience, restricted accounts meant full restrictions. And lastly, every lawyer Nikkie knew received a retainer fee up front; *before* beginning to work a case. Yet, here she was, sitting across the desk from a lawyer, with pee soaked pants, for an added measure of confusion, who was "all in" and actively working Jessica Gracers' case.

"Here's how I see things," Nikkie said, breaking the silence which had crept into its second minute. "We all need each other. Jessica needs you to help her with all legal matters. She needs Derek and me to investigate the case and to explore her alibi—once she gives an alibi, that is. You need us since you aren't in any condition to do any legwork. You also need us for our skills. And we need you to keep us from broaching any legal lines and to feed us information we'll need to work this case. We don't have to like each other or even respect each other, but we do need to work together."

No matter how hard she might have tried, there was nothing Nikkie said that Maryanne could object to. The fact she was sitting in her office, her pants wet with urine and her legs about as trustworthy as the San Andreas fault, drove home the reality of her need for assistance: On the Jessica Gracers case and, perhaps soon, on many things in her life.

"I keep a change of clothes in the trunk of my car," Maryanne said.

"You couldn't have told me that when I was outside at your car?" Nikkie smiled, hoping Maryanne's defensive wall might crumble a bit. Instead of a crumbling wall, Nikkie saw tears welling up in Maryanne's eyes.

"Need to ask you to keep what's between us, just between us. You okay with that?"

"I've always been good at keeping secrets," Nikkie said. "And if you need anything while Derek and I are here in Florida…"

"I don't want Derek knowing, either. You good with keeping secrets from your partner?"

"Not that he'd care, but, sure."

"Then, I think us working together might work out just…"

The shrill of the phone locked Maryanne's words in her throat. Nikkie studied her face as she answered. The conversation was short, consisting of a few grunts of acknowledgement on Maryanne's side and what Nikkie assumed to be a very precise and concise notification from the person on the other end of the phone line.

Maryanne hung up the phone, her face revealing nothing.

"Gonna need you to get my clothes from my trunk."

"What's happened?"

"Jessica is ready to give her alibi."

Chapter 7

Maryanne and Nikkie arrived in the Pinellas County Jail a full twenty minutes before Derek. At first, Maryanne suggested to Jessica as the three women sat together in the cramped interview room, that her alibi be given to her and Nikkie first. Once they had an opportunity to hear her alibi and provide a bit of coaching to clarify any points in need of clarification, they would call in Detective Mathers, and whomever his partner-of-the-day might be, for the police to take the official account of the alibi.

"No," Jessica answered. "I want to give my alibi directly to Derek. I don't mind if you two sit in, but I insist that only Derek Cole asks me questions. Once he feels my alibi is as solid as it should already be, then, and only then will I talk to the detectives."?

"In my experience," Maryanne said, her voice controlled, soft, "those convicted often make grievous errors when first stating their alibi. Emotions run high; details that can't be readily recalled are doused with a heavy layer of creative license. This leads to gaps, to errors, which the police will uncover."

"You know what I did last night?" Jessica said, her face fixed with determination. "You know what I've been doing since you two and Derek left a few hours ago? Waiting. I've been waiting to see if *he* would show up. Waiting for a guard to walk up to my cell, unlock the door and tell me *he* called and cleared everything up. But he didn't call and he didn't show up and no guard unlocked my goddam cell and I wasn't allowed to walk out of this god forsaken place."

"Who is *'he,'* Jessica?" Nikkie asked.

"He's not going to show up and he's not going to call. He can't because I know he was involved in Sam's murder. I was set up from the start." Jessica paused to wipe an errant tear which had escaped the hold of her eyes. "When I was arrested, at first, I only thought about him. About how I needed to protect him. I knew as soon as he heard what happened to Sam and that I was being held, possibly charged, that he'd take some time to work things out. It wouldn't be easy for him, but he'd figure it all out, somehow. He'd tell the cops that I was with him since Friday evening. He couldn't explain how my gun was the murder weapon, but he'd hire the best in the world to figure it all out.

"I didn't sleep at all that night. I kept waiting for him to show up. But by the morning, I knew he wasn't going to show up. So I just sat and thought. And I kept on thinking until I figured it all out. Not all, but enough. I still had a glimmer of hope that he'd show up the second day, but, of course, he didn't. I called him, you know. Before I called for any of you. His number was disconnected. No message, nothing telling me about his new number. So I called his home number. Same thing. Disconnected.

"I was fooled. No, I was played for a fool and I need you to fix this for me. When Derek gets here, I'll tell you everything."

Nikkie sat, ready to begin writing line after line of notes while Derek sat across from Jessica. He listened to her insistence that he, and only he, ask her questions.

"I need you to guide me. Make me tell it like a story. It's how my mind works."

"Sounds more like you're asking me to help you write a fictitious story with you," Derek said.

"Everything I say, every word that comes out of my mouth, will be the truth. I'm not good at just spilling out chronological events. I've never been good at that."

"Okay," Derek said through a deep sigh. "Where do you want to begin?"

"I think you need to understand where Sam worked first. Whom he worked for."

Derek said, "Fine. Where did Sam work?"

"No. Not just questions like that. It has to be me telling a story. Not just answering questions. My God, this shouldn't be so hard for you to understand."

Derek's head turned slowly away from Jessica, towards Maryanne then stopping when his eyes met Nikkie's.

"How about this," he said with his gaze still set on Nikkie. "Tell me about your husband, Sam. Tell me about his job, where he worked. Whom he worked for and with."

"That's better." Jessica shot a small smile that was more of an apology than an expression. "Sam worked for himself, for the most part. He ran his own business. He did since before I even met him. But, around six years ago, he joined a group headed by FJ DeNuzzio. I didn't understand what FJ's company was all about, but once Sam was 'made,' things really went well for him."

"Made?" Derek asked. "Sounds like this FJ DeNuzzio is some type of a mob boss."

"No, not at all. It's just an expression, but one that really makes sense once you understand everything. See, Sam ran an outsourcing business. He worked with companies around the country, and even some in Mexico and Central America, to help them fill temporary positions. He did well. When we married, Sam's business was pulling in well over two million in profits. Since he only employed three people, well, you can imagine his income was substantial. At least we thought it was substantial until he joined FJ's company.

"Sam joined FJ and the others and really started to make things happen financially for us. He was a success before, but the day he joined FJ, he was truly a success. He wasn't just 'making' it any longer; he had made it. He was made. Understand?"

"Sure. Kind of weird, but, sure, I get it. Sam became a 'made man' once he joined forces with FJ."

"And not just FJ," Jessica continued. "There are seven others in FJ's company, making eight 'made' partners. They all own their own companies and all are part of the FJ DeNuzzio Company. Like the FJ DeNuzzio Company is the parent company and the other seven—those owned by the seven 'made' partners—are the children. All work together to support the other businesses. All share in profits and losses. All take the same risks, too.

"Every year, all the profits from all the companies are blended together, then shared nine ways."

"Nine?" Nikkie asked.

Jessica shot an angry look at Nikkie, who immediately apologized for asking the question. Jessica then fixed her sights on Derek, and waited.

Derek's eyebrows dropped in confusion. "You need me to ask the question Nikkie just asked?" he questioned.

"I know this may be different from what you're used to, but, yes. I only want to answer questions from you."

"Okay," Derek said. "Nine ways?"

"Each 'made' partner gets one equal share of the profits and FJ takes two shares. Adds up to nine. Same way all company votes are counted. Each partner's vote counts once except FJ's, whose vote counts as two. With nine, there's never a tie. And since he started the business, set the rules, chooses the direction the company takes and is the only one who interviews potential new partners, him taking twice as much and his votes counting twice as much as anyone else, makes sense.

"Since everything is shared equally…"

"Except for where FJ is concerned," Derek interrupted.

"…Each member benefits from the success of every other member. That's why they all help each other out, in whichever way they can. Sam spent as much time helping some of the others as he did running his outsourcing company. And he also received plenty of help. Especially from Brian Hilton."

"I'll ask about this Brian Hilton in a second. But first, what else is important for us to know about this FJ DeNuzzio and his company?"

"Each member of the team is expected to bring in a certain amount of profit each year. They have quarterly meetings that are meant to give updates about where each 'made' member of the FJ DeNuzzio team is with regards to their forecast. Once a year, around Christmas time, the eight go away for a long weekend. I've never been invited to any of them. No one but the partners are allowed, but Sam told me the meeting is all about year end results and then voting on whether the lowest two producers keep their positions or not. Since Sam became a member, I've only seen three members excused from the company."

Derek pulled his eyes off Jessica and onto the flashing blue light of Maryanne's digital recorder. Normally, Derek was able to give his client undivided attention, but the way Maryanne seemed obsessed over her digital recorder was distracting. At least six times during Jessica's strange sharing of what she promised to be her alibi, Maryanne had reached for the recorder, checked to make sure it was doing what she needed it to do, before placing it back down in front of Jessica, each placement a bit closer to Jessica.

It was only the second time Maryanne had used the digital device, choosing it over her tried and true practice of handwritten notes. But Iron Lou was ripping away her ability to write legibly. The flashing blue light on the recorder reminded Maryanne of the ravaging disease inside her body. Each pulse of the light, it seemed, marked her steady progression to her death.

"I don't honestly know much more than what I've already told you. Sam told me once he signed some legal agreements that prohibited him from sharing too much about FJ and the company. What I do know for certain is that FJ is a very wealthy man and the partners who get through the first couple of years are also wealthy."

"Fair enough. Strange, but fair enough." Derek stretched back against his chair, his arms reaching above his head. "So, you mentioned a Brian Hilton, and, based on the way you said his name, I have a feeling Brian is an important piece of your alibi."

"He and I were having an affair. We were lovers. I met Brian at a company party. There weren't many parties, only when a new partner was named and introduced to the spouses and assistants of the other partners. I was attracted to Brian from the start. He was single, young, in amazing condition and had a kindness in his eyes." Jessica sighed. "It was stupid. Crazy, actually. Sam was a wonderful man, a good husband and was well respected in the company. Me even thinking the way I was about Brian was cause enough for both him and Sam to be removed from the company. Very strict rules, FJ set. Very strict.

"Brian felt the same for me, too. Though he didn't say anything at first, eventually, we ended up in each other's arms. His first year with the company had ended and I guess he did really well. At the next announcement event, I remember FJ kept smiling at Brian and patting him on the back. Like he was gushing over him. I slept with him that night."

"If Sam was a partner with FJ before Sam, why didn't you meet Brian when he was announced as a new partner? You said FJ threw parties to announce new partners, right?"

"Brian was made a partner during the year end meeting. The one only partners can attend. I didn't meet him until he was with the FJ company for over a year."

"Okay," Derek said, forcing his attention away from Maryanne and her flashing blue light. "So, you met Brian Hilton at a new partner meeting and slept with him during the party. Go on."

"It was at a country club. Not sure if FJ is a member or if he owns the place. I remember two things about that day more than I can remember anything else about that night. First is that on at least three occasions, an employee of the county club assured FJ the entire kitchen and dining areas were completely free of peanuts. I guess FJ has a severe allergy to them. The way the employees were falling over themselves to let FJ know about the whole place being peanut free, made me think he owned the place. The second thing I remember vividly is that while the party was going on downstairs, Brian and I were having sex on a desk in one of the upstairs offices. We walked back into the main room, separately of course, after being gone for thirty minutes. No one seemed to notice that we were even gone. Sam just walked up to me, kissed me and said that he needed to meet with FJ alone for a few minutes and asked if I'd be okay alone for a little while. He had no idea I had just had sex with one of his partners one floor above where he was standing."

"This Brian, you said he's single but did he ever have a wife?"

"No," Jessica said sharply, almost like she was jealous of a wife Brian didn't have. "He's single. Never been married."

"Go on."

"Brian and I kept getting together when we could. We needed to be extremely cautious, as you can imagine. I have no idea how much money Sam, Brian and the other members were earning, but it must have been in the millions each year. If anyone found out about us," Jessica paused, shook her head and fixed her sights on an imaginary and distant possibility. "Let me just say if we were found out, things would get very, very ugly."

"Violent?" Derek asked. "You think something would have happened to you and Brian?"

"I don't know about that," Jessica answered. "But there was a member who was fired right before Sam was hired. Sam took his spot, actually. I never met the man and have no real reason to suspect anything happened, but I remember watching the evening news one night, shortly after Sam was 'made.' There was a short story about a businessman who was found floating in the Bay. Shot in the head, apparently. As soon as the reporter mentioned the man's name, Craig Washburn I think his name was, Sam's face went blank. Pale, as if he'd seen a ghost. I asked what was wrong, if he knew this Craig Washburn, but he dismissed me. Said he'd never heard of the guy and that he wasn't even listening to the reporter. But I didn't forget the look of terror on his face for those few seconds.

"I can't say FJ was behind the Washburn murder, but something told me from that moment on that there was more to the FJ DeNuzzio company than just eight businessman earning millions of dollars."

Derek stood, stretched his back with a deep, backwards bend.

"Okay, I'll get back to your relationship with Brian Hilton in a minute. But I'm still not clear on what this FJ DeNuzzio group is all about. What do they do?"

"They buy and they sell. That's it. Nothing romantic. Nothing exotic. They buy things, then they sell them."

"Like what 'things?' What do they buy and sell?"

"You name it. Real estate, businesses, fleets of cars, boats, ships, yachts, islands, stocks, bonds, and foreign currency. Whatever is for sale, they buy."

"They're flippers? They make millions and millions of dollars flipping things?"

"Each member has an area of specialty, or so I believe. Brian buys and sells medical equipment. Sam buys..." Jessica paused. "Sam *bought* outsourcing companies, made them better, then sold them for a profit. He once bought a company that specialized in placing mobile home repair specialists in Arkansas. Bought it then sold it three months later for twice what he paid for it."

"So these eight members, each has an area they specialize in?" Derek said.

"As far as I can tell."

Derek asked, "What's FJ DeNuzzio specialty?"

A look of confused anger screwed across Jessica's face. For a moment, Derek confused the look for one of terror. The type of fear one displays when a terrible realization is made. If there was terror in her countenance, it was fleeting. Gone like sea vapor driven by the force of a hurricane. What was left to spill across her face was unmistakable anger. Hatred, perhaps.

"Apparently FJ DeNuzzio specializes in arranging murders."

CHAPTER 8

"Brian surprised me, actually. I never expected him to take such a risk." Jessica's face had brightened at her mentionioning of Brian's name. After the sour, spiteful look that marred her face when she suggested FJ DeNuzzio might have had something to do with her husband's murder, Derek redirected her conversation to focus on her alibi, and not on her suspicions. "When he sent me that note, asking if I could get away for a weekend with him, I felt like a teenager in love."

"You communicated via notes?" Derek said. "Through the mail?"

"No," Jessica replied. "Never through the mail, or email or text messages. Never through any means that might expose our relationship."

"So you passed notes to each other?"

"Sort of. Brian lives on Snead Island, about forty minutes south of where I live. There's a tiny library on the island. Not really a library, actually. It's just an outside bookcase where people can borrow and donate books. Someone just puts in a book they no longer want and someone else can borrow it for no charge. Probably around twenty to thirty books circulated through that little library. Brian and I passed notes in a raggedy old Lee Child book. Paperback. Torn cover and coffee stained."

"Title?"

"*One Shot*. I actually read the book when I held on to it longer than usual. I was having trouble coming up with a response to one of Brian's notes. Book was pretty good. Not my usual genre but it was a very explosive ending. They made a movie out of that book. Tom Cruise? Have you seen it?"

"Sure," Derek said. "Five foot seven actor playing a six-five character. Bad casting."

"Wednesdays were our message days. I drove down to the island the week before, saw the book and took it. Always on page one hundred and fifty, we'd tuck a note written to each other. His note that day asked about going to his lodge outside of Tallahassee the following weekend. Friday to Sunday morning. I tore up the note and wrote one of my own, saying 'Yes. Details please.' The next Wednesday, I drove back down to the island, found the book and note. Brian told me where to park my car and what time he'd meet me."

"Two things," Derek interjected, "did Brian always have control of the book and, where did he tell you to meet him?"

"I don't read those types of books. If Sam ever saw it in our house, Brian thought he might get suspicious. So it was always in his house."

"Good enough. And the meeting place?"

"A parking garage in downtown Tampa. We had met there a few times before. Brian liked the place since, according to him, it wasn't a place people in our circles ever used for parking and the garage didn't have security cameras. Brian was very careful with our rendezvous."

"Okay, so you met Brian at the garage the Friday before your husband is killed. Drove to Hilton's lodge outside of Tallahassee right from the garage? Make any stops along the way?"

Jessica's face blushed as she looked down at her folded hands on her lap.

"We made one stop, but not at a store or anything. We stopped and made love in the backseat of his car. We really were like two teenagers in love."

"We'll need directions to the lodge," Derek said, pushing Jessica's story forward. "What time did you arrive at the lodge?"

"Around three. No, closer to two, I think. It's a long drive and, honestly, I wasn't paying much attention to the time. I know I met Brian at the garage around nine and we left right away."

"You said you had sex with Brian in his car on the drive up, so I assume you left your car in the garage?"

"Yes. Third floor. Right in the middle of the lot. The more conspicuous, the better."

"Fine. What happened at the lodge?"

"We hardly made it inside before we were all over each other. We had sex on the couch right inside the lodge. I think we even left the door open." Jessica smiled the type of smile that only pleasant memories can create. Derek knew that smile would be wiped off her face when he eventually asked her about finding her husband dead on their kitchen floor. But for the time being, he let that smile play across her face.

It was a good face. A little ragged from her time behind bars and away from her makeup, but, still, Derek considered Jessica's face a good one for a woman to have. Soft cheeks, warm, brown eyes and a nose that turned up the slightest degree at the end. A cute nose, he'd say. Not snobby. Not too pointed or too flat or too anything. Just a nice nose on a nice face.

"We spent most of Friday in bed. Just laughing, talking about things, and, of course, having sex. I'd bet Brian was able to perform five times that day. Once on the couch, once on the kitchen floor," she paused, as her face blushed red, "in the shower off the master and in the bed. And, of course like I've already mentioned, in the car on the way up to the lodge. Brian is a very healthy man."

It seemed that Jessica wanted a reaction from Derek to her last comment about Brian. Like she was either bragging about him or wanted to compare Brian's vitality against Derek's. Derek wasn't interested in either feeding into her pride or comparing notes. His wife had been dead nearly six years and Derek remained faithful to his dead wife. He paused the briefest of moments when an image of Lucy flashed into his mind. In his mind, his dead wife was wearing that look he remembered so well. The look she used to give when she wanted Derek to stop being stubborn. The look told Derek Lucy would want him to move on.

"It's been six years, sweetheart," he imagined her saying. *"It's time to let me go."*

He wasn't ready yet. Close. But not today.

"Great," Derek said. "Brian's a healthy, horny man. What happened the rest of the weekend at the lodge?"

Jessica screwed her face up a bit, then relaxed it.

"We slept till almost eight Saturday morning. Brian went for a run on the trails around his property and I showered and made breakfast. The rest of Saturday, we just spent sitting on the front porch, went for a walk through the woods, made love, ate and drank a few bottles of wine. It was a wonderful day. Relaxing."

"Talk about work? About Sam? FJ?"

"None of that. Not a word about anything important. We just talked about our pasts, our futures. We didn't talk about any shared future, just about things on our bucket lists."

"What's left on the bucket list of multi-millionaires?" Derek said.

"Brian wants to write a book someday. A fictional book. He reads a ton. I have no idea where he finds the time, but I know he loves to read."

"And your list? What's on it?"

Jessica let out a long, exaggerated sigh. Her shoulders slumped a bit and her posture, which had been much too straight for someone sitting in an uncomfortable chair inside an uncomfortable room inside a very uncomfortable and slightly foul smelling jail, collapsed a bit. Her slouching made her look instantly older to Derek. Bent the way people of advanced age often get.

"I always wanted to do something big and have no one ever know about it. Weird, but something like a tremendous random act of kindness which then makes people wonder who was behind it for years."

"Sunday. Tell me about Sunday."

"We woke up around eight again, fooled around, ate breakfast. Brian went for a run while I showered. A little more fooling around, then we drove back to Tampa. Got to the garage around four. Then, we went our separate ways."

"You drive straight home from the garage?"

"Not directly."

Derek could sense a building tension in Jessica's body. Her face pulled back the slightest amount and she wrapped her arms around her torso. She knew Derek would soon ask about finding her husband dead. She was preparing herself to tell that part of the story.

"I drove around town a little. Brian thought it would be a good idea if we pulled out of the garage ten minutes apart, went separate ways and drove around to make sure no one was following either one of us. I drove by Derek Jeter's home on the bay, not sure which direction Brian took."

"What time did you get home?" Derek asked, his voice taking on a sterner tone. Pressing. Urgent.

"Around five. I pulled my car into my driveway around five."

Jessica's voice was softer, quieter. Cut with nerves. Each word was short and proceeded with a bit of an extended pause.

"You have a garage at your house?"

"We do. But I had plans to meet some friends for dinner around six. I left the car in the driveway since I knew I'd be leaving soon."

"Walked in the front door?"

"Yes."

"Notice anything about the door? Opened? Closed. Have an alarm system?"

"Yes, we have an alarm. And there was nothing unusual about the front door. Nothing I noticed, anyway."

"You walked inside. Say anything?"

"I called out to Sam. I told him I was home."

"But he didn't respond."

"He couldn't have."

•   •   •   •   •

"I saw his legs first." Jessica's voice was damp sounding but steady. The type of voice which could go either way. Either erupts into a sob-filled, unintelligible voice or a voice that finds control. It wasn't the type of voice that stayed as it was. It was going one-way or the other. That was for damn sure. "He was lying in the doorway between the den and the kitchen. All I could see were his legs but I knew something was very wrong. As soon as I walked a few feet into the den, I heard my dad's voice telling me to prepare. A million thoughts raced through my mind. One of those thoughts was Sam had gone out the night before, got drunk and passed out."

"Your husband have a drinking problem?" Derek asked, his voice controlled. Dry as a desert.

"He had been drinking more lately. Last few months, I'd say. I asked him if something was bothering him but he wouldn't say if anything was."

"So, you kept walking closer to him?"

"Yes. I saw his hips and his stomach. His shirt was pulled up, like he had either fallen while taking his shirt off or…or his shirt was pulled up when he fell. Then I saw the pool of blood beside him. That's when I knew he hadn't simply passed out."

"What did you do next?"

"My father's voice came again. He was telling me Sam had been murdered and that the killer may still be in the house. I pulled my gun out of my purse and walked further till I could see all of Sam's body. His eyes were half open. I saw a small, black hole right in the middle of his forehead. He was dead." Her voice found purchase on solid ground. "I backed away, holding the gun up in front of me. I was afraid the killer was still in the house and had heard me when I called Sam's name when I first walked in the door. I backed my way to the front door as silently as I could. I remember stopping when my back hit the door. I just stood there, looking at Sam. I called his name again, hoping I'd see him move his legs. That maybe, I didn't see what I saw. That he was okay. Not dead."

"He didn't move, did he?"

"No." Jessica dropped her head. Fell silent. A few moments later, she wiped her eyes with a tissue Maryanne handed her. "He wasn't going to move ever again."

Derek was still standing, hands braced against the back of the chair in front of him. He spun the chair around, sat down. Gave a long, hard look at Jessica. He waited several minutes before she lifted her head and matched his gaze.

"Then what?"

"I ran outside, screaming for help. A neighbor must have seen me or heard me screaming. I don't remember how everything happened. I just remember sitting in the passenger's seat of his car, shaking and crying hysterically. My neighbor called the police."

"And that's how they found you? Sitting in the car, crying and shaking?"

"Yes."

"Where was your gun?"

"I must have dropped it outside. I remember watching the policeman picking it up and taking it away."

"Did the cop have gloves on? The one who took your gun away, was he wearing gloves?"

"I don't remember. I do remember seeing him hold it with two fingers then drop it into a plastic bag, though. Does that matter? Him not wearing gloves?"

Ignoring Jessica's question, Derek continued.

"How long were you outside screaming?"

"I don't know. A minute or two."

"Gun was in your hand the whole time you were outside screaming?"

"It must have been but I didn't have it when the police arrived."

"So after you dropped the gun and got into your neighbors car, did anyone beside the police officer pick up and hold the gun?"

"No. No one."

"Did you have any of Sam's blood on you? Did you feel for his pulse? Check his body?"

"No." Jessica's voice was failing her now. The dampness was increasing and the purchase her voice once had loosened its grip. "I never even checked if he was still alive."

The tears burst forth.

Chapter 9

His day had started like every other: Up at 5:15, fifteen minutes of meditation followed by a room temperature cup of unflavored, fat-free yogurt. After ten minutes for digestion, he was stepping along the same four-and-a-half mile-walking path he took every day. Rain or shine. Four and a half miles. Out the back of his home, to the hard-packed sand framing the ocean, left around the point which marked where the Gulf began and the bay gave way.

He allowed no more than sixty-three minutes to complete the walk. Then, he entered his fitness room on the second floor of his home. He had the entire house designed and built to his specific instructions. The fitness room was no exception.

"It needs to be a fully interior room. No windows. I do not want it wired in any particular fashion. Just electric outlets to power a treadmill, so ensure you accommodate for a high quality, professional treadmill. I want seven lights, recessed into the ceiling. No other lighting. There will be iron weights in the room, approximately a full ton. So the flooring needs to be reinforced. The walls are to be coated with whatever substance you feel will best prevent staining. The walls must also not absorb odors. Lastly, I do not want air conditioning in the room but, instead, I require an air circulation system, complete with dehumidification capabilities."

The architect had asked, "Why no windows?"

To which he received the answer, "Distractions of the mind cause weakness in the body. Design and build it as I have spelled out, or I will find someone who is capable of following simple, clear directions."

After lifting dumbbells and barbells for thirty minutes, he toweled himself dry. Stretching was next. Nineteen specific stretches, each position held for sixty-seconds before he slowly released the stretch and flowed into the next stretch.

He journaled the details of his workout, including his pulse rate upon waking, after finishing his walk and again after the final stretch was released. Precise times were recorded. The leather bound journal was then closed and placed atop the treadmill. It would be opened again the next morning, as it had been every morning that found FJ DeNuzzio waking up in his Anna Maria Island home.

As she did occasionally, his wife, Maria, had his breakfast prepared for him by seven. He had showered, dressed in clothing appropriate for the meetings he had scheduled for the day, and came downstairs for breakfast, greeting his wife with a kiss on her cheek and a quick pat on her backside.

"Busy day, today?" she asked.

"Good busy and bad busy, I'm afraid. Not sure when I'll be finished with my tasks."

"More work to be done with that awful Samuel Gracers murder? What a tragedy. And to think, his wife is accused of killing him."

"I'm afraid so," he answered. "Need to find his replacement before too much time slips between the future and Sam's death."

"I'm sure he'd want it that way," Maria said in a voice fully lacking any emotion.

"And you? What's your day look like?"

"Slow day, for the most part," she said. "I need to pay a visit to a few people in Tampa. I hate driving all the way up there. I hate driving over that damned bridge."

"I know you do. You mention it all the time."

Maria looked sideways at her husband of thirty-three years.

"And yet, I still make the drive whenever it's needed to be made, don't I?"

"Benefits always outweigh your imagined risks."

"As far as I know."

FJ stood five foot six inches, weighed one hundred forty-two pounds and maintained a body fat percentage of no more than seven percent. What he lacked in height, he made up for in fitness and in his commitment to leading a disciplined, controlled and successful life. Born and raised outside of Andover, Massachusetts, FJ was the only child of second-generation Italian immigrants. His father, who had worked for the US Post Office for close to forty years, had died six years ago. His mother, now aged ninety-three, was still active; though a series of small strokes had limited her ability to maintain the lifestyle she had grown accustomed to.

FJ loved his father but it was his mother who had inspired him. She was the driving force in his youth. His mother was the one who demanded that he never settle for what others felt was "good enough."

"Freddy," she would say most nights when, after completing his homework and chores, she tucked him into bed, "good enough is for the rest of the world. Good enough is for those who are happy with leading lives of adequacy. But that's not for you, Freddy. Not for my Freddy. You know why I treat you the way I do?"

"Because you love me?"

"Because you deserve more than what your father can provide. Because the greatest things in this world should lay themselves at your feet. The greatest people should recognize your abilities. I burn you with my love so that the strappings of the weak will never maintain a hold on you. And my boy says, 'Thank you, Mother.'"

"Thank you, Mother."

"If you have a busy day, shall I expect you to eat dinner elsewhere and for me to eat all alone, or should I plan to not serve dinner until…any idea when I can expect you?"

FJ removed his black-rimmed glasses, rubbed the bridge of his nose for several seconds. It was a habit he had developed since first being fitted for glasses when he was nine. While he had forced himself to overcome most every other one of his habits that served no obvious or useful purpose, this one was so innocuous and often afforded him a moment or two of reflection before responding, he consciously chose to keep the habit as a part of his life.

He rifled his open fingers through his crew cut short gray hair, pausing at his head's crown before reversion direction. With his glasses back in place, he tilted his head a bit to his right.

"If you want to say something to me, I suggest you do so. Playing some passive-aggressive, neglected wife character is not only foolish considering the lifestyle you lead, but rather unattractive."

His words were tight, perfectly spaced and emphasized the way one might do so when conveying a message both suggestive of accusation and intended to reveal a specific amount of contempt. Only the word "rather" came out the wrong way. He knew it the moment the word passed his lips. "Rather" sounded more like *"rathuh."*

"Your Boston is showing, dear."

Before FJ could respond, Maria stood, walked to the sink and deposited her dirty bowl.

She knew how hard her husband had tried to remove any trace of his Boston accent. Why? She didn't understand. Perhaps he thought it made him sound too casual. Too common. Too mundane. And, to his credit, his "Boston" only slipped out on occasion, usually when he was angry or growing towards anger. Hearing a weakened *R* sound—drawn out a bit longer when starting a word and truncated into more of an "eh" sound when ending a word—told her she had either succeeded in her seemingly never ending quest to remind her husband of his original roots or that she had better move on before all *R*'s were dropped and replaced with a temper she had seen enough times to know it was better left alone to sleep.

"Either way, home for dinner or not, please do me the courtesy and call?"

His leg bounced up and down in rapid succession. The soft heel of his slipper, knocking against the polished marble floor. He laced his fingers together and placed his hands behind his neck. Smiled a small grin, then shook his head.

"Assume I won't be home," he said. "I'm unsure of how busy I'll be and wouldn't want to promise a call and be unable to fulfill that promise. You do know how I feel about broken promises?"

"That I do, my dear. That I do."

•   •   •   •   •

It was close to eight before FJ was dressed and ready to make the drive from his home on Anna Maria Island to the office building he owned in Tampa. He felt no obligation to arrive at a certain time. The only employee of FJD Company was his personal assistant, Karen, who worked most days from her home. Karen wouldn't be in the office today. No one would be. In fact, he made it clear to all seven members, their personal support staff and to Karen that today was a day not to be in the office. He had work to do there and wanted no interruptions.

When his car reached I-4, FJ turned his cell phone on. He never turned it on before he left the island since he insisted that mornings were uniquely his own. The fact he had to share them with Maria was disturbing enough. But some mornings, this morning being one of them, Maria insisted on engaging him in conversation. Their talks never amounted to anything and served no purpose in his mind. Part of being married, he assumed.

As expected, a few seconds after his cell found its signal, the message-waiting indicator flashed. He pressed a few buttons and dialed his voice mail.

"FJ. Hope your morning has started off well. Just confirming our ten o'clock. Do me a favor, will you, and give me a call at the office?"

He didn't believe in keeping any of his contact's information on his phone. *"Doing so only serves to weaken the mind,"* he would say when asked about his phone habits. He dialed the number from memory, asked to be connected, and waited less than ten seconds for his call to be answered.

"Congressman Wiggins. So good of you to answer my call. Ten o'clock is confirmed and I hope you carry positive news with you today. I do want things behind us as quickly as possible."

"As do I, FJ. We all do."

"Good. Ten o'clock."

Chapter 10

Derek and Nikkie left the jail, headed out to get dinner. Maryanne stayed back with Jessica.

"I know the judge personally," she said. "I'll call the detectives down here right away so they can take Mrs. Gracers' alibi. Then I'll let the judge know we need another bail hearing."

"What will a lower bail amount matter?" Derek asked. "If Jessica's accounts and access to funds are locked up, doesn't matter how low bail is set."

"Just so happens I have an emergency stash of bonds I use in situations such as these." Maryanne nodded her head at Jessica. "You do understand I charge interest for the use of my money, don't you?"

"Roll it into my bill," Jessica said with a dismissive wave of her hand. "And why the heck would getting me out on bail be so damn difficult? They can't think I'd run away to Neebish Island and disappear into Canada or stow away on some slow boat to China. My whole life is here. I'd never run away."

"Severity of the crime you're accused of," Maryanne answered sharply. "You running away is just one concern. You committing another crime is what really scares people."

·   ·   ·   ·   ·

As they sat eating dinner at an area chain seafood restaurant, Derek summarized his meeting with Rachel Gonzales.

"She's the one who will help us. Not sure how much she can, since she's not assigned to the case. But she suspects something, or someone, is behind the murder."

"And this Congressman Wiggins and his ties with the DA? Does she think that has something to do with Sam Gracers getting murdered?"

"She didn't say, but she did bring his name up."

"I tell you who I want to talk with: FJ DeNuzzio."

"Guy like him," Derek said as he spilled the last swallows of his glass of scotch down his throat, "don't meet with people like us. They have people for dirty work like that."

"He sounds the type who has people to do all sorts of dirty work for him."

"Don't jump to any conclusions," Derek cautioned. "Truth may be he's a hard working, honest success story. Sounds like he's built a hell of a company at least. He may be as clean as they come."

"Or as dirty," Nikkie said back. "But," she fluttered her hands over her head as if they were single-winged birds, "my mind is wide opened. So, what's our next step?"

"Brian Hilton. We should wait till tomorrow. See if Jenkins can get Jessica out on bail. Showing up at his home with her in tow would make more of an impression than just you and me showing up."

"Detectives will call him in to the station, right? Take down his story, see if Jessica's alibi holds water?"

"Sure," Derek said. "They'll do that first thing. May even be driving out to have a chat with him right now. But he won't admit to anything. Better for us if he doesn't?"

"Why the hell is that?"

"Think about it from two angles. First, if he says he was with her the whole weekend, then we have a guilty client and he's complicit in the crime."

"Come again?" Nikkie asked.

"Evidence is too powerful. Her gun, her prints on the casings, no forced entry and her two-day delay in giving up her alibi. If he says they were together, those two days were to give *him* time to cover up anything needing to be covered. If she's guilty, our case is done and we go home on our own dimes. Didn't you think it was strange Jessica was able to have access to pay our fees upfront, and probably pay Jenkins a retainer but the only thing we heard about her funds was that they were locked down till her husband's murder was solved?"

"Hadn't thought about that, but people accused of a crime have to be given access to any locked funds in order to pay for legal representation. Right?"

"Not always. Not in Florida without a court mandating a release of funds. Jenkins took the case without getting a dime in advanced payment. I guarantee it. If Brian Hilton confirms Jessica's alibi, she's guilty, he was involved and he paid us our initial fee. No doubt about it."

Nikkie ordered another beer for herself and another double scotch, "low shelf, cheapest stuff you got, two cubes of ice," for Derek from the waitress.

"That's one angle," Nikkie said. "What's the second?"

"If he denies the whole thing. Says he was never with Jessica and wasn't having any type of an affair with her, then, she's innocent and we go to work. Till then, we don't have much to do."

"What's your gut telling you?"

Derek smiled at the waitress as she placed the drinks on the table.

"My gut is telling me it wants more scotch inside of it."

"That's a great sign," Nikkie said. "What's your non-alcoholic gut telling you about what Brian Hilton will say?"

Derek brought the glass to his lips, took a shallow draw, and then placed the glass back on the tablecloth's dampened ring.

"My gut says he'll deny everything. If that happens, you and I won't have time to go looking at alligators or manatees. Jessica is innocent but I don't know yet if we'll be able to help her."

"And what, may I ask, will determine if we can help her or not?"

"I'll let you know."

· · · · ·

August 20

It was close to four in the afternoon before Jessica Gracers walked through the back doors of the Pinellas County Jail. Out of jail and into an entirely different expression of prison.

Since Brian Hilton had denied every last word of Jessica's alibi and his involvement with her story when questioned by Detectives Mathers and Gonzales, Maryanne Jenkins was able to position her plea for bail on the grounds of her client's "urgent need to assist in the physical collection of material evidence to support her alibi."

Jessica had been given conditional bail, meaning four things.

Maryanne Jenkins posted a bailer's bond in the amount of $100,000 which would be forfeited should Jessica Gracers not respond, with a maximum allowance of three hours, to the court's or the sheriff's department's request for a meeting. Should Jessica need to travel or to "otherwise be engaged in legal activities which would potentially compromise her ability to respond in person within the three hour time frame," she needed to first obtain permission from the court. In addition to the bond amount being forfeited, Jessica would also be remanded back to the custody of the Pinellas County Sheriff's Department, where she would remain until "her appearance in court or additional and substantial justifications were presented to the court, which demanded or excused remand." Jessica was disallowed to "visit in person with, attempt unwarranted or unrequested contact via electronic or pedestrian means, or otherwise engage in any manner, with Brian Hilton, his direct associates or place of employment."

"It isn't the best bail agreement I've seen, but you're out." Maryanne Jenkins sat behind her desk in her office. Jessica and Nikkie sat across the desk, Derek stood leaning against the wall off to the left. Maryanne was feeling strong today though the learned "telltale" sign of a coolness streaking up the backside of her legs and underside of her arms was suggesting the evening might turn out to be entirely different. Her spine and midsection felt strangely and comfortably numb. She could feel when she pressed her fingers against her skin, but the touch seemed muted. Quiet and without any radiating echoes.

"So, now what do we do?" Jessica asked, her voice and eyes clearly displaying urgency. And fear. "Do we speak with Brian?"

"There isn't any 'we' involved in anything we do involving Brian Hilton," Maryanne snapped. "You go back to your home, sit your ass down and wait till I tell you to move it. Understand?"

"I can't just sit and do nothing. Especially in that house. My husband was murdered in that house and despite my affair, I did care for him. I'll never go back inside there again."

"Is there a funeral?" Derek asked. "Any arrangements been made?"

Jessica's face fell slack.

"Oh my God. I...I don't even know." Tears welled up in her eyes, collecting in shimmering pools before giving way to gravity. "What a terrible person I am."

"That may be accurate," Derek said, "but I don't think so. Hard to think about details when something like this happens."

"Then why did you ask?" Maryanne said. "You trying to break her down, or something? Trying to make her feel worse than she already does?"

"Because if there aren't any arrangements, they need to be made. If there are, we need to find out who made them and make damn sure Jessica attends."

"He has a brother," Jessica said. "In Houston." Her voice was staggered. Weak and damp sounding. As if it was slowly being surrounded by a flood. "That's where Sam was born and raised. He's the only one who would make arrangements, I'd think. Him or me."

"And you haven't. So, it's either your brother-in-law or no one, right?"

"I'd think. I can't believe I don't..."

Derek cut Jessica off. He figured she wasn't going to add anything of importance to the conversation. Figured she just keep piling on to her own guilt. He'd gotten what he wanted; what he'd hoped for from the conversation.

Guilt was a good thing, Derek believed. Good when the guilt is over something different from whatever crime someone was accused of. If Jessica wasn't feeling guilty about not having even thought about putting her husband to rest, he would have second guessed feeling she was innocent.

"Write down your brother-in-law's contact information and give it to Nikkie before we leave here tonight. She'll find out if anything has been set up. We'll let you know tomorrow."

Beyond the tapping sound of Maryanne's pen as it hit against the solid wood of her desk, the room was silent for a long minute. A few damp, staggered sniffles from Jessica added their sound to the broken, syncopated rhythm of the tapping pen. Derek kept leaning against the wall, arms crossed over his chest, waiting. Nikkie, having worked with Derek for a year, and having seen how he operates with clients, waited in solidarity with what she assumed to be Derek's intentions. Nikkie had a few hundred questions racing through her mind, so quelling her desire to ask them wasn't easy.

Derek would say he couldn't hold a candle to Nikkie's investigative skills, but she knew otherwise. She was good, of that she was confident, but Derek had a talent she could only observe and recognize. His skills couldn't be taught. Someone either had them or they didn't. End of story. For Derek, his skills—largely unidentifiable and wholly unable to be described—were not the result of his upbringing, his six years in the Army or from the few years he spent as a cop in Columbus. His abilities were forged into his being from the intense fire of emotions. He had seen his wife killed. He had held her body, lifeless, void of any hope of recovery. He had sunk to a level of hopelessness and depression very few manage to crawl back from. He had stuck a gun into his mouth, pulled the trigger and, but for a flash of memory of his wife's face filling his peripheral vision, causing him to, *slightly, just enough, thank God,* turn his head, sending the 9mm bullet ripping a path through his cheek and not his skull.

His failed attempt at suicide had changed him, even someone like Nikkie who hadn't known him before his attempt could recognize the change. She knew he still loved and grieved for his wife and for the life he shared with her. But the tragedy of her death and the spiral of depression and despair he suffered through after she was murdered left scars on Derek. The three-inch scar on his left cheek may have been the only visible scar, but there were others. Deeper. Hidden. But these scars were what she could see. And the scars she could see told her as much about the man Derek was as they did about the person he had become.

As she sat in the silent office, wondering how much longer Maryanne would be able to tap out a rhythm and how much longer Jessica could hold back the flood of emotional pain which was surely demanding release, Nikkie let her mind wander to the feelings she held for Derek.

She had taken the first step, a few months ago, while they were working a case in Upstate New York. She told him of the growing and expanding feelings she held for him. It was Nikkie that had reached out to him as they sat alone in his hotel room, inviting him to allow her to show how strongly attracted she was for him. And while her affections were far from unrequited, he wasn't ready. He still felt married. Still attached, despite knowing his wife had been lying still and cold for six years.

He apologized when he refused her advances, which told Nikkie everything she had yet learned about him. His scars were deep and might never fully heal, but she had never met a man, never met *anyone,* for whom she was more willing to patiently await the healing process, no matter how long that process took.

"So, what's next?" Jessica had scribbled down her late husband's brother's information, as best as she could recall, and was leaning towards Nikkie, arm extended and the slip of paper held deliberately in her outstretched hand. "I mean, I'm happy to be out of that horrible, horrible place, but unless we do something about Brian denying everything, I have a feeling I'll end up back there again."

"And if that happens," Maryanne, who had finally stopped tapping the pen against the desk, said, "you should plan on being in there a hell of a lot longer."

"Well that's a pleasant thought."

Derek pushed off from the wall, arms still crossed against his chest. He walked to the front window, pulled apart a slat of the drawn blinds, and spoke without turning around.

"You said you and Mr. Hilton were alone in his lodge around Tallahassee for two nights, right?"

"Yes," Jessica answered.

"Had sex in a few different areas?"

Jessica's face burned with blushing embarrassment.

"Yes. On the couch, the kitchen floor. The bed, obviously. And the shower."

"Busy weekend."

"I'm not proud of being unfaithful, Mr. Cole. Not proud in the least."

"Unprotected?" Derek asked, ignoring Jessica's comments.

"What?"

"The sex? Was it unprotected?"

"I hardly think that is important." Jessica was boiling with embarrassment. Derek could almost feel the heat in the office pouring off her face.

"Did Mr. Hilton use a condom? Yes or no? Very simple question. You were there, right? You were with him in the lodge. Alone. Just the two of you. No other visitors. Had sex at least five times, based on your rundown of places you said you two had sex. You should know if she was using a rubber or not."

"He wasn't," Jessica yelled, her voice trailing off at the end, giving way to emotion.

"Then we go to the lodge." Derek turned away from the window and faced the trio of women in the office. "Funny thing happens when a man and a woman have unprotected sex: They leave evidence. No matter how damn hard they may try to keep things where they put them, drips, spills and gravity always win out. We find that evidence, date it with whatever the hell lab techs use to date bodily fluid with, and if those dates match the days you said you were with Brian Hilton having unprotected sex on his couch, in his kitchen, bed and shower, then Hilton will have some questions to answer."

"And if we don't find… any trace of evidence?" Jessica asked, back in control of her voice and emotions.

"I have a few other ideas."

"And they would be?" Maryanne asked.

"Hopefully unimportant. No reason to discuss possibly unimportant ideas." Derek pulled out his phone, checked the time. "I'm going to call Detective Gonzales. Ask her to meet us up at Hilton's lodge. I want her and not Mathers to be there with us. Maryanne, I'm sure you need to do some lawyer stuff to make Hilton allow us to check out his lodge, so we'll leave you to take care of those tasks. The sooner, the better. Tomorrow morning if at all possible."

"I highly doubt a judge will move on my request *that* quickly," Maryanne said.

"It's quarter after four," Derek said. "If you start the legal wheels turning now, and if you're as good a lawyer as I believe you are, you'll be able to pull something off. Tell the judge we need to collect possible bodily evidence that degrades quickly in this goddam heat. Tell the judge whatever the hell you want, just get us in that lodge as quickly as you can."

"You know something we don't?" Maryanne asked. "You seem to have an urgency."

"Two things: One, fluids can be cleaned up. Two, this Hilton guy, he's pretty rich, right?"

Jessica looked at Maryanne, then Derek, back to Maryanne before deciding the question was, after all, intended for her to answer.

"Very. Why?"

"Rich people don't have any more rights in this country than do poor people, but they can afford to have those rights defended and protected while poor people can't. If you're telling the truth about being with him while your husband was being killed, the fact he's denying the whole thing means he has something to hide. Meaning he was probably involved in your husband's murder."

Jessica stood straight up, fast as an arrow.

"That's not true," she demanded. "The only reason Brian denied being with me is because of his job. His position with FJ's group. I can't say that I'm happy at all about him denying everything, but I'm not surprised, either. FJ is a very powerful and very wealthy man. He can make things happen, and not only good things. I told you about how Sam responded when he heard about Craig Washburn. He never said he suspected FJ, but…just the way he looked when he heard Craig's name."

"So, you think Brian denied everything out of fear? Not only of losing his position but possibly his life as well?" Nikkie's eyes darted between Jessica and Derek. He had suggested their first stop after getting Jessica out on bail would be at Brian Hilton's home. But now he seemed to have changed gears. It wasn't any doubts she harbored about Derek's abilities, it was more her feeling Derek was running this investigation on his own. She made a mental note to approach the subject with him as soon as they were alone.

"I can't say for sure," Jessica said, her voice softer, more sullen. She sounded confused, struggling with competing thoughts.

"You might be right," Derek said, causing Jessica to relax even more. Her body softened, seem to almost collapse in on itself. "But, you may be dead wrong."

Just as Jessica's face began to grow still, a sudden flash of terror raced across it.

"He borrowed my gun!" she said. "He borrowed my gun."

"What are you talking about?" Maryanne snapped at Jessica. "Who, where, when and why?

"Brian. He borrowed my gun while we were at the lodge." Jessica's voice with charged with energy. Her eyes were wide with both fear and hope. "He goes for runs almost every day and, like I told you when I gave my alibi, he went for runs while we were at the lodge. He told me he forgot to bring his gun and asked to borrow mine in case any wild animals crossed his path." She paused, seemed to emotionally collapse into herself as the realization that it really might have been Brian Hilton who, somehow, killed her husband.

"And you didn't think that little gem was important enough to share with us before now?" Maryanne, whose disappointment came through loud and clear through the tone of her voice.

"I didn't think anything of it when it happened," Jessica said, her voice softer and her eyes smaller. "I'm working on pure emotion, here. There's probably a hundred things about that weekend I can't remember at will. Is it possible," she said, staring at Maryanne, "that I can get a break if things pop into my mind whenever they do, even they're not on your time schedule?"

"You want a break?" Maryanne shot back. "Keep delaying important clues and you'll get a 'twenty to life' break."

Derek said, "So, you're telling us that the man who denied he was with you while your husband was killed also borrowed your gun, went running and was, I assume, out of your eye sight with your gun while he was running?"

"That's what I'm saying. Yes."

"Jessica?"

"What?" Jessica replied in a voice so soft it was more of a whisper.

"Ever been hypnotized?"

"No. Why?"

"Because we need to learn about whatever memories aren't popping into your mind, as soon as possible."

CHAPTER 11

Maryanne Jenkins demanded to be told everything. Every last detail. But she agreed with Derek and stayed behind in her office while Derek, Nikkie and Jessica went to Gulf Coast restaurant for drinks and an early dinner.

"I'll make some calls," Maryanne said. "See about getting a warrant to inspect Hilton's cabin. But, y'all had better assure me you'll tell me everything you three discuss. Jessica," she said, ignoring Derek and Nikkie, "you come up with any other memories about your weekend with Mr. Hilton, and you call me straight away. You hear me?"

"Yes," Jessica answered. "Of course."

"That little gem about him borrowing your gun is a hell of a thing to have left out of your alibi."

"I know. I...I didn't think anything of it at the time. It was stupid of me."

"It may be enough to persuade the judge to get us into that lodge, right quick."

The first thing Maryanne did after waiting a full sixty-seconds after the three had left her office, was to stand up. Her legs still felt stronger than they had yesterday, but the chilled trace running up the backs of her legs and arms hadn't warmed, despite the outside temps hovering in the mid-nineties. She stood, felt lightheaded enough that she needed to brace herself against he desk. But she didn't fall. She felt strong enough to walk around, and did so without any struggle. Still, that cold feeling! Icy and so confined. It felt like just one of her veins in each leg and in each arm was filled with frigid water. It wasn't spreading, yet.

She had read about how some ALS patients felt pins and needles across their limbs, even on days when they were able to get around fine. She read about one patient—a dentist from Oregon, if she remembered correctly—complaining about feeling like his limbs were fluid, lacking form and substance. He had said there were times when he would have sworn he felt waves rippling up and down his limbs, like they were tidal rivers.

But she couldn't recall reading anyone presenting with the feeling of ice water in her veins.

"Maybe the docs got it all wrong," she thought. *"Maybe old Iron Lou isn't coming to take me away, after all."* But she knew. And she knew what she was doing in her thoughts: *"I'm just running through the stages. What's this one? Denial? Anger? Sure as hell isn't acceptance. That's a long way off for this Southern girl."*

•　　•　　•　　•　　•

There wasn't a whole lot of conversation between the three for the first hour or so. Small talk, mostly. About how Jessica met Sam and what things they enjoyed doing as a couple. About the positions he held and the type of work he did prior to being "made" a member with the FJ DeNuzzio Company. They danced around talking about Brian Hilton, the affair Jessica had with him and the probability, or possibility, their secret affaire de cœur had been discovered. But eventually, the reasons for them all being together overwhelmed whatever uncomfortableness they felt sitting down for dinner and drinks.

"You and Brian Hilton, how long?"

"A little over a year. Closer to a year and a half."

"See each other a lot during those twelve, closer to eighteen, months?"

"Not at first," Jessica said. "Maybe once or twice over the first couple of months. More often after we started thinking we were covering our tracks pretty well. Sam never suspected anything and all seemed to be going well for Brian at work. Better than okay, actually. He and Sam never told me much of anything about their work, but I could tell things were going really well for Brian. Just the way he carried himself. He was so confident."

"After the first few months, were you and Brian careful about your rendezvous?"

"We were as careful as we could be," Jessica said, her voice low, her eyes glazing over with mist. "I mean, as careful as we could have been, I suppose. Guess we could have made mistakes. Why does it matter?"

"Leverage," Derek answered. "Is there anyone in the FJ group who might better their position if Brian's and your affair was made public?"

Jessica paused a beat, seeming to consider Derek's question. Then she softly shook her head.

"No one I can think of, but, again, I suppose it's possible." She took a deep breath in before continuing. "There're eight people in the company, but I couldn't tell you more than four names. Brian, Sam, FJ and Martin." She let out a gruff of a laugh. "Hell, I don't even know Martin's last name."

"All men?" Nikkie asked. "Any women on the team?"

"Distractions. I never heard FJ come right out and say it, but I've heard him say, the few times I actually was in the same room with him and listened to him speak, that a significant part of his duties to the company are to ensure all members are fiercely self-driven, loyal to the company's objectives, dedicated to the success of all members and do not present any form of, *how did he say it?* 'Distraction, temptation or an attractive pull away from the business initiatives.' Some BS like that, anyway. So, no, there aren't any women members. FJ has a female assistant, as do most of the other members. Support staff. No voice in the company. Only seen when a new member is made."

"I still think 'made' is a strange choice of a word to use, don't you think?" Nikkie asked as Derek worked at his scotch in contemplative sips. "It's a mafia term."

"I thought the same thing, actually. I remember asking Sam what the hell kind of company he was joining. He just laughed at me. Said being 'made' had nothing to do with the mafia or organized crime or anything illegal at all. He said being 'made' had everything to do with becoming an entirely different businessman." Sounded like some cult-crap, if you ask me. But, it makes sense, being called 'made.'"

"How so?"

"Some people say they've made it big when they reach a certain point in their careers. For the FJ Company, just being part of the company is reaching that point. They become 'made'."

"And the one who makes you, also owns you," Derek said. "Like the mob."

Jessica considered Derek for several long seconds, appraising him, perhaps challenging him with her sturdy, confident glare.

"FJ absolutely had control over the other seven, no doubt about it. Again, I only heard him speak three times during new partner receptions, but I could tell he ran a very tight ship. Each time he spoke about the importance of 'moral character,' about 'the unforgivable act of a weakened commitment to integrity.' Remember that old commercial? The one about the brokerage house, EF Hutton?"

"Can't say that I do," Nikkie said.

"Maybe a bit before your time," Jessica said. "Anyway, in the commercial, a bunch of men in stuffy shirts would be sitting around, gabbing about whatever stuffy shirts talk about, but as soon as the EF Hutton character said a word, the entire place went dead silent. The tag line was, 'When EF Hutton talks, people listen.' Same thing with FJ. When he cleared his throat, everyone would shut up, in case he was about to say something."

"Does sound a bit like a cult," Nikkie added. "Either that or this FJ guy has the biggest ego in the world."

"And the power and authority to back it up," Derek said. "If we wanted to speak with FJ, how would we…"

"Forget it," Jessica said, waving her hand dismissively. "FJ is almost a recluse. Doesn't see people. Lives in a beautiful home on Anna Maria Island. Right on the Gulf. Must be worth at least ten million. He has an office in Tampa, but it's not the type of office you can walk into, ask to see the boss, then wait in the reception area till the boss can see you."

"But he does see people?" Derek questioned. "He has an office. Must go there from time to time. No sense having an office unless you need a place to meet with others."

"Recluse was too strong a word. Maybe, too nice a word. The thing is, FJ wouldn't see someone like you, Derek. Nothing personal."

"A person like me? Meaning an investigator?"

"Meaning not wealthy. Meaning having little to no influence over the way things get done in the business and political worlds. I'm sorry if that offends you. It's just FJ is very selective about who he spends his time with."

"Takes a lot more than being told I'm not rich or influential to offend me."

"I'm glad I didn't offend you. Really, I am."

"Will FJ see you? If you scheduled an appointment? Go through the right channels? You're wealthy. Influential."

"And also a suspect in the murder of one of his 'made' employees." Jessica shook her head then took a long draw from her martini. "He wouldn't see me even if all this hadn't happened. I'm only wealthy and influential because I was married to Sam. Now," she let out a quick laugh, "I'm about as influential as the character who plays Ronald McDonald is to the Academy Awards."

"You lost a lot when Sam died," Nikkie said, her voice soft, dripping with true compassion. "More than just your husband."

Jessica held her soft brown eyes on Nikkie's dark brown eyes. A small amount of liquid was building up in Jessica's eyes. Small but growing. It was really the first time Nikkie looked closely at Jessica. Though the lighting in the restaurant wasn't brilliant, it was brighter than what was in the visitor's area of the jail and much softer than the harsh lighting in Maryanne's office.

Jessica was in her early forties. She was thin with what were certainly medically enhanced breasts. The lack of any discernible lines across her forehead or around her eyes, suggested Botox and in frequent use. Recent use, as well. Despite Nikkie's feelings about plastic surgery, she considered Jessica to be quite beautiful. Her brown hair reached a bit lower than her shoulders and found a way to shine even in the less than brilliant lighting of the restaurant. It was clear Jessica spent time in a gym: Her arms were toned, midsection flat and her chin still held the shape of that of a twenty year old.

There was something about her face, the soft cheekbones, the pouty lips and the near perfectly shaped nose, which really set Jessica Gracers out from the crowd. If lined up among super models, she might not be the woman who draws the eyes and attentions of onlookers. But among virtually any other crowd, Jessica would demand an awful lot of attention.

"I haven't even begun to think about what I've lost," Jessica said. "I mean, right now, I hate myself because I'm more worried about what might happen to me than I am about poor Sam. I'm more angry and confused at Brian than sad about losing my husband." She paused, looked at Derek, then back at Nikkie. "I know what you must think of me. Poor, rich white girl couldn't be happy with her adoring, rich husband. Runs out and has an affair. Shallow, pretentious, conceited woman, always getting her way and doing whatever feels right in the moment."

Derek's face remained stoic. If he agreed or disagreed with what Jessica had said, his face wasn't showing it.

"But that's not who I am. Who I am, really. Yes, I cheated on Sam, and I can give you a thousand reasons why I shouldn't have and a thousand more about why I should feel terrible about what I've done. But I loved Brian. I still love Brian. My marriage to Sam was loveless. It wasn't always that way. But over the last five or six years, especially since he joined FJ's company, he and I were more strangers than partners."

Nikkie grinned a little, and then leaned back against her chair. Jessica's face clenched a bit, Derek could see the ripples of her jaw muscles beneath her flawless, smooth skin.

"I didn't tell you that Sam and I had grown apart to justify my affair," Jessica said in a tight, controlled voice. "I know how it must sound and I know how you must feel about me."

"Actually," Derek said, "you have no idea. And it doesn't matter. The only thing that matters is whether or not we believe you're innocent or guilty. I couldn't care less if you slept with kangaroos. All I care about is your innocence or guilt. That and your ability to pay our fees. That's all."

"Well?" Jessica responded without missing a beat. "Do you?"

"Do I what?" Derek said.

"Think I'm guilty? Do you think I made up the whole story about being with Brian in his lodge up north? Do you think I shot and killed my husband? Do you think I'm guilty, Mr. Cole. Yes or no?"

"I think you're guilty of a lot of things. Bad judgment. Questionable character. A healthy dose of being a spoiled, rich, white lady. But you didn't kill your husband. Not with your own hands, at least."

"Are you suggesting I played a role in Sam's murder?"

Derek could tell Jessica was offended. More than offended. She was pissed right off. Insulted, infuriated, and a few other harsh adjectives that wouldn't pop up into his mind as he sat across the oval table from Jessica Gracers.

"You may have not pulled the trigger and you probably had nothing to do with the planning or execution of his murder. But you killed your husband, Mrs. Gracers. That's for damn sure."

CHAPTER 12

Derek was quiet as he drove back to the hotel. Nikkie was sitting next to him, legs crossed, arms crossed and a cross look on her face to complete the ensemble. She assumed he would explain his comment about Jessica killing her husband.

She was wrong.

She assumed Derek would talk about his feelings, thoughts and ideas about the case.

She was wrong.

She also assumed he would apologize for keeping her largely in the dark about how he was running the case. She knew it was his name in bold type on the business cards, that Derek Cole and Associates was, after all, his agency and he should be able to run things as he saw fit. But she was never one to take a backseat. She was good, damn good in fact, at private investigating and felt she was more than deserving of being included into each and every step of any investigation.

She sat, crossed up and down, for most of the fifteen-minute drive from the restaurant to their hotel. When the lighted sign for their hotel was in view, she ended her vigil waiting for Derek to start talking.

"Well?" she said.

"Well what?"

"Are you kidding me? You have nothing to say? Don't feel compelled to at least try to explain what you said to Jessica?"

"What did I say?" he said.

"That while she didn't pull the trigger or plan the crime, that she killed her husband. Remember that little nugget? Sure left an impression on me and I'm sure didn't make our client feel all warm and fuzzy about hiring us."

Derek turned left into the hotel's parking lot, drove around to the side closest to their rooms. He put the car into park but left the engine running. Air conditioning doing its best to keep out the oppressive heat and humidity of the Florida summer.

"I have a bad feeling about this case," he said, keeping his eyes straight ahead. He started shaking his head in quick movements. "Hilton denying everything was expected, but there's something else behind his denial. Someone else, probably."

Nikkie sighed, started feeling a bit better. She trusted Derek's intuitions and understood how their last case affected him. During that case, their assistant, Victoria Crown, had her skull crushed by a madman, causing a traumatic brain injury which would create challenges for her the rest of her life. Another associate working for Derek had abducted Nikkie. That associate turned out to be an illegal drug supplier. He not only abducted Nikkie when she and Derek were getting too close to discovering his involvement, but also tied her up, gagged her, and put her in a bedroom of a house he then lit on fire. If it weren't for the local volunteer fire department, she would have died.

Derek had already watched his wife get shot in the head. He held her seconds after she had died, felt the life leave her body and, along with it, a significant part of his own. And since Derek and Nikkie had expressed their growing feelings for one another, she understood why Derek could feel a bit more protective for her. Losing someone else in his life may turn his one time failed suicide attempt into a successful one.

Nikkie glanced out the side window and laughed when she realized they were staying at a hotel chain that shared names with their client's lover.

"You think this FJ is involved somehow?" she said, releasing the last ounces of her anger and resentment at Derek.

"That I don't know," he said, turning his body to face her. "If Jessica is telling us the truth, the whole truth and…Well, you know how the saying goes, then Hilton borrowing her gun twice during the weekend affords him the means to have her gun used to kill Sam."

"That also means someone else was involved, obviously."

"Unless he can run as fast as a jet plane, you're right."

"So, the question is, who else is involved?"

"And, *why* was Sam Gracers killed. We figure out *why* he was killed, I have a feeling we'll find out who did the shooting."

"Then it's all about the *how*," Nikkie added.

"Already got that part figured out," Derek said. "Again, if Jessica is telling us everything she knows—something I doubt, by the way—her weekend getaway with Brian was all part of the plan. He, and whoever else was involved, needed to get Jessica away from the house, to a place and with someone who would refute her alibi. He borrows the gun, telling her he forgot his and needs a gun to protect himself against rabid raccoons or overly aggressive squirrels. Must have arranged to meet an accomplice during his run, gave him or her Jessica's gun in exchange for a duplicate. Jessica doesn't seem the NRA type, so Hilton was betting against her inspecting the switched gun. The next day, Sunday, the day of the murder, he borrows her gun again, meets his accomplice and gets Jessica's real gun back."

"The gun that fired the fatal shots," Nikkie said with an air of understanding.

"Exactly."

Nikkie thought for a few seconds, and then started shaking her head.

"Time frame doesn't work, though."

"How do you mean?" Derek asked.

"Drive time from the lodge to Jessica's house is close to five hours. She said she arrived home around four in the afternoon but the medical reports list the time of death closer to two. How could her gun be used to kill Sam if she had it with her since eight or nine that morning?"

"Great point, and one I'm hoping Jessica can solve for us. Because, based on the time frame alone, my theory is shattered."

Derek switched off the car and both walked into the stale, damp air. It was still close to ninety degrees, with humidity levels almost as high. The pair walked inside through the hotel's side "Guests Only" entrance, to the elevator.

"One more thing I wanted to ask," Nikkie said as the doors opened to the fourth floor. "At first, you wanted to go to Brian's house, meet him face to face. You even suggested we bring Detective Gonzales along with us. But now, all you seem to want is to get up to his lodge. I understand what you're looking for up there, but why not just send a forensics team and local cops while we visit Hilton's home?"

"Two reasons. First, I want to get a lay of the land. I want to walk the running trail, see where he might have met an accomplice. I want to see how Jessica responds emotionally and physically when she walks back into the lodge."

"So, she's coming with us to investigate a possible crime scene?" Nikkie asked.

"Yeah. We need her with us and we need to make damn sure Hilton doesn't know she'll be joining us. He might meet us up there if he thinks it's just you, Maryanne, the authorities and me. I want to see his reaction when she walks through the door."

Nikkie's thoughts went back to Maryanne, her condition and how unlikely it would be she'd be able to make the trip. Not telling Derek about Maryanne's condition felt like she was hiding something from him. But she had promised Maryanne to keep her condition a secret. She would, at least as long as it was possible to do so.

"Makes sense," she replied. "This is of course assuming Maryanne can get a judge to agree to allow us access to the lodge."

"I have a feeling she'll get a judge to agree, based on Jessica's alibi and the 'recently recalled' bit about Brian Hilton borrowing her gun."

"Okay, that's the first reason you have about going to the lodge instead of to Brian's home. What's the second?"

"I'm thinking we should consider relocating the agency. Been thinking about the panhandle area. Figured it would be a good chance to check the area out."

"My little multi-tasking partner."

CHAPTER 13

August 21

It took more pressure, and a few threats disguised as assurances, than Maryanne expected to get a judge to issue a warrant allowing The Law Offices of Maryanne Jenkins, Esq. and her team of forensic experts and investigators — not to exceed a total number of five people — access to Brian Hilton's lodge. Though she had pressed for the warrant to allow immediate access to her team, the judge dragged Maryanne's request through the muddy legal process, delaying access to the lodge for a full twenty-four hours.

Derek, Nikkie and Jessica drove in one car and Fred Amasini, the court approved forensics specialist, drove up in Detective Rachel Gonzales's county-issued unmarked car. Maryanne had told the team she needed to work on a few "matters of critical importance" and wouldn't be able to join them for the lodge trip. Nikkie wondered if those important matters involved working the Gracers case or dealing with her disease.

As expected, the drive took close to five hours and had traffic not been so light, Derek could have easily imagined the drive taking closer to six. As they neared Tallahassee, they turned off Route 19, onto Route 98 and made their way towards Port Leon and Brian Hilton's lodge. The closer they drew to the lodge, the fewer cars they saw. During the final stretch of twenty miles, Derek saw only one motorcycle, a Ford F-250 trailering a thirty-foot trailer, a twenty-four foot, white box truck and three nondescript cars. It seemed the lodge was in a rather remote and secluded area.

"They're turning here?" Derek questioned, following Detective Gonzales as she turned down a narrow, tree-lined dirt road. "Looks more like a trail than a driveway. Figured this lodge of Hilton's would have a custom brick-lined driveway."

The hard-packed driveway wound its way over low rolling hills, twisting its sinuous path for nearly a quarter of a mile before reaching the single-story, yet very expansive log cabin.

"Not the view I was expecting," Nikkie said as she took in the view of the area.

"It's more of a hunting lodge than anything else," Jessica said, after noticing the disappointed look on Nikkie's face. "A place away from it all, I suppose. Brian's not much of a hunter. At least, not that I knew about."

There were two other cars parked near the lodge, both Mercedes and neither one belonging to Brian Hilton. Before the team could reach the front porch steps, the main door of the lodge swung open. Out walked two men, both dressed in thousand dollar suits, both well overdressed for the heat and the occasion.

"Unless you've had some remarkably successful reconstructive surgery," one the overdressed men said to Nikkie, "I'd say you are not Maryanne Jenkins."

Derek stepped forward, introduced himself and each member of his party.

"Maryanne was unable to join us. And you would be?"

"Someone whose name is unimportant," the man said. "Let's just get this charade of an investigation going so that we can get it over and done with." He looked over Derek's shoulder and directly at Jessica. "Time to put this puppy to sleep, doncha think, Derek?"

If Derek had declined to take Jessica's case, he wouldn't have thought about her, her case or the events which had brought him to Tampa for more than a few seconds on the plane ride home to Columbus. He might be interested to hear how the case turned out, but wouldn't even go as far as to ask Nikkie to check her news stream to see if the case ever went to court and if a verdict had been reached.

He wouldn't be interested enough to invest the energy.

It wasn't that he was cold or uncaring. The exact opposite was more the case. Derek gave everything he had to every one of his clients, squeezing out thoughts or concerns for cases he didn't take. He knew in order to give his "all," he had to cut off other concerns. That usually meant divorcing himself from caring about rejected clients.

But Jessica *was* his client. He *had* accepted her case. So when the overdressed man standing on the porch of Hilton's lodge tossed a probable insult at Jessica, Derek took it personally. He double stepped up the stairs, putting himself belly to belly with the man whose name was unimportant.

"Funny you should mention dogs," Derek began. "Because finding which dog shit on carpets is my specialty."

There was a stare down, lasting no more than ten-seconds, before Detective Gonzales joined Derek on the deck.

"Okay, boys. It's too damn hot out here. Let's get this investigation started so we can figure out which dog needs to be put in the kennel, shall we?"

"Wait a minute," Nikkie said. "Isn't someone from the DA's office supposed to be here with us? Something about 'full disclosure'?"

"The DA's office has waived its right to be represented in your snipe hunt," the other overdressed man said. Derek figured his name was equally as unimportant as the fat, sweaty man standing off to the side of the door. "My associate and I," he said, gesturing to the man standing beside the door, "are here to protect the contents of Mr. Hilton's belongings. DA's office is aware of our presence and is expecting a full and detailed report of your walk-through from us by tomorrow morning."

"You lawyers?" Derek asked.

"Do we look like lawyers?" the fat, unnamed man said.

"You look like a few Ding Dongs away from a heart attack, since you asked."

"You look like you're one more smart-ass comment away from a busted face."

"Okay boys," Rachel Gonzales said. "There's a lot of work to be done. Either you two agree to hate each other but end your little pissing match, or I'll make one of you sit in my car till we're done here. And I'm not sure I'll keep the air conditioning running."

The overdressed man—who must have been at least sixty pounds overweight and was beginning to pour sweat from his hairline as if sprayed with a hose—smiled a broad smile. He stepped aside, gestured with a sweep of his hand towards the front door of the lodge, and said, "Be my guest. Just know, my associate and I will be behind you every step of the way."

"Great," Derek said. "Nothing I need to see inside. I'll let my client guide our forensics specialists through the lodge, since she knows her way around so well, and I'll hit the trails. Which one of you fat asses is planning on joining me for a little hike?"

•   •   •   •   •

Derek headed out alone on the trail, after Jessica told him which trail and which direction she believed Brian had taken during his two runs. The two overdressed and over-fed men, neither of whom Derek believed he would ever share a scotch with, decided their services, whatever those services were supposed to be, were better delivered inside the air conditioned lodge.

Based on Jessica's recollection, Brian's runs each lasted around forty to fifty minutes. Considering the rough condition of the path, the exposed tree roots, numerous areas where there were more rocks than smooth dirt on the path, Derek figured Brian's pace was at most six miles per hour. That meant if he ran for fifty minutes—twenty-five out and twenty-five back—he would have made it around two and half miles before turning around. The forensics specialist suggested he needed at least two hours, assuming there was enough evidence to collect, to complete his duties inside the cabin.

Plenty of time for Derek.

He didn't pay much attention to his surroundings for the first mile of his hike. He figured if Brian had discarded any important evidence, he wouldn't have done so till he was at least a mile from his lodge.

When Derek reached what he figured to be the one-mile point of his hike, he slowed his pace. He started paying close attention to the ground, the trees and the general lay of the land. He wasn't exactly sure what he was looking for but trusted his instincts that he'd know what to notice for when he found it. Unfortunately for Derek, and more so for his client, there was nothing on the trail or in the general area of it which sparked his interest.

The closest the trail had come to the main road heading into the lodge was well over a hundred yards. He was hoping to find a spot where the trail and road were close, creating an easy and convenient location for Brian to have met with his accomplice, exchanged Jessica's gun for a replica and possibly exchanged information. He wanted to come across an obvious place where a careless participant in Sam Gracers' murder may have dropped evidence. If Brian had met with someone during his runs on the trail, Derek had no clue as to where that spot was. Still, he ventured off the trail near the area the trail and road were the closest, scoured the ground for clues and came up empty.

He headed back to the lodge, disappointed but not entirely surprised at his lack of luck.

He was less than a few hundred yards from the lodge when he heard the yelling. A woman was screaming, near the top of her lungs. He didn't hear screams of terror but of anger. Of accusations. Of possible despair.

Derek doubled his pace and was soon had line of sight of the lodge. Jessica Gracers was standing beside Derek's rental car, yelling at the two overdressed men standing on the lodge's deck. In response to Jessica's yells, the two men stood smiling, occasionally nodding their heads in exaggerated, mocking agreement. Nikkie was trying to guide Jessica into the car and was standing, facing Jessica, with one hand on the frame of the open rear seat of the car and the other on Jessica's shoulder.

"Problem here?" Derek asked when he reached within a few yards of Jessica.

Jessica turned sharply towards Derek, her face streamed with tears. Her eyes widened as if she had seen something which had either terrified or enraged her. Derek assumed the look was one of rage.

"They cleaned everything! Everything is different. Those bastards," she said as she pointed a shaky hand and extended finger towards the two men standing on the porch, "got rid of everything inside."

It was clear to Derek, Jessica wasn't in the proper frame of mind for him to get details.

"Get inside the car, shut your mouth and calm the hell down," he said.

Jessica, perhaps shocked at Derek's dismissiveness, grew instantly still and quiet. She said, in a much more controlled and quiet voice, "Everything is new. Everything is gone."

Seeing the change in his client, Derek asked, "What the hell are you talking about? What's gone? What's new?"

"They took the old couch out and now there's a new one in there. New bed, new area rugs, new everything in the bathroom. Every piece of furniture inside was replaced."

"The place is spotless," the forensics specialist added as he walked up closer to Derek. "Smells of bleach, too. I tested a few areas in the kitchen and bathroom but don't hold out any hope. Whoever cleaned in there, did one hell of a job."

Derek turned and walked towards the lodge. He walked up the three steps to the deck where the two full-bellied men blocked his path.

"This little circus is over," one man said. "Your puppy's outburst has been duly noted. Time for you to pull up stakes and caravan back home."

"You like the circus, huh?" Derek said. "Let me guess, your mom was the fat lady? Thought you looked familiar."

Rachel Gonzales appeared by Derek's side almost the second after he had finished dishing out his insult.

"Seriously, boys?" she said. "Let's break it up." She took Derek's arm, gripping him right above his right elbow. She had a firm grip, firmer than Derek expected. Firm enough to distract his attention away from the fat lady's offspring.

"You go inside?" he asked Gonzales without moving his eyes from the man in front of him.

"I did," Rachel said. "Looks all new and clean to me. Nothing to see inside.

Let's go back."

"How many of our side went inside?"

"All of us," Rachel answered, a bit confused with Derek's odd question.

"The number. How many went inside, not counting these two inflated assholes?"

"Me, Jessica, Nikkie and the whatever the hell the forensics guy's name is."

"Four. Right? Four of us walked inside. Got a lay of the place. Probably took a bunch of pictures?"

"Yes, but…"

"Warrant allowed us five people. I'm the fifth."

The two men looked at each other, smiled then stepped from Derek's approach through the front door.

"Be our guest," one said. "We certainly don't want to obstruct justice."

But before Derek could take a step towards the door, Rachel increased her grip on his arm and pulled him to the side. She dragged him nearly all the way across the front of the porch, stopping only when the wrap around porch made a slow arch to the side of the log cabin.

"Is there a reason you're dragging me across the porch?" Derek said.

"Listen to me, and please listen good. There is no reason for you to go inside. All it will do is piss you off. Trust me, trust Nikkie, and trust your client. The place was scrubbed clean and all the furniture was replaced. There's nothing to see inside."

It may have been the way Rachel had said *"inside"* that caught Derek's attention.

"Well I just walked a few miles outside and there's nothing to see outside either. What are you trying to tell me?"

"We should leave. All of us. Let's get out of here, find a place to eat and discuss what happened at this lodge."

"I don't even know you," Derek said, relaxing his body, "but I'm going to trust you on this one."

"Thanks. I need you to do two things for me."

"And they are?"

"One, get Fred Amasini to leave on his own."

"Who the hell is Fred Amasini?" Derek asked.

"The forensic specialist I just spent five incredibly boring hours driving up here with. I swear, the man may be good at what he does, but he is the least interesting man in the world."

"Okay. I'll tell him his services are no longer needed for the time being. I'll let him drive my car back to Tampa. I'll need you to take me to wherever he leaves it."

"Fine. No problem. What's the second thing you need me to do?"

"I told you there's nothing to see inside the house, right?"

"That you did."

"When you walk down the steps, take a look at the ground to your left. Near the shrubs."

Chapter 14

It was close to three in the afternoon before Fred Amasini reluctantly agreed to drive Derek's rental car back to his home outside Tampa alone.

"Five hour drive is a long time for someone as tired as me to be driving alone," he was saying as Derek closed the car door on him. He didn't have anything against Fred; he just no longer needed his area of specialty. Add to that his intense interest in sitting down with Rachel to learn what she had felt was so important to discuss.

Nikkie and a quite distraught Jessica Gracers climbed into the back of Rachel's county-issued Chevy Caprice, while Derek took the passengers seat.

"Did you see it?" Rachel said as she put the car in gear and headed back down the driveway. "Did you see what was in the shrubs?"

"A blue shoe cover. Cloth. The type doctors wear."

"And moving men. And anyone who doesn't want to track dirt or mud into a house."

"Well," Derek said, "considering Jessica said all the furniture in the place was new, it really doesn't surprise me that one of the delivery men accidentally left a shoe cover behind. What's the big deal?"

"How many cars did you pass during the last twenty miles driving here?" Rachel asked as they neared the end of the driveway.

"Didn't keep count. Noticed a few, I suppose."

"Notice the white panel truck?"

"As a matter of fact, I did. You're thinking the movers finished moving in all the old furniture right before we arrived."

"And taking out the old furniture," Nikkie said.

"You didn't happen to catch the license plate, did you?" Rachel asked as a smile played across her lips.

Derek twisted his body in the seat towards Rachel.

"Why, Detective Gonzales, I think you trying to tell me something."

"It was an Alabama plate. Commercial. I have a strange thing with plates and remembering them."

"You call it in yet?" Derek asked.

"Sure did. And based on my information I received just a few minutes before you finished your little nature walk, I have a pretty good idea where that truck is headed."

"Brilliant!" Nikkie said. "Absolutely brilliant."

"The old furniture," Jessica said, after a bit of a delay. "The old furniture will be on that truck. Right?"

"Unless they burned it somewhere on Hilton's property. You didn't notice any smoldering leather couches during your nature walk, did you Private Investigator Cole?"

"I prefer 'Freelance Detective,' and, no, no smoldering leather couches, mattresses, rugs or anything one might expect to find in a lodge."

"So, where are we headed and what are we planning to do when we get there?" Nikkie asked.

"Dothan, Alabama. I have the address of the moving company. Small firm named 'Southern Boy's Moving Company.' One of the deputies back at my station is contacting the local cops in the area. I expect to hear back from them soon. They have at least two hours head start on us, meaning the truck is probably damn close to Dothan by now. The deputy is asking the local cops to contact me as soon as they see the truck arrive at the moving company's parking area.

"I highly doubt Hilton told the movers to destroy the furniture. That would have been a red flag for them. Not that movers for a company called 'Southern Boys Moving Company' would give two shits about red flags, but, if Hilton went through the trouble of getting all new furniture delivered just in time before we showed up, I'm thinking he wouldn't do anything else to raise suspicions."

"So," Nikkie started, "when we get there, then what? We can't just demand to see the furniture in the back of the truck. Plus, we sent our forensics specialist home."

"We get a judge to issue a warrant for us to take possession of the furniture," Derek said. "Actually, Maryanne will need to handle that."

"So?" Rachel said, "Why aren't you calling Maryanne Jenkins yet?"

•　　•　　•　　•　　•

Rachel pulled the car into a truck stop just south of the Alabama border. The place seemed buzzing with activity. More cars than trucks in the parking areas.

"Busy place," Derek said as he climbed out of the car.

"This truck stop is well known in the area. Big place for gay men to connect."

"Like a pick up place?"

"More like a place for members of the gay community to get together to talk, meet, share the challenges of being a gay man in the south."

"Can't say I know much about the gay culture but I would have thought a truck stop wouldn't be the most accepting place for gay people to use as a community hall."

"Did cause plenty of trouble at first. But after a while, the community kept growing and wasn't going to be bullied into staying away."

"Economic boom for the place's owner, I'd bet."

"I'm sure that helped the owner grow more accommodating."

Derek asked Nikkie to call Maryanne about getting a warrant for the furniture in the truck. He sensed they she and Maryanne had formed a closer working relationship than he had formed with Maryanne. While Nikkie was explaining what they'd found at the lodge and the details of the missing furniture, Rachel received a call from a police officer from the Dothan Police Department.

"We're all set," Rachel said as she ended her phone call. "They have two squad cars at two different locations, looking for the truck. Turns out Southern Boys Moving Company is run out of the two owner's homes. The truck will end up at one of their houses soon. The officer will call me as soon as the truck arrives. Any luck with Maryanne?"

"There may be a problem," Nikkie answered. "Since the moving truck with the possible evidence in the back is crossing state lines, getting a search and seize warrant is a matter for the feds. Maryanne is making some calls, but isn't hopeful she can get this turned around all that quickly."

"Then we sit and watch the truck until the feds come through with the warrant."

"Well, Derek, if things with the feds take as long as most things with the feds do, waiting and watching will be a problem for me. I need to be back on duty tomorrow by nine."

"How many hours back to your department?" Derek asked.

"Depending on traffic, I'd say around seven."

"We'll give you an hour buffer. If we get nothing from the feds by one, you head back and I'll stay."

"We'll stay," Jessica said. "That furniture and whatever evidence we find on it, is my way out of this horrible mess. I'm not leaving till we do whatever it is we need to do to clear my name."

• • • • •

Finding the moving truck was easy. Simple, actually. An officer from the Dothan Police Department spotted the truck pulling off the main highway leading into the city. He followed the truck through the city and parked behind it when the truck driver and his passenger climbed down from the cab. The officer instructed the men to leave the contents of the truck untouched and that there would be "people from Florida" showing up to take possession of whatever was in the back of the truck. The truck driver and his passenger simply nodded in cooperation, then walked into the house.

Simple.

Things got more complicated when Derek, Nikkie, Rachel and Jessica arrived.

As Rachel exited the car to speak with the Dothan Police Officer, Nikkie called Maryanne to tell her they were at the scene with the truck and to ask about any progress getting a warrant.

"Nothing yet," Maryanne had told her. "And I have a feeling getting the warrant is going to take a while."

"We may not have a while," Derek commented. "I have a bad feeling those brothers are making phone calls right now."

As Nikkie ended the call, the truck driver and his partner walked out of the house. They walked directly to the truck. When the driver pulled the keys out of his front pocket, Derek shot out of the car.

"You boys planning on going somewhere?"

Neither man answered. They continued towards the moving truck.

"Hold it right there, gentlemen," the Dothan cop called out. "I have orders to make sure this truck stays exactly where it is and that nothing is removed from the back."

"Y'all need to see my driver's license, or my proof of ownership?" the driver asked.

The driver was in his mid-twenties; greasy hair, greasy black t-shirt and a brown-tooth of a smile. He spit out a load of brown saliva.

"My brother and I have more work that needs to be done and the people paying us have given us what they call a 'deadline.' So, pardon my lack of respect for you, officer, but our client has informed us that unless you have a warranty to show us, we are free to finish our duties."

"You mean a 'warrant'?" Derek asked.

"Whatever you want to call it. Y'all got one of them or, can my brother and me be on our way?"

"We're expecting to have a warrant any minute now," Rachel said.

"I am not a college educated man," the driver said, "but it sounded like you said you do not have either a warranty or a warrant on your person. Is that what I heard you say?"

"Do you know what you're hauling?" Derek asked.

The driver turned his tobacco stained smile towards Derek.

"Well, seeing as how my brother and me drove to where our client paid us to drive, and then loaded up the contents in this truck with our own hands, I'd have to say that we are aware of our haul. Ain't that right, Bobby? Ain't we aware of what we're hauling?"

"Yup," Bobby said. "We are aware."

Bobby looked like the polar opposite of his brother. He was clean shaven, wore his hair styled by a professional and not by a plastic comb and the clothes he wore, though a bit dirty from his day of manual labor, were well fitting and only a whisper away from what those familiar with "working class" fashion would describe as "current and sharp."

"I'm willing to bet neither of you gentlemen are aware of why we are interested in taking possession of the contents of your truck," Derek said, taking a few steps closer to the driver.

"Now that would be a very true statement. And what is also a true statement, is that we don't give a rat's ass about you or your interests." The driver turned towards the Dothan cop, and said, "Officer, are we free to go about our business?"

The cop shrugged his shoulders, looked at Detective Gonzales.

"Don't suppose you have the warrant yet?"

Rachel shook her head.

"Then, I'm afraid if these two Dothan citizens want to be on their way, nothing stopping them."

"How much?" Jessica, who had stepped out of the car to better hear the conversation, asked. "How much for whatever is in the back of your truck? Name your price. Five thousand? Ten? Name it?"

The driver smiled, glanced over at his brother. He kicked a few pebbles sitting at his feet. He pulled off his *"Roll Tide"* hat, scratched his head before answering.

"Thing is, we've already entered into an agreement, which included payment for us to keep everything in our possession. Now, you seem like a nice lady, so I can imagine you'd understand the importance of my brother and I keeping our word."

"Twenty-thousand dollars," Jessica said. "I'll write a check out for twenty-thousand if you just give us one hour to do what we need to do with the furniture in the back of your truck."

"Checks bounce."

"Mine don't."

The two men looked at each other, obviously considering Jessica's offer. After several moments, the driver started shaking his head.

"I think that hour would cause us to miss our deadline. We do thank you for your offer, but it's a 'no can do' on our part. We free to leave, Officer?" he asked the Dothan cop again.

"I suppose so."

•　　•　　•　　•　　•

They followed the moving truck north through the city. Though he had no way of being certain, Derek had the sinking feeling if Maryanne wasn't able to encourage the feds to "hurry the hell up," the furniture along with any and all evidence it contained, would soon be destroyed.

For nearly an hour, the truck headed north with a Dothan City Police car behind it and a Pinellas County issued, unmarked Chevy Caprice not far behind. Inside the Caprice, Derek and Nikkie were calling everyone they believed might be able to help them.

Derek spoke at length with Ralph Fox; a retired chief of police in a small, Upstate New York town whom Derek had met while working a case. The two had become friends once the case was closed and Derek often relied on Ralph's experience and wisdom when dealing with challenging situations.

"Now Derek," Ralph said after listening to Derek detail the complexity of the situation, "you call yourself a 'Freelance Detective,' still I assume?"

"Yes."

"Sounds to me like you're gonna need to go all freelance if that warrant from the feds doesn't come in."

"I'm with two cops. One is driving the car I'm in right now and the other is fifty feet in front us in his marked car. Not sure how they'd take me going freelance."

Rachel gave Derek a sideways look, frowned, then shook her head.

"Immediate feedback I've just received suggests the aforementioned members of the law enforcement community would not appreciate any freelancing activities on my part."

The sinking feeling in Derek's gut was getting worse.

Nikkie, who had called Maryanne Jenkins the second after the truck driver had started the engine, was sitting in silence, cell phone pressed to her ear and her eyes darting between the white moving truck and the car's clock. She was pleasantly surprised at how long the drive to wherever it was they were going was taking and dismayed at how long the feds were taking to deliver the much needed warrant.

After they had been following the moving truck for a little over an hour, the truck made a left hand turn onto a dirt road. "Private Property. No Trespassing," signs were posted on either side of the dirt road. The truck pulled up past the signs, then, after stopping, the driver climbed down from the cab.

"Stay inside," Rachel instructed.

She climbed out of the Caprice, walked over to where the driver was speaking with the Dothan City cop. Less than a minute later, Rachel walked back to the car.

"We can't follow any further. The two moron's family owns the land, including the road we're on. The driver told the Dothan cop he expects him to enforce Alabama's private property laws. Cop agreed. Told me we're free to park on the side of the main road but not to step foot on any privately owned land."

Twenty minutes later, from the air conditioned Chevy Caprice, Derek, Nikkie, Jessica and Rachel Gonzales saw black smoke rising in angry twists from several hundred yards down the private road.

"Holy shit balls," Derek said. "They're burning it all."

*   *   *   *   *

"Now what? Now what the hell do we do?"

Jessica was leaning against the front bumper of the car, watching what was certainly the furniture from Brian Hilton's lodge going up in smoke, along with her hopes of getting her name cleared. Her emotions were checked; not showing anger, despair, hope or any emotion besides that which one who feels time is working against them displays.

"I think you three should find the nearest gas station and fast food place. Fill up and get us some food for the long drive back to Tampa."

"You're not including yourself in your suggested plan," Rachel said. "Any reason for that?"

"Because I don't want to put any of you into a compromised situation."

Nikkie walked close to Derek, looked him in the eyes, and said, "What are you thinking?"

"Be nice to know what those two are burning back there, wouldn't it? Be even nicer if we could take possession of anything not burned up already."

"I don't want to hear anymore," Rachel said. "If you really want to stand here on the road, waiting for the brothers to drive back down their private driveway so you can ask them what they burned, then I can't stop you. In fact, I'm out of my jurisdiction as it is." Rachel jiggled the car keys in her hands. "Come on, ladies. Let's fill up and get some food for the drive home. We should be back in about an hour, Derek. Think that's okay for you?"

"I hear fast food places down south aren't as fast as they are up north. Better plan on an hour and a half."

*   *   *   *   *

There weren't enough trees or shrubs to ensure he'd have a place to hide in case a car, or a specific truck, worked its way down the pitted, hard-packed dirt driveway, but Derek wasn't worried about hiding. If the brothers came tooling down the driveway, saw him and decided to dish out the type of hospitality southern Alabamans like to show trespassers, he was ready to demonstrate some of the self-defense hospitalities the Army had drilled into him. He was angry; not only at the two brothers but also about feeling that his client was in trouble. With Brian Hilton denying her alibi and with any potential physical evidence, which would have proven that Jessica was with Hilton in his lodge probably reduced to ashes, Derek was struggling to come up with a logical next move in the investigation.

As he walked on the left hand side of the driveway towards the rising black smoke, he admitted he was acting without any real plan. When he reached the end of the driveway, saw what the brothers were burning, what was he going to do? *"Piss on the fire and hope to save one of the couch pillows?"* Or maybe he'd discover the brothers overlooked the mattress and he'd be able to sneak into the truck and haul the mattress out to the road where Rachel would be more than happy to tie it onto the roof of her car. The truth was, he wasn't expecting to see anything at the end of the driveway and he wasn't expecting to do anything, either. He just didn't think he could sit in a car with his client for five hours after not trying to do anything.

For Derek, not trying was worse than failing miserably. To fail, you had to at least try.

He saw a ramshackle house—single story, weathered with a deeply sagging roof—as he turned what he assumed was the final turn of the driveway. The yard surrounding the house had that "run to riot" appearance often seen at places where homeowners stopped caring. The condition of the house suggested it hadn't seen a resident in quite a long time.

Off to his right, Derek saw two things that piqued his interest. The first was a pile of new lumber, enough two-by-fours and four-by-fours to frame a new house. The lumber was stacked neatly, covered with a series of patched-together blue tarps.

"Renovations or a new build?" Derek thought.

The second thing Derek noticed was what the lumber was placed next to. A newly constructed steel pole barn. Had to be at least forty-by-eighty. Fifteen foot, double garage doors, gleaming in white facing directly at the run down house. On the side of the pole barn facing away from the house, was an entry door. Derek made his way to the door.

The door was opened. Inside, a long stretch of overhead lights in three rows ran the length of the pole barn. The middle strip of lights was turned on; giving Derek enough light to visually inventory the inside of the barn. He walked inside, grateful to be out of potential view of the brothers. He stood looking around the pole barn and wishing he had more time to explore what was inside. He moved back towards the door. He noticed a key ring hanging from a rusty nail to the left of the door. On the ring were two keys. Both looked the same and both looked like keys used to open doors. Long, squared at the end. Deep channel running up the middle. He peered out through the door, saw the brothers busily emptying the back of the moving truck. He grabbed the key ring and worked one of the keys free. He stuck it in his pocket, just in case.

He stepped out of the barn, after checking to make sure no one was keeping an eye on the open door, then slipped back into the cover of the trees.

Parked behind the neglected ranch home, off to the left, was the moving truck. It was parked facing the driveway, meaning the lift gate was closest to a pile of burning debris. The flames weren't very high, he judged them to be reaching no more than eight feet above the pile of mostly charred and reduced to ash pile of fuel, but the smoke billowing out from the pyre was as black as death. It coiled up in a lazy cyclone.

The two brothers were standing with their backs towards Derek. Both were simply watching the fire as if at a backyard bonfire and the contents on the fire were nothing more than some pine logs felled the previous season. He wondered if the brothers knew the importance of the furniture they had assembled into a pile, soaked with gasoline and set a match to. If they did, and if Hilton turned out to be guilty in Sam Gracers' murder, they'd both be looking at prison time for obstruction of justice.

But they probably had no idea. Hilton most likely hired them to deliver furniture he had purchased from a Dothan area furniture store, far enough away from Tallahassee so as to not raise any future suspicions, and haul away the old furniture. Derek imagined the brothers calling Hilton, or whomever Hilton had hired to make the furniture purchase and to hire the brothers for a day's labor, and telling him about the two cops and three other people parked outside the house where they had parked the moving truck. The brothers were probably offered an extra few thousand to make sure the furniture was destroyed well ahead of the feds coming through with the warrant.

"Just two good ole' boys making a living," he thought as he started backing his way towards the road. *"Probably made more money in one day than they had in any month of their lives up to today."* But Derek knew that wasn't the case. He knew, based on what he'd seen in the pole barn that he'd cross paths with the brothers again before he closed the Jessica Gracers case.

He was back at the end of the driveway thirty minutes into the ninety minutes he told Detective Gonzales he needed.

.　　.　　.　　.　　.

"You don't look like someone who accomplished anything exciting," Rachel Gonzales said as Derek sat in the passenger's seat beside her.

"Couch, mattress and box spring, a load of sheets, pillows, towels and two area rugs; all burned. All soon to be nothing but a pile of ashes."

"Son of a bitch," Nikkie scowled from the backseat. "I thought we had Hilton dead to rights."

"Man like that," Derek said, "a millionaire with enough people willing to kiss his ass for the chance at earning favor with him, is one tough SOB to have nailed so easily. I should have gone up to the lodge alone. Shouldn't have told anyone. Just me, a camera and a way to collect evidence."

"And then every last piece of evidence you may have found would have been inadmissible in court," Rachel said. "He had too much time to clean out the lodge. Way too much time. Nothing we could have or should have done differently."

The way Rachel was talking, the words she was using and her obvious interest in Brian Hilton told Derek he had been spot on with his initial impression of her. She may not yet fully believe in Jessica's innocence; there were still too many open questions, but it was clear she wasn't dismissing Jessica's alibi and Hilton's possible involvement. And after Rachel asked a question to Jessica about what, if anything, happened during her and Brian's drive back from the lodge, Derek's remaining doubts about Rachel evaporated.

"We made one stop," Jessica answered Rachel. "I didn't notice it at first, but Brian started getting nervous about a green SUV he believed was following us. I remember he kept looking in his rear view mirror, like he saw something he couldn't quite understand. After a while, maybe fifteen minutes, his body language changed. He seemed nervous, stiff. I asked him if something was wrong. He told me, in a very calm voice, that he thought we were being followed. I looked in the side mirror and did see an SUV behind us, but I have no idea how long it had been there."

"Did you notice the plates?" Rachel asked.

"No. Looking at license plates isn't in my normal list of things to do."

"So, what happened?" Rachel was pressing Jessica. She seemed anxiously hopeful Jessica's story provided a clue. Something she could use to further solidify her belief of Jessica's innocence.

"Brian kept driving for another twenty minutes or so, and kept looking in the mirror. I was getting very nervous, more for him than for me. He had more to lose than I did. After a while, he saw a convenience store up ahead. He pulled around to the side, kept the car running. He got out of the car and walked around to the front of the store. He was gone maybe five or six minutes. When he came back, he seemed much more relaxed. He sat down, told me his paranoia must have gotten the better of him. He said the SUV did pull into the same convenience store as we did, but the driver was a man he'd never seen before. He said the SUV driver pulled up to the pump, filled up and left without giving Brian a single glance."

"So, that was it?" Rachel asked, her voice dripping with obvious disappointment and, perhaps, a trace of contempt.

"I guess so. He did suggest that I use the bathroom to freshen up a bit."

"You walked into the store?" Derek said. "If so, there'll be security footage."

Jessica sighed. "No, not into the store. The bathrooms were on the side of the store. Almost right in front of where he parked. I just ran in quickly while he did something with my phone."

"What do you mean? He did what with your phone?" Rachel was back to being anxious.

"Well, he said I should wipe out my history from my…I don't know…my location tracker, I think? Does that make sense?"

Nikkie jumped into the conversation.

"Where was your phone? In your purse or on your body?"

"In my purse."

"Did he know that?"

"I guess so. He picked it up from the backseat, told me it would only take a few minutes to clean out my phone. He bet me he'd be done with my phone before I was done in the bathroom."

"And I bet when you got back into the car, your purse was sitting on the backseat again." It wasn't a question Nikkie presented.

"Yes. Why?"

Rachel glanced at Derek first, then, using the rear view mirror, shot Nikkie a knowing smile.

"Because, if everything you told us so far is the truth," Rachel said to Jessica, "Hilton swapped the gun he gave you at the lodge with your real gun. The one he borrowed from you the first day he went for his run. The gun that killed your husband. He made the switch back when you were in the bathroom."

"And I bet the driver of the green SUV was following you two," Nikkie offered. "Except he wasn't following you to catch you and Brian doing something you shouldn't have been doing"

"Timeline all fits now" Derek said. "If the driver of the green SUV did give Hilton your actual gun, the murder weapon, then it puts Hilton front and center in this murder investigation."

It was clear Jessica was struggling to wrapher head around everything being said in the car. She was tired, scared about her future, grieving for her husband and probably a bit heartbroken over Brian Hilton.

"So, Brian borrows my gun when he goes for a run on Saturday. But the gun he gives back to me after his run wasn't really mine?"

"How close did you inspect the gun when he returned it to you?" Derek asked.

"Not at all. Just had Brian put it back in my purse. I never use the thing. I only carry it when I remember to. Haven't even fired it in at least a year."

"Rachel," Derek said as he turned slightly to face Detective Gonzales, "Jessica's gun? Locked in the evidence room, I assume?"

"Has to be. This really isn't my case, so I didn't witness it being logged, tagged and locked away. But that's the only place it could be."

"We need Maryanne to have the gun inspected for prints. Probably a long shot. But if Hilton or whoever did the shooting left a print on the gun, Jessica's alibi gets a whole lot stronger."

• • • • • •

The car was silent for a long stretch of highway. The bag of Taco Bell sat near Derek's feet; growing cold and filling the car with a smell only greasy fast food can generate. A few times, Nikkie asked a few questions to Jessica about any other place she and Brian had gotten together.

"Any place besides a hotel or public place. Your house? His house? An apartment you may have? Anywhere?"

"Hotels, for the most part. Really, only hotels till he suggested he go to his lodge last weekend. Never in my or his house."

"You said you two had sex on the way up to the lodge," Nikkie's voice revealed her excitement. "You two repeat that event on the drive back from the lodge?"

"Doesn't matter if they did," Derek said, knowing the track Nikkie was taking. "We'd need a warrant to inspect his car."

"Meaning he'd have time to arrange a fiery accident with his car." Jessica sounded defeated, as if the walls of whichever prison she was likely to be sent to were beginning to close in around her.

Derek reached down, opened the Taco Bell bag, pulled out a taco and took a bite that made half the taco disappear.

"If the gun was wiped of prints, we may need to turn our attention away from Hilton. Unless you all can come up with another avenue of approach, he's a dead end."

"Won't the fact he borrowed my gun prove anything?"

"Circumstantial, at best," Nikkie said. "With Hilton denying every part of your alibi, him borrowing your gun would be a matter of he said, she said. The fact he already denied he was with you that weekend, makes him borrowing your gun an impossible event. He couldn't borrow something from you if he wasn't with you."

Derek, who finished his first taco and was ready to attack the second, said, "And, no offense, but people are less likely to believe the word of someone accused of murder than they are some rich, white guy."

"Then…if the gun was wiped clean…what defense do I have?"

"That's why you're paying Nikkie and me. To find your defense. We're not going to create one out of thin air, but, if you're innocent, we'll find your defense. Honestly, I'm not holding out any hope that we'll find any other prints on your gun but yours. And I didn't think we'd find anything at the lodge, either."

"Then why the hell did we waste an entire day driving there? You could have been investigating other things."

"Two reasons," Derek said. "One, there's nothing else to investigate on your case, yet. Two, I needed to make Brian Hilton sweat a little. Turns out, he sweated a whole lot. He's nervous as shit, right now. That's for damn sure. And nervous people sometimes make mistakes. Nervous people who are guilty of murder always make mistakes."

Jessica said, "You think he's sweating? Are you kidding me? He denies everything, gets rid of any trace of me being at his lodge and probably has the best lawyers in the country on retainer, just waiting to jump into action. He's not one to sweat; he's one who prepares. And why the hell do you keep saying *if* I'm innocent? If you think I killed Sam, then I don't need your services a second longer." Her anger was building slowly, like a steam engine, the pressure was rising. "As a matter of fact, you said to me over dinner yesterday that I killed my husband. You said I may not have pulled the trigger, but that I killed him." The pressure had reached the point of explosion. Jessica was yelling at Derek in a high-pitched, hatred and anger driven voice. "So, once and for all, do you think I killed Sam or not? If you do, then you're fired. If not, then, for God's sake, stop suggesting I may not be innocent."

Derek was quiet for several seconds. The air in the car was charged with nervous energy, as Rachel and Nikkie waited with their emotions held in abeyance for Derek's reply.

"You said Sam's and Brian's boss, FJ, ran a tight ship, right?"

Derek's response was unexpected, causing Jessica to swallow her anger and force herself to think outside of her raging anger.

"Yes. Very tight. As far as I know. I only heard him speak a couple of times and neither Sam or Brian talked about him much."

"But you knew enough, or at least you believe you knew enough, to say Brian's position would be in jeopardy if FJ found out about the affair you and

Brian were having?"

"Yes. I don't understand where you're going with this."

"You knew having an affair with Brian put him in a compromised situation. Probably put your husband in a potentially tough spot as well. But you had the affair anyway, didn't you?"

"That's…It's not like I planned to fall for Brian. Sam and I…our marriage was, I don't know…falling apart. Slowly. Painfully. I felt so lonely. The thing with Brian just happened."

"Lot of people in the world. Lots of men. Most of who don't work for this FJ guy, but you chose one of the seven people in the world who do work for him. You chose to put Brian and your husband at risk. You said Sam reacted pretty emotionally when he heard about a guy who FJ fired was found murdered. Don't you think your husband may have been wondering if FJ was somehow involved in that guy's death?"

Jessica's anger was melting into humiliation. Into a deeper sense of guilt.

"I'm sure he was," she said in low, weak voice.

"You probably wondered about it as well. You saw how Sam responded. That had an effect on you. You don't trust FJ and probably think he's capable of almost anything. You even suggested FJ's speciality is arranging murders. So, you asked me what I think. I'm gonna tell you. You didn't murder your husband, but your affair with Brian did. That means, you caused the death of your husband."

Chapter 15

Brian Hilton went to bed a little after eleven the night before Jessica Gracers team of investigators went up to his lodge. He figured he wouldn't be able to get much sleep. The DA, Julia Steinberg, had stopped by around eight that evening, telling him a judge had issued a warrant for the search of his lodge and for the collection and seizure of evidence. He had thanked her, almost dismissing any concern of the news she delivered, then, as soon as the DA was pulling her car out of his driveway, he went to work.

He had several people who had completed sensitive jobs for him in the past: Men who understood the value of a hard earned buck and realized when those bucks were in an abundant supply, expediency and secrecy were part of the job.

He dialed a number from his cell.

"Place needs to be spotless. You understand? Spotless. Couch, area rugs, towels, sheets, pillows, mattress, chairs, everything needs to be gone."

"You know how good we can be when properly motivated."

"I don't want the place barren. Everything gets replaced. Top shelf shit. Don't go to some chain furniture store, thinking it will have time and money. Do it right. All the way. Every detail."

"Got it. You use a cleaning service down there?"

"Can't use them. Find some off the radar cleaners. Don't hire anyone established. Find some illegals, just make sure they're damn thorough."

"Got it. Time frame?"

"You're on the clock as soon as we hang up. Everything needs to be done by one tomorrow. One-thirty at the absolute latest."

"That is one hell of a tight time frame, considering we have to buy all new stuff, move it down to your place and take everything out. Damn tight time frame."

"I'll pay you enough for you to make time stand still. Figure it out. Make it happen."

There was one snag; an issue that cost him an additional $50,000. It was a small price to pay but a large enough price to make sure Jessica Gracers didn't outbid him. His hired hands confirmed his investment was well spent by sending him a video of the pile of his furniture burning. He watched the video a couple of times, making a visual inventory of each piece of furniture he remembered being in his lodge.

Brian Hilton ended up sleeping much better than he expected.

CHAPTER 16

August 21

"So, what's the plan for today?"

Nikkie and Derek were in the downstairs lobby of their hotel, drinking coffee and eating some less-than-fresh pastries from the complementary continental breakfast. Seems they had arrived during a convention, the Regional School Teacher's Union, which made the breakfast area much too crowded for them to find a seat.

"I'm going to tail Hilton for a few hours. See how he spends his day. If I get a chance, I'm going to talk to him as well. He probably won't say a word to me, but I need to make sure he doesn't think his stunt at his lodge crippled us." Derek took a long swallow of coffee, stood and gestured towards Nikkie's half-empty mug. "I need more coffee. You?"

"I'm fine,"

She watched him walk away, twisting his way through the crowded lobby and into the even more crowded breakfast area off of the hotel's lobby. She counted at least a dozen turned heads as he made his way to the coffee station; the female teachers in Florida, it seemed, had good taste in men. At six foot even, close enough to 200 pounds to call it even and an obviously well conditioned body, Derek had a "head-turning" physique. And Nikkie knew that when those heads turned and saw his strong face, dusty blonde hair and striking blue eyes, women's knees got shaky and their minds went racing to places they would never want their husbands or significant others to know about.

As she watched him fill his cup of coffee and while she noticed small groups of women begin to whisper to each other while looking at Derek, Nikkie felt a twinge of jealousy. She wondered how Lucy, Derek's dead wife, had dealt with the obvious interests other women held for her husband.

"Was Lucy jealous?"

"Come again?" Derek said as he sat down beside Nikkie on the padded windowsill. The morning Florida sun was already making its intentions for the day clear and was beating on their backs through the slightly tinted window.

"Lucy, was she a jealous woman?"

"Of me?" Derek said, his face twisted in a mixture of confusion and curiosity. "Not of me. Why are you asking?"

"You're thirty-eight, right?"

"For a little while longer, yes."

"You and Lucy were married when you were in your mid-twenties?"

Derek nodded his head, still wondering where Nikkie was taking this conversation.

"I was in the Army still. We were married when I was twenty-five. Still had a two years left of service."

"How did you look when you were married? I mean, you're still in great shape, amazing shape, actually, but seeing as how you were still in the Army, you probably were in even better condition."

Derek smiled a broad smile, showing his perfectly straight, white teeth.

"You're telling me I'm letting myself go, aren't you? Suggesting I need to lay off the cheeseburgers and scotch and spend more time in the gym, right?"

"Not at all. Just noticed that almost every woman in this lobby is checking you out. They watched you walking towards them when you went to get coffee and they watched you walk away from them. Now, they're checkin' you out sitting next to me. If you, at thirty-eight years old, still have the ability to turn every head in a place," Nikkie paused, breathed deeply through her nose then slowly shook her head, "then I feel bad for Lucy."

"I don't notice stuff like that," Derek said, nodding his head sideways towards the center of the crowded lobby. "Doesn't really mean anything to me. Sure, I get propositioned once in a while, but it's just not my style. When I was with Lucy, she knew I was only interested in her."

"And now?"

"I'm only interested in finding out where you and I end up, not in whether other women want to spend time with me." He smiled again. "That sounded a little conceited, didn't it?"

"Based on the looks you're getting, I'd say you are spot on accurate."

There was a long, somewhat awkward silence between the two. Derek worked at his coffee while Nikkie, a woman from whom the feeling of jealousy was entirely foreign, darted her eyes around the lobby, occasionally meeting the eyes of one of Derek's admirers.

"We need to start having sex," she said without looking at Derek.

"May be a bit awkward with all these people around."

"Let's solve this damn case then take a little vacation. Just you and me. We deserve it after all we've been through."

"Fine with me," Derek said. "Have any place in mind?"

"I know this lodge south of Tallahassee. I have a feeling it will be up for sale or rent soon."

"I heard about that place. All new furniture and clean as a whistle."

Their laughter started out laden with nervousness but soon morphed into the type of laughter which brings people together. Their laughter, though it last only moments, pushed their past even further away from their minds and evaporated the stresses of the Gracers case.

"Okay," Nikkie said, now ignoring the continued lustful glances towards Derek that the teachers were still lobbing his way, "I know what you're doing today. Want to hear my plans?"

"Absolutely."

"Jessica said Brian and everyone at the FJ Company is in the business of buying and selling, right?"

"That's what she said."

"Real estate, businesses, everything."

"Yup."

"You can't buy so much as a cup of coffee without there being a trace of the transaction left behind. I'm going to do some research on Brian Hilton today. Probably on the whole FJ Company, but specifically on Brian Hilton's dealings."

"What are you looking for?"

"A reason for murder."

•   •   •   •   •

It was getting close to the end of August, meaning the final month of the third quarter was soon to start. For the year, Brian had delivered on his promised revenue numbers, but the fourth quarter—beginning in October and ending on the last day of December—was looking weak. He needed either two or three average-sized deals to flip or one whopper. Since the size of the deal really didn't alter the amount of work or persuasion needed — in fact the smaller deals often were more taxing — Brian settled on giving everything he had to one potential deal.

It was a big opportunity: Depending on how quickly he could acquire the targeted business, he could flip the business to already identified buyers by mid-December. But if the current owner wasn't motivated properly, or even worse, had weak decision making muscles, the identified buyers may send their interest and their capital elsewhere.

That would mean Brian would miss his quarter revenue promise and, more than likely, miss his yearly commitment. Both were wholly unacceptable possible outcomes.

"No time like the present to get things moving more quickly," he thought as he sat in his custom-made, leather desk chair, picked up his secure phone, and dialed a Tennessee area number.

"I'm hoping you have some good news for me, doctor," Brian said, feeling no need to introduce himself. "Pretty sure we discussed and agreed on having this wrapped up by the end of August."

"It's only mid-August," the doctor said.

"It's August twentieth. The fifteenth is mid August, not the twentieth."

"He's scheduled to come in tomorrow. I have the test results and I'll deliver them to him then. After that, my job is done."

"That's probably not true, and it bothers me you may actually believe it to be true. You deliver the results tomorrow, making damn sure you do so with impact. Then, when he asks for a second opinion, which we both know he will, you direct him to our partner. Then, our partner will send him back to you to have the conversation about treatment. So, doctor, your job is far from done."

"You can do your part of this agreement the second after he leaves my office. If you're as good at closing deals as you say you are, my job will be done. Hell, I may be able to start on another job for you before August ends."

"One at a time, doctor. One at a time." Brian paused, letting the doctor's imagined smile fade away. "How convincing is the report?"

"It's not only convincing, it's so specific he won't know where to get a second opinion. We'll force him our way."

"And you'll make the suggestion before he leaves your office?"

"Like the other one, I'll suggest he get his affairs in order. I wouldn't be surprised if he calls you on his way home from my office."

"That would be perfect. Didn't turn out that way last time, though, did it? Took longer than it should have."

"If I recall, the last time we worked together, things worked out well for you in the end."

"And for you, too. This one needs to go smoothly and quickly. Be convincing, doctor. And be impactful."

"A terminal cancer diagnosis usually is."

CHAPTER 17

Matt Steel didn't flinch at all. True to his surname, he sat with his face set as still and as cold as ice. As he sat on the visitor's side of his doctor's desk, Steel listened to his diagnosis, prognosis and suggested course of treatments.

"I'm sure this is hard for you to hear. It always is. And, I'm sure you're going to want a second opinion. I took the liberty of doing some research and I found a doctor who specializes in your type of cancer. He's outside of Tampa, which, I know isn't all that convenient, but he's the best in the south. I can have my office set up an appointment for you.

"Listen, Matt, I'm really sorry. I'll do whatever I can to help you through this and, honestly, I think you're going to be fine. But it's going to take everything you have. Treatment and recovery for this type of cancer is a real bear, and you're going to need all your focus on getting better. I can't make any decisions for you, but I can suggest you clear your calendar for the next six or nine months. At least. Maybe a year. The specialist in Tampa will know better.

"Go home, try to relax and figure out what's most important to you. I know your company is your baby, but, for considering the severity of your diagnosis, I think you should consider stepping aside and letting your son run the business for a while."

"My son has no interest in the business. I think I told you that."

"Probably did. Sorry. Someone else, maybe? Someone you trust?"

"Like I said, it's me or no one. I built it from the ground up and no one knows how to keep it running but me."

The doctor steepled his fingers, nodded his head, then took a long, deep breath in.

"Your health is what's important now."

"I know. And I know what I need to do. This specialist in Tampa? How quickly can you get me an appointment?"

"I'll have my office staff call him right now."

"Thanks, Doc."

"Go home. I'll call you personally when we have an appointment scheduled for you. You going to be able to be flexible with your schedule?"

Matt Steel nodded his head.

"I'll be damn flexible real soon."

"Good for you. You deserve to focus on yourself after how hard you've worked. And, before long, you'll be right back making your competition nervous again."

"We'll see about that. First things first. Thanks, Doc. Call me at home when everything is set up."

. . . . .

Doctor Timothy O'Connell walked his patient out of his personal office, through the waiting room, down the hall and right to the double exit doors. He held his face in a stern countenance the entire way. He stood and watched Matt Steel amble across the parking lot like a man who had just lost his best friend, watched him find his car and pull out of the medical complex before he turned and quickened his pace back to his office. He could hardly contain his excitement. If things went as they had the last time he partnered with Brian Hilton, Doctor Timothy O'Connell would be seeing a lot more zeros at the end of his offshore bank account.

He told his head nurse to cancel all of his one-on-one appointments scheduled for the rest of the day. He made his way to his private office and sat down after pouring himself a large tumbler of whiskey. O'Connell thought about calling Brian Hilton to let him know he should be expecting a call from Steel any minute now, but decided instead to keep hold of the upper hand he felt he possessed.

"Let that son of a bitch find out for himself," he said softly enough to ensure his spoken words didn't creep outside the walls of his office.

Timothy O'Connell assumed Hilton would want to partner with him at least one more time, which he was fine with. The first partnership yielded the good doctor over $350,000. If Hilton didn't screw up, the Steel partnership should almost double his take.

"One more time," he said in a whisper. "But next time, my fee will be enough to set me up for life."

He drained the whiskey, poured another, then began scanning his patient files for a possible third target.

He identified two possible targets. Both wealthy, in their mid-fifties and with a family history of cancer.

"Perfect candidates," he thought to himself. And if he had lived another week, he might have tried to run the "Hilton Scam" on his own. But of course, Doctor Timothy O'Connell was just a day away from the end of his life after he closed his computer down, finished his second double whiskey and decided to call it an early day.

Chapter 18

Snead Island, Florida may not have the allure Anna Maria Island claims, but those who call Snead Island home wouldn't trade a thing in exchange for the attraction Anna Maria has. Though the island is fairly heavily populated, with million dollar homes squeezed into small lots, the lack of tourists and renting transients makes the island more of a community. Neighbors know each other. Help one another out. Take care of each other.

It surprised Derek how easy it was for him to find Brian Hilton's address. Though it wasn't listed in any phone book, not that he could have found a phone book had he even attempted to look, a simple database search on his iPhone revealed a Snead Island address as belonging to Brian Hilton.

He parked outside Hilton's palatial home, sitting with the air conditioning blasting away in his rented Nissan Altima. He didn't care if Hilton noticed his car, grew suspicious and called the local authorities to have the car checked out. He would have preferred it, actually. If a cop car pulled up behind his car, Derek would know Hilton was home. For as it was, he had no idea if the house was empty or occupied.

At one point, Derek climbed out of his car and went for a walk, looking for the "library" Jessica told him about. He found the small, white painted case a quarter mile from Brian's house. He walked up to the case, which was nothing more than a three-by-three wooden-made box with sliding glass doors, and checked the inventory. Nothing by Lee Child.

Though Derek was in excellent condition, the short walk in the oppressive heat and humidity drove him back to his car. He walked slowly, admiring the beautiful homes, the spectacular views of the bay while breathing the heavily salted air.

He waited nearly two hours — waiting, doing nothing was the part of the private investigator job Derek disliked the most — before he decided on taking a different approach. He pulled his car into the driveway, shut the car engine off, and then walked up the immaculately maintained walkway to the front door. He rang the doorbell and listened as the customized doorbell played the

Mozart piano concerto number twenty-four inside the house.

Less than a minute later, a man with short brown hair, graying at the temples, swung open the door. He was shorter than Derek by two inches and had a thin body; like the body of a long-distance runner.

"Can I help you?" the man said.

"I'm looking for Mr. Brian Hilton."

"You found him. And you are?"

"Just a guy hoping you can tell me a place I can buy some furniture in a hurry. Maybe the name of a good moving company, not afraid of burning the replaced furniture. Any ideas?"

A look of utter confusion crossed Brian's face. His eyes pulled into squints and his eyebrows squeezed together. Then, as if a light was switched on inside his brain, his face relaxed. He lowered his head, then slowly began shaking it.

"You must be that investigator Mrs. Gracers hired."

"Pretty formal, calling a woman you were having sex with Mrs."

Brian's head shaking increased speed.

"I'm sorry, I don't know your name."

"Derek Cole."

Derek had been trained and had learned to expect anything. The Army had taught him any person, no matter how calm, could instantly turn into a threat. His years as a cop with the Columbus Police Department solidified that belief. Derek was ready for any turn of events. He prided himself at being able to respond to most situations with little to no delay. What kills people are delays. Delays in reacting to threats. Delays in responding to life or death decisions. A man pulls out a knife or a gun on someone, and that someone freezes. Maybe only for a second or two, but a second or two is all it takes to give the overwhelming advantage to the aggressor. Derek's reflexes were finely tuned. Expecting everything and anything meant very few people would ever gain that second or two-second advantage. But what Brian Hilton did set Derek back on his heels. He was taken completely by surprise. Had no idea it was coming.

He invited Derek inside his home.

· · · · ·

"I'm expecting an important business call to come in," Brian said as he showed Derek into a marble-tiled living room, which overlooked a screened in pool, and, beyond that, the bay of Tampa. "Can I get you anything to drink, eat? I have a full bar, plus the best sweet tea this side of Alabama."

Derek was still a bit surprised to be inside Brian Hilton's home. It wasn't that he was actually inside the home of the person who he believed was behind the murder of Sam Gracers; it was that he didn't need to break in. Instead, he was instead invited in which was what had set him off.

When he was sitting in his car outside Hilton's home, Derek decided, one way or another, he needed to get into both Hilton's lodge and his home on Snead Island. Though the lodge had been cleaned, probably sterilized, nervous people always made mistakes. As for getting into the home he was now welcomed inside of, Derek figured if Brian Hilton had possession of any evidence linking him to the Sam Gracers murder, it would be somewhere in this very house.

"I'll take a cold water, if that's on the menu," Derek said.

As Brian turned towards what Derek assumed to be the kitchen, his cell phone rang.

"Damn."

Brian looked at his phone's screen, then said, "Derek, I'm sorry, but this is the call I'm expecting. Seriously, make yourself at home. Kitchen is off to the right, bar and media room to your left. This should take no more than five to ten minutes."

He slid his finger across the phone.

"Brian Hilton…Matt Steel! How are you, my friend?"

Brian gave a "thumbs up" sign to Derek, then climbed the staircase. A few seconds later, Derek heard the muffled voice of Brian Hilton, then a door close shut.

Time to explore.

Brian's call lasted less than ten minutes, giving Derek enough time to quickly explore each room on the first floor. After grabbing a bottle of Dasani from the refrigerator, he walked silently through each room, pausing only occasionally to flip through a thin stack of papers and to rifle his hands through end table drawers. He looked on every bookshelf and every flat surface for the Lee Child book Jessica suggested the two used to pass notes back and forth to each other, but didn't see the book. In fact, Derek didn't see any fiction books at all.

He found nothing of interest. Nothing indicating Hilton was involved in anything suspicious and absolutely nothing tying him to Jessica Gracers.

"Things go well on your call?" Derek asked. He had heard Brian's tone of voice changing and determined the tone Brian had been using was the type people use right before ending a call. He quickly made his way back to his original spot on the couch. When Brian reappeared in the room, it was as if Derek had only gotten up to grab a bottle of water.

"Very well, actually. Thanks for asking." Brian shot a puzzled look at the bottle of Dasani in Derek's hands. "Water? I thought you private investigators were more whiskey type of guys?"

"Cheap scotch, actually."

"Well, if it's all the same to you, I just closed the biggest deal of my life and feel like celebrating a bit. I have some of the finest scotch in the world. Care to join me?"

"Expensive scotch would be wasted on me. I'm more of a bottom shelf type of guy."

"That's crazy." Brian smiled, shook his head a bit. "Listen, I know it's hot as hell outside, but my patio is climate controlled. You head out and I'll bring you a scotch that will make you never want to drink another brand for the rest of your life."

"Climate controlled outdoor patio?"

"Cool mist and air circulation system. The mist is so fine, you won't even feel it against your skin. Cost a fortune but I love the view from the backyard. Please, head out and I'll be there in two minutes."

As he stepped through the sliding glass doors and onto the covered patio, Derek realized two things. First, despite it being close to a hundred degrees, the patio's air was perfect: Humidity was low and whatever the hell a "cool mister" was, he liked it. The second thing he realized was if he wasn't investigating Brian Hilton for framing his client for murdering her husband, Derek would have liked the guy. Hilton was unassuming, welcoming. He had an air of confidence and openness about him that was disarming.

"You're not here to make friends, Cole," he thought. *"You're here to find out how this asshole framed your client."*

Brian came out through the sliding glass doors, which, it turned out, could be opened automatically by placing a foot an inch from the motion sensor located near the door jam, carrying two tumblers filled with brown liquor and two large ring-sized cigars.

"Deanston Highland single malt. Twelve years old. Not the most expensive, by far, but, damn this is good scotch." He handed Derek a tumbler. "Wasn't sure about your ice preference, so I added two. Figured people either like one cube or three, so I split the difference. And, if you're one of those purist who drink it straight, I'll pour you another and will have that as my second."

"Two cubes is fine," Derek said.

"And, not sure if you smoke cigars, but I always have one after I land a big deal. Join me? They're Cubans."

Derek snipped the end off the cigar, lit it using a torch flame Brian handed him and drew in the smoothest, silkiest cigar smoke he'd ever tasted. And when he followed the cigar draw with a pull of the scotch, Derek figured he could spend the rest of his life on Brian Hilton's cool misted patio, smoking cigars and drinking scotch, and be absolutely fine with how his life ended up.

Before Derek could grow upset with himself for devoting more of his mental energy towards being amazed at how great the scotch and cigar were, Brian started up the conversation.

"So, I know you're not here to talk about good scotch. You want to talk about Jessica Gracers. Am I right?"

"Yup. You seem pretty open to talk about her."

"No reason not to be. I mean, actually, there are probably a thousand reasons why I shouldn't be speaking with you about her, or about anything. But, I really feel bad about what happened to Sam and…Jessica has some issues you may or may not have noticed yet."

"Issues?"

"Let me guess. She told you she and I were having an affair. She told you she was with me at my lodge when her husband was murdered. That much I know for certain since you all showed up with a search warrant in hand to inspect the place. She probably told you some story about how Sam wasn't a good husband, that they had grown apart and getting involved with me was not intended at all. It just happened, like she and I had no control over our emotions."

"So far, so good."

"Well, let me tell you the truth: I met Jessica at a company party a year and a half ago. As I'm sure you know, Sam and I work for the same group."

"FJ DeNuzzio's group."

"Exactly. She and I met when FJ introduced a new partner. We talked a little but no more than I spoke with any of the other partner's wives or girlfriends. A couple of days after the party, Sam calls me. He asks me what his wife and I spoke about at the party. I told him we didn't talk about anything important. I couldn't even remember a single topic. Hell, I barely remembered her name, to be honest. I asked Sam what the heck he was getting at. He said Jessica hadn't stopped asking questions about me. He wondered if I made a suggestive comment to her. If I came on to his wife at the party. Listen, Jessica is an attractive woman, but she is *far* from being my type."

•   •   •   •   •

"So, have you been converted?"

Derek shot Brian a puzzled look.

"Are you asking me if I believe what you're saying over what my client is saying?"

"No," Brian said, laughing and waving off Derek's question with his hand. "I mean, has that delicious glass of scotch converted you to being a fine scotch connoisseur instead of a rot-gut scotch drinker." Brian stood up, bending forward at his waist. "Or, do you need one more to find out for certain?"

Derek considered him for a beat. Then only drained the last bit from his glass and nodded his head.

"One more ought to do it," he said.

When Brian returned with two more heavily poured glasses of scotch, Derek was ready with questions.

"Why the hell did you get all new furniture in your lodge and have your old furniture burned by the two movers?"

"Last month, I had a partner meeting at the lodge. Partners with their spouses or significant others. Jessica and Sam showed up, of course, even though I was pretty damn nervous about having her in the place. Hell, I was nervous as shit just letting her know where my lodge was. Anyway, the party was fine. No issues, but Jessica was wandering all over the place. She went into every room. I guess that's not a big deal but I found her lying down on my bed at one point, just before the party was breaking up. Just lying there, like she owned the damn place. When I found out you were bring a forensics specialist to inspect my lodge, I figured I had better do some serious cleaning. Last thing I wanted was for you guys to find one of her hairs left on my pillow. Or, I don't know, some of her DNA on my couch.

"Sam called me the day after the party to apologize. He told me he was concerned about his wife, thought she might have some mental illness. He also told me he had been speaking with his lawyer about getting a divorce. Sam and I weren't the best of friends, but close enough to share some personal matters, anyway. If you're interested, I can give you the name of Sam's lawyer. Talk to him yourself. See what he says."

"I may just do exactly that," Derek said in a low, somewhat muffled voice.

"I know what Jessica said in her alibi. I was read the whole damn story. Beginning to end. I know what she said about she and I having sex all over the lodge. I wasn't taking any chances. Plus, and this may have been pure paranoia, if she really is as mentally sick as Sam and I believe her to be, I didn't put it past her to have driven up to my lodge, found a way in, and to plant evidence all over the place. I wasn't taking any chances."

Derek puffed away at his cigar, spilling bluish smoke into the air, as he considered Brian's story. It was so different from Jessica's. Told in such an absolute and confident manner that Derek was seriously challenged not to believe Brian's story over his client's. He decided making a call to Sam Gracers' lawyer would go a long way in helping him decide which story was accurate. If Sam Gracers was about to file for a divorce, Jessica had motive. And the one critical thing missing from the Gracers case thus far was motive.

"What can you tell me about FJ DeNuzzio and his company?" Derek asked.

"What do you want to know? Most disciplined and intelligent man I know. Gets up before the sun every day. Workday or not. Same time, every day. Works out then goes for a beach walk around his place on Anna Maria Island. He has a fantastic home on the island. As close as you can get to the westernmost point. Beautiful.

"He keeps everything simple, really. Simple and brilliant. FJ is a true genius. A business genius and a genius when it comes to understanding how people tick. His grandfather started a vacation rental business back in the 1930s, which he handed down to FJ's father, who then handed it down to FJ. But FJ took the business to a whole new level. Instead of just renting homes owned by other people, he started buying homes and renting them himself. He bought tracts of land on Anna Maria Island, well before the market went through the roof. He bought condos, hotels, resorts…you name it. Took his grandfather's business that, in today's dollars, produced a couple hundred thousand a year in revenues and turned it into a worldwide business that brought in millions each quarter.

"About six years ago, FJ was approached by a team of investors from London. He sold them the whole business for over a hundred million. But, after five or six months of retirement, he got bored. Came up with an idea where a very selective group of business professionals all work together, pooling resources, sharing risks and profits and each focusing on their own area of specialty. He formed a group of eight, including him, and the idea just took off. I was fortunate enough to be asked to join a couple years ago and I haven't looked back since.

"I won't tell you too much about how FJ has the partnerships arranged. It's proprietary. Literally, if other business owners knew how the hell FJ does it, how he arranges the seven different businesses and how each of us seven work together but also completely independently, there would be hundreds of other partnerships like FJ's. FJ treats his 'formula' like KFC keeps their secret recipe."

"But partners have left or have been asked to leave over the years," Derek questioned. "You'd figure one of them would leak the recipe. Maybe start his or her own similar partnership?"

Brian shook his head.

"Each of us signs a whole stack of legal agreements. There's a lot more than these two, but two of those agreements are non-disclosures and non-competes. If a partner leaves or is asked to leave, they have about fifty-million reasons to keep their mouth closed."

"So, what's your story? How did you get to where you are?"

"I was eighteen years old. Just graduated from high school up in Vermont and getting ready to head off to a local community college. Typical story for plenty of kids that age: I had no idea what I wanted to do with my life. I was good at fixing things but had no interest in getting paid to fix stuff.

"About a month after graduation, I broke my arm playing football in my parent's backyard with a bunch of friends. Had a cast from my wrist past my elbow. When I went to have the cast removed a month or two after I broke my arm, I saw a box of tools behind the receptionist's desk. I asked her what the tools were for, and she told me they were old and broken cast saws. When I was with the doctor, I asked him about the saws. He told me they buy new ones every so often and throw away the old ones. Said the last thing they needed was for a saw to malfunction and end up causing damage to one of their patients. I asked the doctor if I could take the saws, he said yes, and I brought them home. I took them apart, cleaned them, fixed them and made them like new. A couple of weeks later, I got dressed in the only suit I owned, and ended up selling the cast saws to another orthopedic medical practice. I sold six saws that day for three hundred and seventy-five dollars. My total cost, not including labor, came to fifteen dollars."

"That's a hell of a profit margin," Derek commented.

"I was hooked. I made the rounds every quarter to every doctor's office and hospital in the Vermont, Massachusetts and New York areas. I took a loan from my dad for start up money and was able to pay him back every cent within six months. I started small, but grew to a point where I was buying million dollar MRI machines from hospitals, having them remanufactured and selling them back to the same hospital or a different one for two to three times what I paid for them.

"I have no idea how FJ heard about me—finding talent is part of his secret formula—but I was pulling in close to two million in personal income a year when I decided to join FJ. I ended up selling my business for six point four million and got into buying and selling other entrepreneurs businesses. Now—and I hope this doesn't sound like I'm bragging or think I'm better than anyone else—I'd consider two million a year in income to be my poverty line."

Derek liked this guy, and he was pissed that he did. Hilton seemed so genuine and down to earth, despite being a multimillionaire and partner with a company shrouded in secrecy. But maybe FJ's group was exactly how Brian had described it: A group of business people, sharing risks and rewards. Helping one another out. All above board. Fully legal. Legit.

Derek drained the remnants of his glass and stubbed out the majority of his cigar.

"I think I'll let you get back to work, Brian. I would like to get the name of Sam Gracers' lawyer from you before I leave."

"Absolutely."

Brian walked Derek back inside and to the front door. He bolted up the stairs, leaving Derek alone downstairs once again. He wasn't sure if the scotch had numbed him or he no longer felt the need, but Derek didn't even consider having one last unmonitored look around Hilton's first floor.

"Here you go," Brian said, extending a business card to Derek. "I don't know the guy but Sam recommended him to me a while back. Tell him I gave you his card. He might be more willing to talk with you knowing a friend of Sam's sent you."

Derek took the card, then shook Brian's hand. He turned towards the door when a few more questions popped into his mind.

"What can you tell me about a man named Craig Washburn? Used to be part of FJ's company, or so I've been told."

"Never met the guy, but, yeah, he was a partner with FJ. Shady character, from what I heard. Ended up with a bullet between his eyes, floating in the bay.

"Just like Sam, except for the floating part."

Brian squinted his eyes in thought, wondering, then discovering Derek's meaning.

"If you're trying to somehow tie Sam's murder into Craig's, forget about it. The only connection I could make, and this would be a real stretch, is Sam took Craig's spot with FJ. That's it. Craig was shady, like I said. FJ doesn't talk about why he removes partners, but I heard in the business community that Washburn was involved in some illegal operations."

"Such as?"

"Don't know. Just heard he was running with some so called 'business professionals' who solve disputes with baseball bats and handguns. If I were a betting man, I'd say Craig Washburn was killed and his body dumped in the bay by some questionable associate he wronged."

Derek moved on to the next question sitting in his brain.

"I hear you love to read? Have an idea about writing a book someday?"

Brian let out a cackle of a laugh. Short, loud.

"An old dream of mine. I suppose Jessica told you that?"

"She may have mentioned it."

"And you're thinking if she knows about my dreams that I must have shared them with her during some pillow talk?"

"A man doesn't usually share dreams with strangers," Derek shot back.

"When I was introduced to the FJ partners, FJ talked about my past, my present and three interesting facts about me. He does that with every new partner. Two of those interesting facts was I love to read and want to write a book someday. Not exactly 'pillow talk,' wouldn't you agree, Derek?"

Derek simply nodded his head, added what Brian had said to his growing list of questions he needed to ask Jessica.

"One last thing. You said something outside that got me curious."

"What did I say?"

"Well, it wasn't really *what* you said, it was more *how* you said it. You said Jessica was an attractive woman but she wasn't your type. What did you mean by that?"

"I'm gay, Derek. Knew I was gay since I was thirteen. Never tried to hide it or deny it. So, Jessica, as attractive a woman as she may be, is really far from being my type."

Chapter 19

Nikkie was doing research in her room for less than thirty minutes. She had found what she was looking for much easier and much more quickly than she could have even hoped for. In March of that year, a business owned by a Donald Reagan, was sold to a company called "Advancement Solutions." The listed owner of Advancement Solutions, according to the State of Florida Public Records database, was Brian K Hilton. Reagan's business exported medical devices to developing countries. The database listed 2015 annualized sales revenues for "Reagan Medical Devices, Inc" at $5.25 million.

Another Internet search provided a Sarasota address for Donald Reagan, along with a phone number.

"Whatever happened to privacy and unlisted numbers?" Nikkie thought as she dialed the listed number for Reagan.

He answered on the third ring and seemed more than happy to meet with her, after Nikkie explained the reasons behind her call.

She pulled into the driveway and was knocking at the door of Donald Reagan's home by eleven in the morning.

"I really had no intentions of selling my business," Donald had said. "Hilton had contacted me a few months before, I'd say...five or six months before. He tossed out an offer which sounded a bit low, but, still, not an insulting offer. I told him even if he doubled the offer, I wasn't selling. He seemed fine. Sounded like a sharp businessman."

"So, what changed your mind?" Nikkie asked while sipping a cold, tall glass of iced tea.

"I lived up outside Nashville at the time. Used to like living in a bigger, busier city. Anyway, I went in to my doctor's office for a little issue I was having. He ran a bunch of tests then called me about a week later. Told me he needed to see me in his office. He told me I had a histiocyptic reticulosarcoma tumor. He said it's usually fatal but, with proper treatment and plenty of rest, I had a fighting chance.

"He sent me to a specialist in Tampa, which worked out well since I owned an apartment near the Tampa ports. The specialist started me on chemotherapy and suggested my type of cancer may have been caused by stress. Said there was 'plenty of evidentiary support' to back up the whole stress angle. Those were the words he used. *Ver-fucking-batim.* I'll never forget those words of his. Set me on my ass. Running my business was stressful as hell and getting worse with all the governmental regulations they keep introducing and the constant changes in international business law. Turns out, my business was killing me. At least, that's what I thought.

"I called Hilton a couple of days after I started chemotherapy. Sold him my business for five million dollars. Happy to be rid of it at that point. If stress caused my cancer, I wanted my company out of my life.

"I went through treatments for three goddamn months. Made me sick as a dog. Then, one day, I'm sitting in the specialist's office. He walks in, all smiles. Tells me the latest PET scan showed zero trace of my tumor. Fully healed. A hundred percent gone. A fucking miracle."

"Must have been a tremendous relief for you. Congratulations."

Donald fixed Nikkie with long, intense stare. Though he looked healthy to her untrained eyes, she could see something deeper was affecting him. Something beyond the horrible cancer treatments. A deeper side effect than what any disease could have left as its scar.

"Hilton turned around and sold my business, the business I built from the ground up, the business I thought caused my cancer, three months and seven days after he bought it from me. Sold it for twelve and a half million."

"You think you could have gotten more for your business? Like he knew something was about to happen which made the value more than double?"

"Me selling it for five and him selling it for twelve is on me. I didn't know what the business was really worth. That's on me. What gets me is that I don't think I ever had cancer. I built in an 'out-clause' into the sale contract. I had ninety days after signing the sale agreement to back out. That specialist in Tampa told me I was cured exactly ninety-one days after I signed the agreement. One fucking day past my drop-dead date.

"I don't like coincidences. Don't believe in them. I called my doctor up in Nashville. Read him the riot act. He said some shit about how chemo can have an effect on the brain. Said I'd feel more like myself after a few more months. Basically, he blew me off and got me off the phone as quickly as he could. Said I was suffering from paranoia and that I should see another damn doctor about it. Probably had someone he could recommend, if I gave him the chance to. So, I drove over to that specialist's office in Tampa. Son of a bitch told me the same damn thing. That chemo messes up the brain for a while. Said all the tests were conclusive and the treatments he prescribed were all fully approved and fully supported by the American Oncologists Society."

Nikkie tried to read Donald's face. She looked hard to see how certain he was in his beliefs. She tried, impossibly, to read on Donald's face any indication of "cancer brain." Looking to see if he was suffering from paranoia.

She could see nothing but anger and an abundance of pain.

"No offense," Nikkie said, "and I get the timing of the out-clause and finding out you were cured, but it's a bit of a stretch to believe two doctors would lie about a cancer diagnosis, put you through unnecessary treatments, all the while risking their careers, their reputation and your life."

"That's what I thought at first. Thought maybe my brain was clouded up. Jammed up with that poison they pumped into my veins. So, I didn't do a damn thing for…hell, six, seven weeks. By then I figured any chemo shit would be out of my system. My brain didn't seem to be any better or worse than while I was on the poison, but someone going crazy is usually the last person to recognize his weakened hold on sanity. I scheduled an appointment with a lymphatic system specialist in Miami. Didn't tell him anything about my past medical history, just paid him a couple thousand dollars for him to test the living crap out of my lymphatic system and tell me how healthy it is. Guess what he came back with?"

"Healthy system?"

"Damn healthy. I asked about that tumor, that histiocytic reticulosarcoma tumor and whether or not those tumors leave scars or evidence they were once in the system. He told me histiocytic reticulosarcoma tumors always, and he stressed *'always,'* leave irreparable damage. Every damn time. But in my body, the only thing he questioned me about was me being overweight and my blood pressure being on the high side."

"Why didn't you bring that doctor's findings to someone?"

"Not everyone who knows the human body has a medical degree. In fact, some of the best healthcare specialists in the world never stepped a foot into a med school. Or a hospital for that matter. The Miami doc I saw was a Chinese holistic guy. Wasn't anyway in the world any medical board in the US would give two shits about what he found in my body. Or rather, what he *didn't* find."

"Did you ever contact Mr. Hilton again?"

"Tried to. Even went to his home up on Snead Island. Son of a bitch called the cops on me. Got a nice restraining order for my time and troubles. If I could find a connection between Hilton and those damn quacks, I'd sue his ass for every last cent he owns." Donald paused a beat. "Actually, I wouldn't sue the bastard; I'd kill him."

Nikkie paused, giving Donald the chance to calm down. Maybe to retract his threat against Hilton.

He just sat in a silent stare.

"The doctor in Nashville; what's his name?"

"Doctor Timothy O'Connell. His partner in crime, the asshole specialist in Tampa is Mark Ruggerio. I'll add both of them son of a bitches to my kill list if I find that connection."

"So you never filed a complaint with the Florida State Board of Physicians? Or the board in Tennessee?" Nikkie already knew the answer.

"Nope," Donald said. "That's like filing a complaint with the government about a governmental employee. Nothing happens but a shit-ass investigation followed by a whitewash cover up. And with my Miami doc not recognized as being a real doctor, I would have been wasting my time filing a complaint."

"But if there's more than one complaint?"

Donald slid forward on his chair. Leaned in close to Nikkie.

"You find someone else the same shit happened to, and I'll give you five million dirty dollars."

"I don't want your money."

"Neither do I. I haven't touched a cent of that money Hilton gave me. It's sitting in an offshore account. Sitting there, collecting about a half point of interest every year." Donald paused a beat. "How about this; I'll hire you to find out if Hilton and his band of quacks ran this scam on anyone else?"

"Let me see what my investigation turns up. I'll let you know, but, really Mr. Reagan, I won't take a cent from you, no matter what I find."

Donald slid back in his chair.

"If you do find something, come right to me with it. No sense going the complaint route. I'll handle things my way."

"You really shouldn't talk about killing someone."

"You gonna tell on me if one of those fuckers turns up dead?"

"Probably not. But still…"

"You listen to me and you listen good: If you or I find out those three are connected, I will kill each and every one of them with my bare hands. If they all turn up dead, you'll know I done the murders. Tell whoever you want. I'll be long gone before anyone comes knocking on my door."

Chapter 20

In fiscal year 2015, the seven partners of the FJ DeNuzzio Corporation, LLC, realized total revenues of $583.8 million dollars. Of that amount, forty-seven percent was profit. Meaning 2015 was the partnership's strongest year. $235.2 million in profits, after all expenses and foreign exchange rates were factored in. The $235.2 million in profit was divided up nine ways; each of the seven partners getting their share and FJ taking two shares. Each of the seven partners received a bonus in March 2016 of over twenty-eight million dollars. FJ's bonus climbed north of fifty-six million.

But of course, FJ and all seven partners didn't see all of their bonuses. Each had expenses which couldn't ever see a line on any balance sheet. Payoffs to secondary suppliers were always a major expense. So, too, were payments made — usually in cash — to independent contractors. Bribes to governmental officials, both foreign and domestic, were another large draw from the partners' bank accounts. Many of these bribes, payoffs and payments to independent contractors were scattered throughout the calendar. But one particular unrecorded expense was nearly always paid out in September of each year. Election time.

For FJ, the list of politicians holding out their hands was unusually small for the approaching month of September. Despite Clinton and Trump making a mockery out of the national Presidential election and both Senate and Congress races taking place in many states, FJ only expected to dish out ten to fifteen million in off the record contributions.

Chump Change.

There had been years when his payoffs and other unrecorded expenses exceeded his previous year's income. But 2016, despite his wife's efforts to purchase significantly more than she had in previous years, wouldn't follow suit. As he sat behind his modest desk, in his small, quiet, downtown Tampa office, scrolling through a litany of spreadsheets, FJ estimated his fifty-six million dollar plus yearly income would survive the year. More than likely, his reported income statement when 2016 gives way to 2017 would be north of twenty million.

Not a bad year. Not bad at all.

But settling for any number, no matter how impressive, was a sign of weakness. Twenty million would be a fantastic number, but adding another one hundred-eighty five million, from a source FJ had already identified, would be even better. Wouldn't make even a single change in how he lived his life or in the lifestyle he lived. Wouldn't alter the course he wanted his business to take. Wouldn't convince him to add more partners, make more contributions, donate to whchever damn charity his wife insisted the couple support, or get him thinking about cashing out, selling his business and to find out what retirement was all about.

That wasn't for him. Not his style at all.

FJ's greatest attribute—according to him—was that he never compared himself to anyone else. He had no competitors. Didn't care if someone he knew, and whom he knew was less skilled, reached the billionaire status. For FJ, staying off any list was significantly better than any benefits of being on any list.

"Let those of weak character strive to have their names listed among others of equally weak character," FJ had said during a past year-end partner meeting. "The less people know about you, the more influence you can have. Familiarity is almost as expensive as maintaining a public image. Have neither. Strive to go unrecognized. To remain anonymous. Accomplishing those objectives will allow you greater power than even the wealthiest people in the world could imagine possessing."

And for FJ DeNuzzio, anonymity also afforded him flexibility.

Congressman Wiggins had a press conference scheduled for the upcoming Monday to announce he was retiring from Congress and would be throwing his full support to Julia Steinberg. FJ wouldn't be in attendance. He may decide to watch the press conference on TV, but had absolutely no interest in seeing Wiggins make his big announcement.

Steinberg would be there, of course. Sitting to the Congressman's left, wearing the outfit FJ had suggested. She'd smile when she sat down, a few times while Wiggins spoke and then flash a broad smile when Wiggins told the press, "I cannot think of anyone more qualified, more prepared or more capable of serving my beloved district than District Attorney Julia Steinberg. Now, many of you are familiar with Julia and the excellent work her office has done during her tenure as the DA. But for those who don't recognize her name, I'm going to tell you why. Julia Steinberg is no politician. She doesn't run around, shaking hands, kissing babies. Yes, she currently holds an elected office, but just being elected to a political office doesn't make her a politician. The second she took office, Julia Steinberg went right to work. Cleaning up the crime, locking criminals away and making this district safer for all who call this wonderful part of the world home.

"Now, I'm not one to say too many things about someone interested in taking over my job in Congress," he would pause for the crowd's laughter, "but the only reason I was able to finally persuade myself to retire was knowing Julia Steinberg was willing to serve our district in an even greater capacity."

FJ had written the speech Wiggins was going to deliver. Wrote every word of it. Even choreographed when Steinberg should smile, clap her hands, laugh, pretend to jot down some notes. He even demanded Wiggins kiss her on the cheek when facing the cameras.

"If she initiates the kiss," he said to Wiggins when the two sat in his office earlier that day, "then the appearance is you are doing her a favor. Your kissing her tells everyone you respect, admire and appreciate that she is making it easy for you to ride off into the sunset."

The Monday announcement was fast approaching. So, too, was the need for District Attorney Julia Steinberg to understand her responsibilities.

CHAPTER 21

"You understand the importance of delivering a swift conviction I assume?"

FJ DeNuzzio hated politics. The false claims, the ridiculous lies, the pandering to groups of people for the sole purpose of persuading them to check off their name when they enter their assigned polling place. He had strategically decided to work closely with a select number of politicians, chosen for the positions they held and, more importantly, by how easily the politician could make the distinction between the few who mattered and the masses who only needed a smile, or a serious look of concern, some professionally chosen words or to be told the politician "had a plan" to solve whatever public issue was the most talked about on the faux news morning shows.

As much as he hated politics, his hatred was dwarfed when compared to his utter disdain for politicians. To FJ, a disturbing majority of politicians were people equipped with such an anemic set of skills that he wouldn't have one working as an intern for a landscaping concern he owned.

But, politicians had value solely based on their positions.

Once a politician could no longer claim ownership of a particular position, they fell into a unique category of people FJ referred to as "the spent waste." Meaning ex-office holders were garbage; having fully served whatever specific use he had for them. Should they make a triumphant return to an "FJ recognized" position, they were promoted from the waste heap and back into the group of the hated but useful.

He never chose a politician but rather chose the position held. The elected public servant could be brilliant or a complete and total moron; it didn't matter. Only the position mattered. Didn't matter if the politician holding a particular office was a republican, a democrat, independent or any one of the other minor parties: All that mattered was the position and FJ's ability to influence the person holding the office.

District Attorney was not a position he valued, but Julie Steinberg was not long for the DA's position. With Congressman Walter Wiggins agreeing that his time, and his usefulness, was reaching the finish line and with him further agreeing it was time to allow FJ to handpick his replacement, Steinberg should soon occupy an important position as far as FJ was concerned.

"The last thing you need is to have a murder investigation and resulting court case extending beyond Election Day. In fact, I'd say since Congressman Wiggins needs to announce his intention to retire in a matter of a few days, I'd suggest you tie this case up before primary day. Not that you will have a competitor to worry about in the Democratic primary, but our pesky two-party system will certainly produce a Republican candidate you'll need to defeat. And, if I were consulting your opposition, I would instruct your opponent to attack your lack of dedication to the position of trust the voters of Pinellas County elected you to. How in the world could someone so disinterested in seeing to completion a murder that has so upset the local community ever be trusted to hold the position of a United States Congresswoman? That's what I would advise your opponent to drill into the district voter's tiny minds. So, I'll ask again, do you understand the importance of delivering a swift, and may I add, convincing conviction?"

"Are you suggesting I offer a plea to Jessica Gracers?"

"Please do not answer a question with a question. That practice is better used during public speeches delivered."

Julie stirred in her seat. Though an accomplished lawyer and having earned a reputation for having ice in her veins, sitting across FJ was a wracking ordeal.

"Yes, sir. I do understand how important it is for my office to get a swift conviction."

"Not your office," FJ corrected. He smiled and fixed his gaze on Julie's eyes. He shook his head with quick, subtle movements. "Don't pass off any potential failure on your office. *You* are in charge, aren't you? *You* hold the position of District Attorney, correct?" FJ's smile widened a bit as he pointed his index finger at Julie each time he said "*You.*"

"You're right, Mr. DeNuzzio," Julie said, adding a manufactured smile of her own to mirror FJ's. "So, allow me to rephrase my answer: I understand how important it is that I deliver a swift and convincing conviction in the Sam Gracers murder case. And I will do exactly that."

"No matter the costs?"

"No matter the costs."

"Good to hear," FJ said. "I have some other tasks I need completed once you've put Jessica Gracers in prison and have secured the election. Oh, and don't worry too much about the whole election. Campaigning is for those lacking knowledge in the ways of manipulating the voting sheep. I'll see to your victory. You put Jessica Gracers away where she can't provide any interruptions."

CHAPTER 22

Derek was sitting at the end of the hotel bar when Nikkie strolled in. She had called him during her drive back from Sarasota and her meeting with Donald Reagan, telling him they needed to talk. She had suggested that before they take another step in their investigation, they needed to decide where in the hell the investigation was leading.

"We have too many paths to explore," she told him. "Too many rabbits to chase down holes."

"Not sure what your day produced, but mine sure was interesting. You inviting Maryanne to our palaver?"

"Palaver?" Nikkie questioned through a small laugh. "You've been reading again, having you?"

"The Dark Tower by King. Damn good words in those books. Palaver just so happens to be my new favorite."

"Wonderful. And, no, I won't be inviting Maryanne Jenkins to our 'palaver.' She's one of the topics we need to talk about."

Derek was nursing his drink as Nikkie pulled up a high-back chair and sat down next to him at the bar.

"I think today was a bad day for me," Derek said, his eyes set on the mostly still full glass of scotch in front of him.

"Why? What happened?"

"May have lost my taste for cheap scotch."

"How absolutely horrible," Nikkie remarked, sarcasm dripping from each word. "May as well shut down the agency and get jobs as Wal-Mart greeters."

"Hilton is to blame."

"Come again?"

"He gave me some high-end scotch during our sit down on his climate controlled backyard patio. I'm a changed man, Nikkie. A changed man."

"Wait, you had drinks with Brian Hilton? What the hell did you do to make that happen? Threaten him with your gun?"

Derek spent the next ten minutes detailing his time with Brian Hilton.

About his side of the story. About what Hilton shared about FJ and the partnership. Derek told Nikkie about the tiny public library to confirm its existence, probably to afford at least some amount of validity to the story Jessica had given them. Derek finished by detailing his quick and far from exhaustive search of Hilton's first floor.

"Didn't find anything of interest, and certainly didn't find the Lee Child book Jessica told us about. Didn't see the book in the free library thing, either."

Derek continued, sharing as many details of his time and conversation with Hilton as he could recall. He ended his part of the palaver by telling Nikkie, "Brian's the type of guy you can't help but like. Really wanted to hate the guy, or to at least not trust a word he said. But, that's not how things turned out."

"You think he was telling the truth? About being gay?"

"Wasn't interested in testing his honesty about that subject. Doesn't matter, anyway. If he is gay, he wasn't having sex with Jessica."

"You don't think gay people can have sex with members of the opposite sex?"

"Not sure about woman," Derek said, feeling the warm flow of embarrassment crawling over his face. "But men have certain equipment which needs to be…motivated? Not sure how else to say it. And if Hilton isn't attracted to women, his equipment won't get motivated."

Nikkie just shook her head. What looked to Derek like a very small smile was standing still on her lips.

"The brain is the only equipment which needs to be motivated, Derek. And if given the proper stimulation or motivation, I have no doubt Brian could have performed."

Nikkie was silent for a few minutes, considering what Derek had told her. She contrasted what Reagan believed about Hilton to Derek's impressions. After ordering a white wine, and after Derek ordered himself a twelve year old, single malt, Glenn Fiddich scotch, Nikkie began with her role in their palaver.

"He may be a likable guy, but his explanation for what he did at his lodge doesn't hold any water."

"Questionable, I agree. But, if what he said about Jessica is accurate, about how she stalked him and may suffer from some mental illness, I'm not sure I wouldn't have taken the same drastic measures as he did."

"Did you call Sam Gracers' lawyer yet?"

"Meeting with him tonight at seven. You and I, that is."

Nikkie smiled at Derek, then, playfully, nudged him with her shoulder.

"Glad you're including me, Mr. Cole."

Derek swirled his drink in his hand a few times, with the slightest smile crossing his face.

"I also called Detective Gonzales. Gave her the rundown of my meeting with Hilton and asked her to dig through the archives for information on the Craig Washburn murder."

"She find anything of interest?"

"She was busy. Said she'll get to it tomorrow. Also told me the DA, Julia Steinberg, has been around the police station a lot more than usual as of late. She told me the DA's had at least four one-on-one meetings with the Sheriff and a couple with Detective Mathers."

"Is that unusual?" Nikkie asked.

"DA's and the police work hand-in-hand, especially on high profile murder cases. But, even with Gracers being a wealthy business owner, that many meetings is suspicious in my book."

"Seems to be plenty of suspicious things about this case. More than its fair share."

Nikkie talked for ten minutes, telling Derek about her meeting with Donald Reagan. Derek spent most of the time listening to Nikkie with his mouth partially open and his eyes wide in amazement.

"Holy shit balls," he said after Nikkie finished. "Gotta give some credibility to Reagan being messed up in the head, but, damn, if his accusations are spot on, this case just got a whole lot bigger."

"And," Nikkie said, "gives Hilton motive."

"How do you figure?"

"Jessica and Brian both said Brian and Sam were somewhat close. They worked for this FJ DeNuzzio guy and, according to both, also worked together at times. Let's say Sam discovered that Brian was scamming people into selling their businesses to him by working with crooked doctors and having them convince the business owners they had a type of cancer caused by stress. Sam puts some pressure on Brian, maybe he threatens to go to the police..."

"Or to FJ," Derek interjected.

"Or to FJ, right. Brian gets nervous, devises some plan to kill Sam and pin the murder on Jessica. Not sure how he pulled it off nor how to explain Jessica's story about how long her and Brian's affair had been going on, but, to me at least, it does give Hilton a hell of a motive."

"You're right about the timeline. Maybe Sam was squeezing Hilton to get some piece of the action. Maybe he wasn't going to turn Hilton in but was instead blackmailing him. If that's the case, Hilton may have started putting his plan together a year and a half ago. Damn patient man, if that's the case."

"Like I said, we have too many rabbits to chase down and too many holes to chase them into." She paused a beat. Took a long pull from her wine. "I suppose we now need to palaver about which rabbit we chase first."

"I'm already sick of the palaver word, but I agree And, I have some ideas."

"Shoot."

"You start chasing down the two doctors Reagan told you about. Maybe give them a call. Ask them some questions. See if they get nervous."

"Makes sense."

"Also, while I was with Hilton, he got a phone call from a guy named Matthew Steel. He told me he was expecting an important business call when he first invited me in. After the call ended, he walked out holding a bottle of damn good scotch and two cigars."

"The very scotch which changed your life?"

"Same damn bottle. Hilton said he just closed the biggest deal of his life. Maybe you should track down this Matthew Steel. See if there's any connection between him, Reagan, and, I know this may be a long shot, but to the doctors as well."

"Perfect," Nikkie said. Whenever Nikkie started to feel excited about the progress of a case she was working, or when the case took on a new, unexpected direction, her enthusiasm became palpable. It practically poured out from her skin. No matter what she may be doing at the time the excitement hit, a wave of seriousness and anticipation washed over her. She was practically vibrating as she sat beside Derek. "And you? What rabbit are you going to chase?"

"I want to meet with this FJ DeNuzzio guy. Get a feel for him. Find out if he's someone we need to chase."

"All roads seem to lead to him, don't they?"

"Not sure if they all do, but the ones we're traveling on seem to."

Nikkie grew silent. To Derek, she seemed to collapse in on herself. The excitement and enthusiasm which was pouring out of her just ten seconds ago, seemed to have vanished like the scent of a rose in a hurricane.

"Something else you need to tell me?" he asked.

She smiled a small grin, finished her wine, then slowly started shaking her head.

"Maryanne Jenkins," she said, more like a question than a statement. "What's your take on her?"

"Still think she's Caribbean. Beyond that, she seems capable. Maybe a bit too busy to be handling a murder defense. Why do you ask?"

Her smile widened a bit.

"She's not Caribbean," she said. "That accent you picked up on is caused by her disease. I promised her I wouldn't say anything, but I think you knowing more about her is important to our case. She has ALS. Lou Gehrig's disease."

"That's a hell of a disease, from what I've heard. Fatal, right?"

"Unfortunately, yes. Most patients die within three years of diagnosis. Maryanne was diagnosed over a year ago."

"That sucks, but not sure if you're feeling bad for her or bad about something else?"

Nikkie turned quickly to face Derek. Pulled her long, dark hair from her face.

"Jessica Gracers is a millionaire, right? At least she was married to one, making her, under the law, a millionaire as well."

"I suppose."

"How many millionaires would choose a one lawyer law firm, with one location, which is within walking distance to the local jail?"

"You thinking Maryanne is involved somehow?"

"No. Not at all. I just don't get why Jessica would hire her instead of some high-powered law firm out of Tampa. Why choose a small-time lawyer, who probably specializes in small-time cases, to defend her in a murder charge? It doesn't make sense. At least not to me. Maybe I'm missing something. And I'm not suggesting Maryanne isn't a good lawyer. Maybe the best around. But still, a millionaire hiring a lawyer like her? I don't know."

"Guess we should ask Jessica about her decision."

"You think it's a rabbit worth chasing, or am I thinking too much?"

"I think that I'm not thinking enough," Derek offered. "Really is strange that Jessica hired Jenkins, I suppose. Lots of lawyers in town. Lots of powerful, influential ones. I don't think Maryanne Jenkins is one of them." Derek grew silent for several moments, as both he and Nikkie were lost chasing thoughts around their minds.

When their thoughts were mostly corralled and their drinks emptied, Nikkie turned again to face Derek.

"It's four o'clock now. We are meeting Sam Gracers' lawyer at seven, which leaves us a couple hours to start chasing rabbits. I'm going up to my room to call those doctors Reagan told me about. You do whatever your wonderful little mind tells you to do. We'll meet down here at six-thirty. Okay?"

"I guess our palaver is over."

"For now, it is. Just for now."

Chapter 23

]Brian Hilton had just finished his fourth scotch, *"Big deals demand big celebrations,"* he thought, when his cell phone rang. He recognized the number.

"Doctor O'Connell, I presume."

"We're fucked. We're all fucked and you need to get us unfucked."

"Whoa," Brian said. "Back it up. What are you talking about and please watch the language. It's far from professional."

"That Reagan guy, he met with a private investigator today. She just called me ten minutes ago."

"What are you talking about? What private investigator?"

"Nikkie something or other. I stopped remembering when she started asking about Reagan and how I was connected to you and to Ruggerio down in Tampa."

Brian's thoughts were swimming in a sea of scotch, desperately trying to find solid, stable ground.

"This 'Nikkie' work alone?"

"She mentioned some guy's name. Said she worked for his agency."

"Derek Cole? Did she say the agency was Derek Cole's?" Urgency was climbing into Brian's voice, something Timothy O'Connell picked up on.

"I take it you know this Cole guy? Yes, that was the name she used."

"She told you she met with Don Reagan and that he said what?"

"Said Reagan didn't believe he ever had cancer and that I was working with you and Ruggerio to scam him into selling his business to you. I brushed it off, as best I could, but she was sharp. Kept on asking questions. I had to hang up on her."

"Son of a bitch!" Brian barked.

"That's not all. She asked if Matthew Steel was a patient of mine."

The call went silent. Ten seconds. Fifteen. Inching towards twenty.

"Hilton? You still there? What the hell…"

"I'm still here," Brian said softly. "I'll take care of everything."

•   •   •   •   •

Unlike when finding contact information for Donald Reagan, Nikkie had an abundance of issues getting in touch with Matt Steel. Her first call was to his Nashville based business, where Mr. Steel's personal assistant would only tell Nikkie, "Mr. Steel is out of the office and won't be in for a few days."

"This is urgently important. Can you give me his cell or home number?"

"I'm sorry, I can't do that. But, I will take your name and number and if I speak with Mr. Steel, I'll pass on your information."

Nikkie's sense of urgency was climbing to epic heights. Though Doctor O'Connell didn't say Matthew Steel was one of his patients, she could tell by the waver in his voice her mention of Steel's name registered. Now, with Steel being out of the office "for a few days," Nikkie was convinced Steel was a patient of Doctor Timothy O'Connell.

"Listen to me and listen real, real close: You need to either give me Mr. Steel's number or call him right freaking now and tell him to call me. I'm not selling time-shares or asking for his opinion on the upcoming election. This is, quite literally, a matter of life and death."

"I'll be sure Mr. Steel gets your message, Miss Armani."

Nikkie scoured every Internet resource she had, her desperation growing exponentially by the minute. Despite her best attempts, Matthew Steel's contact information was too evasive. Just about when she was about to give up, to turn her attention to getting ready to meet Sam Gracers' lawyer, her cell phone rang.

It was Matthew Steel.

"Listen, I don't know anything for certain and do not want to give you false hope, but I would strongly suggest you see another doctor, someone not recommended by Doctor Timothy O'Connell or Doctor Mark Ruggerio."

"You're telling me this Reagan saw O'Connell and Ruggerio, had the same diagnosis and was working with Hilton?"

"That's what he told me this morning. Again, I don't want to give you any false hope or…"

"Forget the false hope crap, would ya?" Steel paused a few moments. Nikkie could hear him breathing heavily. "It didn't feel right. None of it. About five months ago, I go in to see O'Connell for a physical. I walk out of O'Connell's with a clean bill of health. Two days later, I get a call from this Hilton guy. No idea who the hell he is or why he's asking if I'm interested in selling my business. I go about my life, forgetting Hilton ever called. Then, he calls me last week, makes another offer. I turn it down and tell him I'm not interested and to stop calling me. Then, I get a call from O'Connell, telling me he needs to see me."

"And he told you that you had a cancer usually caused by stress?" Nikkie asked.

"Damn straight. That was yesterday. I called Hilton today, let him know I've reconsidered and am ready to sell. Son of a bitch had papers sent to my home within two hours of me calling him."

"It's none of my business, but did you sign the papers?"

In a low voice, cutting with anger, Steel said, "Yes."

"Talk with your lawyer, see what you can do." Nikkie paused for a second. "Actually, I don't care if you talk with your lawyer or not. What I do care about is you getting to see another doctor as soon as possible. And, please, let me know what that doctor tells you. It's really critical."

"If what you're suggesting is the truth, I'm going to…"

"Don't tell me you're going to kill, injure or otherwise maim Doctor O'Connell. I've heard that once today already and don't want to hear it again."

"Nah," Matt Steel said. "I'm not going to kill him. Just going to make sure he never sees another patient as long as he lives."

"Mr. Steel," Nikkie continued in her best professional voice, "we really don't know anything yet. God forbid, Doctor O'Connell told you the truth and is an excellent doctor. Please, just go see another doctor and, please let me know what happens."

"You have my word on it. Thanks. If things turn out for me, I'll owe you more than I can ever repay."

"You won't owe me anything."

Strange thoughts go through everyone's mind from time to time. Thoughts that seem to originate out of nothing. No logical reason for them showing up. They don't exist one second, then, *poof,* there they are. Before Nikkie ended the call with Matt Steel, one of those strange thoughts clouded her mind. She trusted strange thoughts and always tried, whenever possible, to act on them.

"Mr. Steel, can I ask you one last question?"

"You can ask me anything you want."

"Your lawyer, the one you use for your personal and business dealings, who would that be?"

"A law firm up here in Nashville called "Jefferson, Pearl and Malloni. Does that matter?"

"No," Nikkie said, feeling the strange thought was only intended to give her another rabbit to chase. "I was just wondering if it may be a different lawyer you sent those signed papers to for the sale of your business."

"Well, I didn't send them to my lawyers," Steel said. "I mean, I sent them copies, but the papers were drawn up by a lawyer outside of Tampa."

Nikkie's heart skipped several beats. Her stomach dropped to her knees.

"Was the lawyer's name Maryanne Jenkins, by chance?"

"That's her name, all right. Another problem?"

"A big one. But, fortunately, this problem is not yours."

CHAPTER 24

The cell phone belonging to the older brother and co-owner of Southern Boys Moving Company rang at seven-fifteen in the evening. The calling number was private, but Jackson Kennedy knew who was calling. There was only one person who called him from a private number. That person had called him three times in just the past couple of days. Probably four or five times prior.

"More work means more money," Jackson thought as he answered the call.

He listened for a minute, nodding his head, grunting his occasional understanding and agreement. Jotted down a name, address and time frame. When the caller paused, after asking if Jackson and his brother Bobby were interested in the job, Jackson scribbled down a number. Several numbers, actually, all followed by a dollar sign.

"Job like this, plenty of risk involved," Jackson said.

"Increased risk means increased reward. Tell me, yes or no."

"I have a number in mind. If we agree to it, then my answer is yes. If not, well, I'm sure you have other people willing and able to handle work like this for ya."

"What's your number?"

Jackson believed the person who didn't reveal a price usually won negotiations. He could have tossed out his fee, it could have been accepted, and he could have left a whole basket full of money on the table.

"You tell me a number you're comfortable with first. I'll let you know if we're close enough to haggle or if you should find yourself some less than professional folks for this type of job."

"Fifty-thousand. Sixty if the job is done tonight."

Jackson raced the pencil tip across the dollar amount he had scribbled down as his target.

"I think we can do business. Yes, I believe my brother and I have a clear calendar tonight and can get the job done for you. Sixty grand, payable by tomorrow morning. Are we in agreement?"

"You'll get paid. You always do."

"You want this doctor to suffer a bit first?"
"I don't care what you do. Just make it clean and certain."

CHAPTER 25

It was a twenty-five minute drive from their hotel to where Peter Maxim, Sam Gracers lawyer, suggested they meet for dinner. Those twenty-five minutes went by much too fast for Derek and Nikkie.

"You have to be kidding me?" Derek said after hearing Nikkie's recap of her call with Matt Steel. "Same doctors, same diagnosis and same Brian Hilton?"

"And you haven't heard all of it yet."

"I have a bad feeling we have more rabbits to chase."

"Guess who the lawyer is Matt Steel said drew up the papers for the sale of his business?"

"You've got to be kidding me?"

"None other than Maryanne Jenkins."

"And we were wondering why a millionaire like Jessica Gracers hired Jenkins! Turns out she's the go to lawyer for the millionaires around here."

"Derek," Nikkie said, "what are we into?"

"I don't know. Something damn bigger than what we thought at first. And, like I said, I have a bad feeling about this whole case."

"Hope you're not planning on keeping me in the dark in order to protect me."

"Thought has crossed my mind, but no, I need you more than ever with this case."

They arrived at The Bay Overlook Restaurant a few minutes before seven. Nikkie sat in silence while Derek scribbled furious notes into his Moleskine notebook. He was streaming his thoughts onto the pages, hoping some of them would connect. He hoped his notes would show him what the hell he needed to do next.

"Ready?" Nikkie asked when she saw Derek raise his hand away from his notebook.

"Not really," he replied. "I'm actually nervous as shit this guy is going to tell us something that makes my head spin in confusion more than it already is."

"If things go the way they have been with this case, he probably will."

.   .   .   .   .

"I really shouldn't be meeting with you, you know. Attorney-Client relationship. Sacred in the world of law."

"Doesn't stand when your client is dead," Derek said.

Peter Maxim was nothing like Derek or Nikkie imagined. Instead of being a sharply dressed, uber-professional looking man, Maxim was dressed in a wrinkled button down shirt and dress slacks that had seen better days. He was nearly bald, with only a few strands of hair hanging on for dear life around his temples. He was short of stature, maybe five foot five, five-six if he was wearing shoes.

"Not true," Maxim replied. "Not when there's a criminal investigation surrounding a client's death."

"So, why'd you agree to meet with us then?"

Maxim leaned in close to the table, a movement Derek thought unnecessary since there wasn't another diner within twenty feet of their table.

"Because something is afoot. And I'm terrified my name and those of my partners will be dragged into this mess."

"Self preservation," Derek stated.

"Call it what you'd like, Mr. Cole. Self-preservation or due diligence or Daffy Duck, I simply do not care. I agreed to meet with you, and am happy to do it, to make sure my law firm's name retains its pristine reputation."

"Well then," Nikkie said. "Let's get to it, shall we?"

"Without ordering first?" Maxim commented. "Despite the underlying grounds for this dinner meeting, I would still believe dinner should be included in a 'dinner-meeting.' Wouldn't you agree?"

The three ordered dinners, drinks and made small talk till their meals arrived.

"You got your dinner, now can we talk about Sam Gracers and what you know about his marriage and anything else you feel might be of importance?" Derek didn't like Maxim. Didn't like him at all. It wasn't about him having issues with lawyers in general, just the issues he had with pretentious pricks. He figured he'd be picking up the tab for dinner, as well. Another thing he didn't like about the guy.

"You ask, and I'll tell you what I can. Okay?"

"Okay," Derek said, "I'll go first. Was Sam's wife, Jessica, being treated for any mental illness?"

"Can't tell you and wouldn't even if I knew."

"Did Sam ever speak to you his concerns about his wife possibly suffering from mental illness?"

"Can't tell you and wouldn't even if the law said I could."

Derek thought the meeting and the conversation with Peter Maxim was nothing more than a game to Maxim: A chance for a free meal and, perhaps, to get back at any private investigators who had pissed him off in the past. It was a game Derek was quickly growing tired of.

"Did Sam ever share with you his thoughts or concerns about Brian Hilton, FJ DeNuzzio or anyone involved, presently or in the past, with the FJ DeNuzzio group of partners?"

Maxim started to say something but was shut down by Derek before the first syllable crossed his lips.

"And if you say you can't tell me or wouldn't even if you could, I'm going to ram that T-bone steak right down your throat."

Maxim, who was much smaller than Derek, puffed out his chest.

"I'd like to see you try it."

"You should think about getting your eyes checked, Maxim."

"And you should compare our business cards, if you even have one. You may have more muscle on your body, but I have the full might and strength of the law as my sidekick." Maxim paused and shot Derek a smile dripping with contempt and arrogance. Wiping that smile off his face was now more attractive to Derek than was shoving Maxim's dinner down his throat.

"Gentlemen, please," Nikkie said. "You two can compare your penis sizes later. Right now, we need to find out how you can help us find your client's murderer. You accepted this meeting for a reason and I don't think that reason was to get a free meal and some drinks."

Peter Maxim grinned at Derek, nodded to Nikkie, then went back to work at his steak.

"I'll forget your little testosterone outburst ever happened, Mr. Cole. Now, please, continue. As I told you during our phone conversation, I will answer any questions I can but will not, under any circumstances, offer any information or direct the aim of your questions."

Nikkie moved closer to the table, mimicking the move Maxim had made several minutes earlier.

"Did Sam Gracers file for a divorce?"

Maxim smiled, his open mouth revealing chunks of meat and traces of the mashed potatoes in various states of mastication.

"He did not *file* for a divorce."

"In your opinion, was Sam Gracers preparing to file papers for a divorce?"

"Since they were never filed and therefore have zero legal standing, I can tell you definitively that my client, Samuel Gracers, was in the process of filing for a divorce from his wife, Jessica Gracers."

"When were the papers supposed to be filed with the court?" Derek asked.

"Today, actually. I assured Sam I would have the articles drawn up by yesterday and would have sent to him for his review by yesterday evening, and filed with the courts, pending his acceptance, by today. Two-thirty, to be exact. I am very prompt with my calendarized events."

"Was his wife aware of your client's intentions to file for divorce?"

"That, I do not know."

"Grounds?" Derek asked.

"Pardon me?"

"Divorce filings have to have grounds. Usually irreconcilable differences or some bullshit reason like that. What were the grounds for divorce?"

"You're learning quickly, Mr. Cole. Learning how to play this wonderful legal game we are engaged in."

"Wonderful, but how about you answer my question and leave the compliments for another time?"

"You are ill tempered, aren't you?"

"Some people have an effect on me."

"Okay then, the grounds for the divorce were to be marital incompatibilities caused by an evolving status of mental decline. I guess just because Jessica was fantastic in bed wasn't enough for Sam to want to stay married to her."

"That would be tough to prove," Nikkie suggested.

Maxim gave Nikkie a sideways glance. "Florida is a 'no fault' state, my dear. Just need a reason, not the evidence to back up the reason."

"Evolving status of mental decline," Derek said, not intending to ask a question but the upward lift of his voice suggested one. "Meaning Sam thought Jessica was going nuts, right?"

"Can't answer what my client thought or may have thought about his wife."

Nikkie leaned back from the table. Hit the back of her chair with an audible *thud*. What Maxim had told her and Derek was adding more to her confusion regarding their client. If Jessica was aware of Sam's intentions to file for a divorce, any court in the land would see that knowledge as motive. But, without the papers for divorce being approved by Sam Gracers and never filed with the court, it would be nearly impossible to prove Jessica had prior knowledge.

Motive was gone. Improvable.

In the silence that followed Maxim's last answer, Nikkie's mind went back to what Derek had told her about his conversation with Brian Hilton. *"Maybe Hilton was being honest about his reasons for denying Jessica's alibi and for burning and replacing all the furniture in his lodge,"* she thought. *"Doesn't make him any less of an asshole if he really scammed people into selling their businesses to him, though."*

Derek was also lost in thought. His thoughts were focused more on questions he wanted to ask but knew Maxim wouldn't or couldn't answer. He wracked his mind until he found a question he felt Maxim would answer.

"Gracers ever use an attorney by the name of Maryanne Jenkins?"

"The ambulance chaser? The fish out of water Jessica Gracers hired? Please."

"Seem pretty confident about that."

"I have reason to be." Maxim placed his fork on his plate, steepled his fingers. "Mr. Cole, my firm provides the absolute best legal services to our clients. From simple matters to the most complex. There is absolutely nothing Maryanne Jenkins could possibly say, do, or promise which would entice one of our clients away. Nothing."

"Lower price for services?"

Maxim laughed a bit too loudly for the quiet atmosphere of the nearly empty restaurant.

"Lower fees are not something people like Sam Gracers shop for."

"Maybe Gracers needed some legal assistance for a matter that fell outside your firm's expertise. Like maybe a matter that fell outside the boundaries of the law."

"Not Sam. He was straight as they come. All above board. Always had every contract I wrote for him double checked by another member of my firm."

"One more question before we leave you."

"I'm not finished with my meal yet," Maxim protested as a piece of poorly chewed meat flew out of his mouth and landed an inch away from Derek's hand. "Haven't even considered the dessert menu yet."

"You're free to stay as long as you'd like," Derek replied as he flipped the piece of meat with his knife back towards Maxim. "My last question is about your client's estate. His money, more precisely."

"I am not going to share my client's personal financial records with you, if that's where you are headed."

"Not at all. Just wondering why his legally married wife doesn't have access to their joint accounts?"

Maxim wiped his mouth with the cloth napkin, and then gently folded it back onto his lap.

"Now that is a question I should not answer but will." He leaned in even closer. "About a year ago, Sam had me make some changes to all the accounts which were in his name. The joint accounts were left as they were. But his accounts, and, yes, before you ask, it is legal for a husband to have complete control over privately owned financial accounts, with certain restrictions, of course. His accounts were to be held in probate in the event his death was of a suspicious nature. Being murdered certainly met that requirement."

"How long are the accounts held in probate?"

"Five days is all the law will allow."

"After that?"

"Jessica Gracers, being the legal wife of Sam Gracers, is entitled to every last penny in Sam's private accounts."

"Any idea how much money we're talking about?"

"I know exactly how much, but we're not talking about Sam's money. At least, I'm not."

"Did he tell you why he wanted that done? To have his personal accounts locked away?" Nikkie asked.

"Not his personal accounts, his private accounts. Big distinction, legally speaking."

"A little play money he hid away from his wife?"

Maxim gave Nikkie a long stare. Followed the stare with a condescending smirk.

"I think your definition of play money and Sam Gracers definition are as different as the light from a lightning bug and from a lighting bolt. But no, he didn't tell me why he wanted his private accounts set up as such and I didn't ask." Maxim lowered his voice. "But strictly between us and completely off the record, I suspected Sam felt his wife was a threat to his well being. He never suggested she threatened him, and again, this is all my speculation. I may be completely off base."

"Makes sense to me," Derek said. "Sam starts to think someone may be interested in getting rid of him to get to his money, so he decides to have the final laugh and has the money unreachable."

Nikkie asked, "And Jessica Gracers never found out about Sam's private accounts and how he had you change access to them after he died?"

"Not that I'm aware. The only person, besides me and two other partners at the firm who were aware of what Sam asked me to do was his alternate power of attorney. His primary power of attorney being his wife, of course."

"Who was his alternate power of attorney?" Derek asked.

"Since it is a matter of public record, for those who knew where to look, I don't mind telling you who served as Sam's alternate. It was the owner of the partnership Sam worked for. FJ DeNuzzio."

Chapter 26

"I think I'm more confused now than before we met Maxim. Just when I thought we should turn our attention away from Brian Hilton and on to Jessica, Maxim drops an FJ bomb."

Derek and Nikkie were too exhausted to conduct their day-end recap in the hotel bar and chose instead to sit together in Nikkie's hotel room. Nikkie was sitting in a chair near the window while Derek was stretched out on the floor; something he did when he felt overwhelmed.

Nikkie glanced towards Derek and responded, "We need another palaver. Need to figure out what the hell we're looking at with this case." She paused, then before giving Derek the opportunity to agree, disagree or to begin his version of a recap, she started in. "We're hired to prove Jessica Gracers did not kill her husband, Sam. Though she doesn't give us anything to go on at first— no alibi—we, for the most part, take her at her word. When she finally gives us the alibi, and if I haven't mentioned this already, the way she gave her alibi to us was just plain weird."

"You mean how she'd only give her alibi to me and made me ask her questions to make her story more like a narrative? Yeah, that was a bit different. May just be her way. I'm not thinking too much into it. Yet."

Carrying on without acknowledging Derek, Nikkie said, "We find out Brian Hilton is a potential player in the murder. At least according to Jessica's alibi. We get a warrant to check out the lodge Jessica said she was in with Hilton at the time of the murders. But before we get there, Hilton replaces all the furniture, has it burned and destroys any chance we had to recover DNA evidence to prove Jessica's claim. Then you—and I have no idea how you pulled this off—get invited into Hilton's home..."

"Where I lose my affinity for cheap scotch. Don't forget that part. Pretty important."

"Where he tells you he's gay and therefore not interested sexually in Jessica, explains why he had the lodge cleaned and furniture burned and suggests Sam Gracers thought Jessica may be suffering from a mental illness. I find out Hilton may be scamming business owners into selling him their businesses by working with a doctor in Nashville and one in Tampa. These ass wipes tell the business owners they have a cancer often caused by stress. You overhear Hilton speaking with Matt Steel, who turns out to have just agreed to sell his business to Hilton after going to the same Nashville-based doctor…"

"Timothy O'Connell."

"…And after being told he has cancer. He's sent to the same specialist in Tampa…"

"Mark Ruggerio."

"…But I called Steel, let him know what Donald Reagan told me, and he tells me almost the exact same story as Reagan's. Steel also tells me the papers for the sale of his business were drawn up by and sent to Maryanne Jenkins."

"Whom our friend, Peter Maxim, described as an ambulance chaser. Not the typical high-powered attorney you'd expect to be working with a guy like Hilton."

"Maryanne Jenkins tells me she has ALS. Not sure if that fits anyplace in this mess of a case, but it might." Nikkie spun her chair around, facing the window. "Sam Gracers has Maxim put a hold on his private accounts—and I have no idea how a private account is different from a personal account, by the way—and has this mystery man named FJ DeNuzzio as his alternate power of attorney."

"When you think back to Jessica's alibi, she suggested FJ might have had something to do with Craig Washburn's death. So, we certainly can't count him out as a potential suspect."

"And I'm not. Not in the least. We just don't know anything about the guy."

Derek sat up, leaned his back against the bed.

"Physical evidence at the crime scene all point to Jessica. Her gun, her prints on the casings and she was the only one at the scene. Add to that what Maxim said about Sam getting ready to file for divorce and we have motive."

"Assuming Jessica knew about Sam's desire to divorce her. No way of knowing that for sure."

"Jessica also said Brian borrowed her gun when he went running at the lodge. Said he forgot his and needed hers in case he ran across any rabid raccoons."

"Has Detective Gonzales gotten back to you with any info on the gun? Any prints found?"

"She hasn't. Hoping to hear something soon, though."

"It's the details of Jessica's story that get me."

"What do you mean?" Derek, who was now standing, leaning against the far wall, asked.

"Details. Like how she and Hilton used a book…"

"*One Shot* by Lee Child."

"…To pass notes back and forth to each other. That's a very particular detail."

"And improvable unless we find that book in Hilton's home. Think we should ask Maryanne for another warrant?"

"Honestly," Nikkie answered, "I don't think we should tell her anything. Not until we find out her story. Find out how and why she was involved with Hilton. She may be involved in this tangled mess somehow."

Derek sighed. Pulled out his Moleskine notebook from his back pocket. Flipped till he found a blank page and scribbled some notes. He finished writing, walked to Nikkie holding the notebook open for her to see. Handed her the pencil.

"I wrote down initials for four people. FJ, for DeNuzzio, JG, for Jessica, BH, for Hilton and MJ, for Jenkins. Unless you can think of anyone else I should add to our list of possibles, circle that your gut tells you killed Sam Gracers. Don't think on it, just let your gut decide."

Nikkie held the pencil in a hovering pattern over the notebook.

"Are you saying we should only concern ourselves with the murder and disregard what Hilton may be doing with those doctors and those poor business owners?"

"Not at all. But we need to focus. There are way too many variables with this case. No way we can chase all these rabbits."

Nikkie moved the pencil closer to the page. She paused, gave Derek a little smile, her face set in a slightly upturned position, then drew a large circle around two initials.

CHAPTER 27

August 22

Derek was awake by five-thirty the next morning. After gulping down two glasses of water drawn from the bathroom sink, he dressed in his running clothes then made his way via the stairwell to the lobby. Running had become more therapeutic than exercise for him over the past few years. It gave him time when no one would ask him questions, seek his advice or demand his attention. For a short while, friends of his with whom he worked along side when he was part of the Columbus Police Force would join Derek for his morning six to nine mile runs, but his pace and penchant for finding hills to run up soon convinced them to find other running partners. In truth, it was more Derek's desire to be alone for the forty to sixty minute run than him wanting to physically push himself so hard which drove his intense running workouts. Since it was against the unwritten, unspoken "man code" for one to ask another to "slow down," Derek's morning runs were almost always time for him alone.

This morning, with nothing more than his jumble of thoughts and his memories of Lucy to accompany him, he ran close to ten miles. He cut his pace back, assuming the day might drag late as the recent ones had, and managed to complete his run in a few seconds under seventy minutes.

When the elevator doors pulled open to the seventh floor, Nikkie was leaning against the wall across from the doors.

"Happy to see you," Derek said, "but kind of creepy to think you've been waiting here for me the whole time I've been running."

"I want to change the initials I circled last night."

"You stood outside the elevator doors waiting for me to get back to tell me that?"

"I've been up since four. I heard you leave and wanted to tell you before you left. But, I know you don't like to talk to anyone before you run so I decided to wait till you got back."

"Why have you been up since four?" Derek asked as they walked side-by-side down the hallway to their adjoining rooms.

"My thoughts woke me up. Couldn't fall back to sleep once they did."

"Your gut telling you something differently than what it did last night?"

Nikkie stopped, put her hands on her hips.

"You kind of forced my gut to make a decision last night. Holding that notebook open in front of me with four people's initials for me to choose from; don't think my gut feelings work that way. So, after a few hours of thinking more about it, I want to change who I circled."

"That's not how gut reactions work, Nikkie. The whole thing about them is they're not arrived at after hours of thinking."

"Well, mine are. And, I want to change my answer."

They spanned the final twenty feet to Derek's room. He slid his key into the card swipe, pushed open the door.

"And," Nikkie said from behind him, "I noticed you didn't circle any initials last night. You without a gut feeling or don't feel like sharing?"

"You and I have been working together for over a year now, right?"

She nodded her head.

"In that time, your gut has been right way more often than mine has. I have a good idea who killed Sam Gracers but not sure I trust that idea fully yet. I wanted to see what your gut was telling you. See if we were on the same page."

"And?" Nikkie said as she inched a bit closer to him. "Are we on the same page?"

Derek fell silent. His eyes fixed on Nikkie's while his gut twisted and leaped in strange acrobatics. He took a small step closer to her, erasing the small space which had separated them. Nikkie reached her open hand up and caressed the side of his face. "Same page or we still a chapter away from each other?"

Derek's cell phone rang. She pulled her hand back, looked at Derek, and said, "Check the caller ID. I have a strange feeling about this call."

"You and your gut," Derek said. "I wish it was wrong sometimes."

He slid his finger across the screen. He shrugged his shoulders, indicating he didn't recognize the number.

"Derek Cole…"

Derek's face fell slack. He plowed his fingers through his hair, took a deep breath in. Whoever was calling him had more to say. Nikkie's eyes grew wide with anticipation. She stood, pressed her face against Derek's and tried to listen the conversation. A few moments later, and after Nikkie picked up exactly nothing from the conversation, Derek thanked the caller then ended the call.

"What? What happened? Who was that?"

Derek stepped to the bed, then fell face down onto it.

"That was Detective Rachel Gonzales," he said, his voice muffled as it leaked out through the mattress his face was pressed against. "Brian Hilton is dead."

"Oh my God," Nikkie exclaimed. "What happened? When?"

Derek rolled over, extended his arms straight out to his sides.

"She found out around two this morning. Explosion in his home on Snead Island."

"Are you kidding me? His house exploded? A bomb?"

"Not sure yet. But, there's more."

Nikkie sat down on the bed beside Derek.

"What? Tell me."

"They've arrested Jessica Gracers. She was seen leaving Hilton's home a few minutes before the explosion."

Silently, Nikkie stood; walked over to the chair she had been sitting in the night before. Picked up the notebook and the pencil, drew a big "X" over the initials she had circled last night and drew a few heavy circles around another set of initials.

• • • • • •

"Sorry I'm so late. Case I just got assigned last night is a real doozy."

It was past two in the afternoon before Derek and Nikkie met Rachel Gonzales at an oceanside bar beside a walking park not far from their hotel. Rachel had asked to meet with Derek and Nikkie during the call she made to Derek and fully expected to make that meeting by nine. But, soon after she and Derek ended their call, she was pulled out on a new case.

After Derek and Nikkie caught Rachel up to speed on what they uncovered the day before, Rachel turned the conversation to what she had been learning and doing in the background on Jessica Gracers' case. By the time they had finished filling Rachel in, Rachel's face was set in a surprised expression.

"Guys," she said, "I hope you're ready for another surprise."

"I seriously don't know if my brain can handle any more surprises," Nikkie said.

"Well, you mentioned a doctor's name up in Nashville during the rundown of your day."

"Timothy O'Connell," Derek said.

"The case I was called out on, the case that made me late for our meeting today, was for a dead body found in the bay. I didn't have much to do at the scene since the body was found washed up on shore. Wallet, filled with ID's still inside. Guess who the victim was?"

"You've got to be kidding me?" Nikkie said. "The doctor? Timothy O'Connell?"

"Absolutely positive. And by the looks of his body, he was killed within an hour or two from when his body was discovered. Whoever killed him, didn't do it quickly. Tortured him pretty bad."

Derek said, "Cause of death?"

"Gun shot to the forehead."

"Caliber?"

"Small. Not sure yet."

"I have a feeling ballistics will come back saying it was a .380."

"That wouldn't surprise me in the least."

"Tell us about Hilton," Derek said. "We'll get back to O'Connell later."

"Details are sketchy. Snead is in Manatee County. Probably wouldn't have heard much about the incident till tomorrow but I have a friend who works dispatch for Manatee who knew I was interested in Hilton. She called me as soon as she found out it was Brian Hilton's home and that he was killed. Like I said, details are sketchy, but the lead investigator believes someone planted a pipe bomb directly under the chair Hilton was sitting in. Remote detonation. Instant death. There's Hilton all over the walls in the room."

"And they like Jessica Gracers for the murder?" Nikkie asked.

"Some neighbors of Hilton gave a spot on description of a woman they saw walking down the front walk and getting into her car. Didn't get plates but the car they described matches Jessica's car. And the description they gave of the woman matches perfectly. She's in county jail down in Manatee County as we speak."

"She admit to the crime?"

"Nope. Said she went to see Brian to try to find out why he denied everything she told us in her alibi, rang his bell but he never answered. Said she left and drove straight home."

"Wait a minute," Nikkie said. "The bomb was planted beneath the chair Hilton was sitting in? How could he not have known he was sitting on a bomb?"

"There was an empty bottle of whiskey on his back patio and another bottle, two-thirds empty, in his kitchen. Best guess is that he got drunk and never knew his ass was about to decorate his walls."

"The sheriffs will find my prints on the bottle out on the patio," Derek said. "My half-smoked cigar may still be in the ashtray, as well."

"I thought of that," Rachel said. "I'll let the lead investigator know I spoke with you and share your story with him. Nothing to worry about."

"With this case," Derek remarked, "there's everything to worry about."

After another round of drinks were ordered and served, Nikkie started in.

"Okay, Jessica is in custody for Hilton's murder, but I don't think she would have killed him and allowed herself to be seen. Hilton dying kills her alibi, right?"

"Sort of," Rachel said. "He already refuted everything she claimed, but with him out of the picture, he won't be able to defend himself if her case goes to court. Not sure if him dying hurts her case or helps it. As for you feeling she didn't kill him, I tend to feel the same way. Jessica Gracers is a pretty smart woman. I don't think she'd casually walk down his walkway after parking her car in his driveway, knowing how easily she could be seen. I think, at least as far as Hilton's death is concerned, wrong place, wrong time."

"What do you know about O'Connell? The doctor from Nashville?" Derek's mind was slowly putting some key things together. He felt he was getting close to knowing which rabbit he and Nikkie needed to chase. There were just a few pieces left. Rachel had one of the pieces, and Maryanne Jenkins had the others.

"Too soon to know much," Rachel said. "We know he was tortured, shot in the forehead and dumped in the bay. Body wasn't weighted down at all. Found him floating face up around a half mile from shore."

"Anonymous person call it in? Someone say they saw a body floating in the bay but, before the 911 dispatcher could ask his name, the caller hung up?"

Rachel screwed up her face a bit. "How do you know that? That's almost exactly what happened. How did you know?"

"That's what I would have done. Probably called from a pay phone north of Tampa. Hard to find a pay phone nowadays, but down in Florida, lots of elderly people still like to use old technology. I saw a few pay phones while driving around today."

"The call did come from a pay phone north of Tampa. But, what do you mean that's what *you* would do?"

"The person who called 911 was the killer. Wanted to send a message to someone. That's why the body wasn't weighted down. He wanted it to be found and found easily and quickly. Also didn't want to take the chance the body would get dragged out by the outgoing tide, so he called it in himself. Gave himself enough time to head back to his home but not too much time for the tides to pull the body out to sea."

"Okay," Rachel said, digging into her purse in search of something to capture notes on. "Tell me what else you would do."

"I wouldn't have done it alone, that's for sure and I wouldn't dump the body within a hundred miles of where I live. You're looking for two killers, neither local. Tell me, you said O'Connell was tortured. What part of his body was tortured the most?"

"Penis was mutilated. Numerous slashing cuts and at least one deep penetrating stab. Right through the testes."

"How about O'Connell's mouth?"

"Busted up pretty badly. Bunch of teeth knocked out. Not sure yet but there's probably a few more cracked and hanging on by a thread. Lips all busted up. Like O'Connell was punched hard and often."

Derek was asking his questions in rapid fire. No emotion behind them. He asked, listened for the answer, then moved to the next question.

"The knife wounds to his groin, were they direct or through O'Connell's pants?"

"Derek, you're beginning to scare me. The crotch of his pants was cut up pretty bad. Like the killer, or killers, stabbed and slashed at his groin while O'Connell was still wearing them."

"The wounds were meant to embarrass O'Connell as much as they were meant to hurt him. The killers wanted to make sure O'Connell understood they were in charge. That *they* were more important than he was. They weren't homosexual or trying to repress some backed up sexual dysfunction, that's why they didn't have O'Connell drop his pants. Didn't want anyone, including each other, to think they were gay. Just wanted to make damn sure O'Connell lost his manhood.

"The focus on the mouth tells me these two didn't want O'Connell to talk. Not after they were done, obviously since they had every intention of killing him, but while they were torturing him. Probably didn't want to feel stupid if O'Connell used some fancy college words they couldn't understand. These killers were contracted to kill O'Connell. They threw in the torture for no charge. Kind of like their own fringe benefit."

"You seem to know more about this than any of us at the department," Rachel said. "So, tell me, who are these guys and who paid them to kill O'Connell."

"Hilton hired them, that's for damn sure. Nikkie called O'Connell and put him on notice by mentioning three names: Reagan, Steel and Hilton. That was a trifecta of doom and despair for O'Connell. As soon as he hung up on Nikkie, O'Connell called Hilton. Check his phone records. You'll find I'm right about that. Probably read him the riot act. Told Hilton he needed to take care of the problem. Hilton contacted two people he uses for off the record jobs, gave them O'Connell's info and told them to be quick about it. Last thing Hilton wanted was for O'Connell to freak out and tell authorities about what Hilton and he had done."

"Makes sense to me," Rachel commented. "Still, it's a long stretch, but it does make sense." Rachel paused as her face slowly displayed the look of an approaching thought. "Wait a minute, those two brothers in Alabama, you think they are the killers?"

"That would be my bet. Hilton used them to take care of the lodge. Probably used them for a whole bunch of jobs. When I was at their strip of land where they burned the furniture, I peeked into a pole barn on the property. Just a quick glance. Inside were four cars, possibly a boat as well. Each covered up with a custom fit cover. Soft material so the cars wouldn't get scratched. I've seen covers like those before. Know how much they cost. People don't spend a grand or more on car covers to protect a Hyundai Elantra. Those cars were high end. They also had enough lumber sitting next to the pole barn to do a full rehab on the house on the property. Lumber like that costs a lot. Got me wondering how two brothers who run a small moving company could afford automobiles like those and have enough left over to spend on fixing up a house. They didn't get their money from moving, that's for sure."

"They could rent out the storage space. Those cars could be owned by other people," Nikkie suggested.

"Not with the same type of covers. All black, all custom and all made of the same material. Whoever owns one of those cars, owns them all. And someone with enough money to own four cars worth spending a grand each to cover, isn't going to store them in some pole barn owned by those brothers. Never would happen."

"Could be," Rachel said in a voice that was streaked with self-doubt, "that the brothers inherited a bunch of money from their parents or a rich uncle?"

"Thought of that, too. While I was waiting for you to pick me up on the side of the road, I sat out of the sun and did some searching on my phone. I'm not very good at the whole Internet thing, but good enough to know how to search public databases. I guess our old assistant, Crown, loaded an app on my iPhone. Gives me access to a whole bunch of public databases. Turns out the owners of Southern Boys Moving Company—which is run under a legally filed DBA, by the way—are Jackson and Robert Trainer. A Mrs. Gloria Trainer, the boys' mother, lives in a trailer park in Mississippi with her second husband. Never changed her last name. The boys' father is off the radar. His name, Thomas Trainer, is listed on both of the boys' birth certificates, but there's no known address for him."

"Sounds like he abandoned his family," Rachel said.

"Sounds that way."

Rachel said, "If I was the DA or a defense lawyer, I'd say all you have are possible connections. Not a thread of evidence."

"I plan on taking care of that in the morning."

Nikkie stiffened her spine, gave a long, knowing look to Derek.

"Whatever you're thinking about doing, stop. I know that look in your eye and I know nothing good ever follows that look."

"I'm going to pay a visit to Jackson and Robert, better known as 'Bobby,' Trainer. Getting a little tired of chasing all these rabbits."

"You're not planning on driving all the way up to their home tonight, are you?" Nikkie asked.

"Damn right, I am. Want to get there before they have too much time to clean up any traces of O'Connell. I figure they drove one of those covered cars for this job. Wouldn't want to use their moving truck. Too easily remembered. They used a car from the pole barn, drove to wherever O'Connell lived. Took care of business then drove him down to Tampa."

"You're thinking they killed him up in Tennessee?" Rachel asked.

"That's what I would do. Don't want to take any chance of him getting away while driving to Tampa. Kill him up in Nashville, then drive the body to Tampa. That's what I would do."

"Then put the car back under covers in case anyone saw it. Makes sense."

"My first stop will be that pole barn," Derek said as he waved to the waitress and mouthed, "Check, please."

"Big problem, as I see it," Nikkie offered. "Time frame issue, again. If it was the brothers in Alabama, how the hell did they get to Nashville then to Tampa in the time frame we're looking at?"

"Not really," Derek said. "Dothan to Nashville is a little over three hundred and seventy miles. Figure six-and-a-half hours. If the brothers got the call day before yesterday, say around eight, eight-thirty, they'd arrive in the Nashville area around four to four-thirty. Great time to kill someone, if you ask me. Probably didn't waste much time. They surprised O'Connell, subdued him, drove him someplace out of the way. Plenty of places like that outside of Nashville. Let's say the brothers finish up their business by six. They probably brought a car with a good-sized trunk. They tossed O'Connell in the trunk, and then drove to Tampa. That's a long-ass drive. Ten hours if you go straight through, twelve if you take your time, which I'm sure they did. Probably took turns driving. One drove, the other slept.

"They couldn't get to Tampa in the daylight. I place them in Tampa around eight-thirty last night. They waited till it got a bit darker, dumped O'Connell in the bay, drove to the north side of Tampa, stopped at a pay phone, called in their sighting of a body, then drove back to Dothan. Time frame works fine."

Rachel checked her notes. Slowly started nodding her head.

"The 911 call came into the center at ten-twenty. Time frame fits."

Nikkie let out a long sigh. "Let's say you're right. Let's say Jackson and Bobby Trainer were hired by Hilton to take O'Connell out to make sure he keeps quiet. If that's true, then we have another killer on the loose. No matter how creative you can get with time frames, there's no way the Trainers could have made it to Snead Island in time to match the explosion which killed Hilton. No way in the world."

"Fortunate for us," Derek said, "we snag Hilton's killer, we snag Sam Gracers' as well."

Chapter 28

When Jessica Gracers learned her recently departed husband's brother had not only planned a funeral for Sam but had already petitioned the Pinellas District Attorney's office for possession of his remains and for the rights to transport his body across state lines, she grew enraged. After her calls to DA Julie Steinberg's office were routed to voicemail or sent to an intern who promised to "get the message to the District Attorney as soon as possible," Jessica demanded she be released from her jail cell on account of extreme emotional distress.

Her request was practically laughed at.

When she called Maryanne Jenkins and again demanded that she get down to the DA's office and get her out of jail, immediately, her attorney matched her rage.

"Jessica," Maryanne barked at her, "you were out on bail after being accused of, and arrested for the murder of your husband. The conditions of your bail were extremely clear. In the best-case scenario, a judge would remand you to the cell you're now remanded to simply because you violated the conditions of your parole when you drove to Snead Island with the full intention of speaking with Brian Hilton. That's the best scenario. But what you're looking at now is more like the worst-case scenario. You admit to driving to Hilton's house. Admit to walking up to his front door. Thirty-minutes after you leave Hilton's house, he's killed by an explosion. And guess what, Jessica? Let's say you had nothing to do with Brian's death. Let's say you are telling the truth and all you did was walk up to his door, but changed your mind before you rang the bell. Let's say you did drive home and had absolutely nothing to do with the explosion and Brian's death. Guess what? It doesn't matter. You're experiencing the worst-case scenario simply because you violated the conditions of your parole and were in the wrong place at the wrong time. There isn't a judge in the country who would let you out on bail again. You're staying where you are till both cases, both *murder* cases, are closed."

Jessica fell silent. Didn't make a sound for close to two minutes. She probably would have kept on saying nothing had the guard not tapped her on her shoulder.

"Time's up."

Jessica took a deep breath, held it then blew it out directly into the mouthpiece of the phone.

"It seems I've reached my phone-time limit. So I'll end with two demands. Since I am paying you, I am comfortable with issuing commands. You get me out of here by tomorrow at the latest. I don't care how you do it, just get it done. If you don't, I'll make sure your business dealings with Brian Hilton are made public. That will certainly raise some eyebrows, wouldn't you think?"

It was Maryanne's time to go silent.

"Yes, yes, that's right. I know all about your role in Brian's business dealings. I'm not a lawyer so I can't say if the services you provided Brian were in support of any illegal practices, but still, the fact you insisted that your dealings with Brian were kept as quiet as possible will certainly raise some eyebrows. Maybe *you* should rehearse your alibi for Brian's murder."

Without a second delay, Maryanne asked what Jessica's second demand was.

"Get Cole up here ASAP. I can't call him myself. Get me out and get Cole here, now!"

•　　•　　•

Jessica shared her cell with a forty-six year old black woman, arrested for assault with a deadly weapon. Jessica's cellmate had been her cellmate when she was first arrested for Sam's murder. The time they spent together was done so without a single word passing between them. But as Jessica sat on her bed—four inch thick mattress, paper thin sheets and a pillow with as many stains as lumps—the anger inside her demanded release.

"So," Jessica said, "what are you in for? That's what convicts say to each other, isn't it? They talk to each other about what they're 'in' for? I'm in because the man I had an affair with—and I'm not telling you that because I'm proud of the fact I cheated on my husband—refuted my entire alibi by insisting he and I had not spent the weekend together."

Her cellmate remained sitting still, head hung low, fingers knitted in a loose grip.

"Well, since you asked, my husband, Sam, was murdered the weekend I was away with Brian. That's his name, the man I was having an affair with. I guess I should say that *was* his name. He was killed yesterday. Someone planted a bomb in his house. Killed him instantly, or so they tell me. Before he was blown up, along with any chance of him admitting he was with me at his lodge the weekend my husband was murdered, I violated the conditions of my parole. I went to confront him. Drove down to Snead Island, walked right up to his front door. Had every intention of insisting he tell the truth. Would have resorted to begging, if it came to that. But I lost my nerve. Honestly, if I had seen him face to face and he acted as if I was crazy and wouldn't even admit to me what he and I had together, I…I don't know what I'd do.

"So, I left. But some of Brian's neighbors gave a description of me and my car to the authorities after Brian was killed. They arrested me even before they told me Brian had been killed. That's two men, two men that I loved, killed within the same week. Do you have any idea what that can do to a woman?"

Jessica sniffed back some tears. Straightened herself and continued.

"I just met with my lawyer. I insisted that she get me out of this horrible place. I even threatened her. That's right, I threatened my lawyer." Jessica crossed her legs, leaned forward at her waist. "See, my husband found out that Brian was doing something terrible in his business. Simply terrible. Sam and Brian work for the same person. Hard to explain the company, so I won't bother you with the details, but the man they worked for was involved in what Brian was doing as well. No, I can't say I know that for certain, but considering how tightly FJ, he's the owner of the company, runs things, I cannot imagine him *not* knowing what Brian was doing.

"I don't know how Sam found out. But he told me one night, probably four or five months ago. Said it was eating him alive to know what Brian and FJ were doing. They were practically stealing million dollar businesses from people. Terrible, simply terrible what they were doing. I couldn't believe it at first. No, that's not true. I knew what Sam told me was the truth; I just didn't want to admit it. I fell in love with Brian and couldn't bring myself to accept what an awful person he was.

"Sam never knew about the affair. At least I pray he never knew. The idea of him knowing and the pain it would have caused would be unbearable to me. Unbearable.

"I know what you're thinking, and I don't blame you one bit. You're thinking if I cared so much for Sam and his feelings that I would have never had an affair. But we had grown apart. We barely spoke to each other the past year. He changed, Sam that is. He changed from the caring, loving man I married to someone closed up. Secretive.

"Thinking back on it now—I've had plenty of time to think as of late—I've come to realize Sam probably found out what Brian and FJ were doing about the same time he started to change. It wasn't that he was changing or had fallen out of love with me. What he found out had caused him to change.

"Anyway," Jessica said as she wiped away a tear which had slid down her cheek, "I started to do my own little investigation. Actually thought about hiring a private investigator at first but ended up finding what I was looking for without much effort." She laughed a bit. "It's kind of funny. When I was thinking about hiring a private eye to found out if Brian was really doing what Sam told me he was, I spoke with a relative of mine who lives in Maine. She told me she and her husband had hired a private eye a little while back. And guess who I ended up hiring after I was accused of murdering my husband? That's right, the private eye I almost hired to investigate Brian. Strange how things work out.

"I won't bore you with the details of how I found this out, but I discovered Brian was using this lawyer named Maryanne Jenkins, who just happens to be the lawyer I hired to get me out of this mess, to draw up paperwork for the purchase of the businesses he was scamming people out of. I can't say she knew all the details of how Brian was convincing these poor men to sell their businesses to him, but I know she must have known enough to want to keep it quiet.

"Remember I told you I threatened her? Well, I did. I told her that if she didn't get me out of his horrible place that I would let the world know she was involved in what Brian was doing. I wish I could have seen her face when I told her what I'd do. Not that she shows any emotion. She's a cold person. But I just know my threat must have just twisted her face all up in a jumble of a mess.

"Not that it matters much now, I guess. Sam is dead and my only alibi is dead as well. I'll probably spend the rest of my life behind bars. The rest of my life."

Jessica wiped her face dry, sat up then leaned back, using her flayed arms as braces.

"Not much of a jailhouse confession, huh? Just a sad sack story told by a sad sack, unfaithful woman."

Her cellmate dropped her hands, picked up her head, titled it to her left a bit.

"I beat my husband with an aluminum baseball bat on account of him raping my sister. That's what I done. That's why I'm in here."

Jessica just stared in silence.

After two minutes of pregnant silence, a female guard walked up to their cell. Rustled keys out of her pocket. Slid open the iron door.

"Gracers, you're out. Bail posted."

Jessica stood slowly. Stood holding her hands clasped across her belly. She took a few steps towards her cellmate, bent down and whispered in her ear. Kept whispering for several seconds.

Her cellmate's eyes slowly grew wide. Then she nodded her head a few times.

"Marcus James. My husband's name is Marcus James."

CHAPTER 29

"You won't get another chance. I need you to tell me you understand. This is it. Last chance. Screw up again, and your butt will be behind bars."

"I won't screw up again. I can't go back into that place."

Maryanne had waited outside the jail for her client to go through the "exiting process." That process took thirty minutes from the time Jessica was told she was being released, again, till her personal belongings were pulled out of inmate storage, checked against the inventory register, handed over to her and being asked to sign on the dotted line to agree everything taken from her had been returned.

"You can't return the time I've lost," Jessica said sharply to the charge deputy.

In response, the deputy only gestured to a closed door.

"Change in there. Your lawyer is waiting outside in her car for you. Have a nice day."

As Jessica approached Maryanne's car, she saw Maryanne fixing her gaze dead ahead. Like the last thing Jenkins wanted was to look at her. Jessica considered passing by Maryanne and walking somewhere to find a different way home. Anything would be better than having to sit next to a woman who hated her as much as did Maryanne Jenkins.

But the heat was pouring down. Sky was heavy with dark, almost mud-colored clouds. The heat was going to break soon. Had to. And Jessica chose getting in Maryanne's car over being stuck in what promised to be a torrential rain.

Once Jessica acknowledged and responded to her admonition, Maryanne put the car in gear and headed south towards Jessica Gracers' home.

"Where are you taking me?" Jessica asked.

"That's what you ask me? That's the most important thing you can think of to ask? How about, 'Hey Maryanne, thanks for getting me out. How did you do it? I know I messed up going to Brian's house. But, how did you get me out?' Instead, you want to know where I'm taking you? My God, Jessica, Brian may have been right about you."

"What does that mean?" Jessica snapped.

"That you have some emotional issues. Mental issues."

Jessica twisted her body away from Maryanne. Folded her arms in a tight knot over her chest.

"Considering the relationship you had with Brian and all the damage that relationship would do to your 'sterling' reputation as a lawyer, I can't believe you'd rather criticize me than beg me to keep my mouth shut."

Maryanne shot a sideways gaze at Jessica.

Jessica was right, Maryanne did hate her. Hated her for not only what she knew about her dealings with the recently departed Brian Hilton, but for everything Jessica Gracers stood for. To Jessica, people were either useful or not useful: No one had any intrinsic value unless they were wealthy or influential. That's how Maryanne Jenkins thought of her client. And damn the day Jessica Gracers called her from jail, telling her she needed to represent her against the murder charge. Damn that day! She could have come clean, right then and there. She could have told Jessica to go pound salt, find another sucker who'd be willing to trade money for insults. She could have walked, as long as Iron Lou permitted it, right into a judge's chambers, spilled out an armful of files regarding her business dealings with Brian Hilton and thrown herself on the mercy of the court.

She could have presented a strong case to support her claim that she was forced into providing legal services for Hilton. Could have talked about the promises Hilton extended to her. Promises of a ruined career. A ruined reputation. And maybe something much worse.

Though Hilton never threatened her directly, she did receive an unmarked envelope, which had been left sitting on her pillow at home. Someone obviously had broken in, took nothing, did no damage, but left a poorly clasped, manila envelope for her review. Inside the envelope were two pictures and an article cut out from the local newspaper. The photographs, grainy, black and white, printed on the cheap type of paper most people use in their home printers, were of a man she later learned to be Craig Washburn. The first photo showed Washburn as an obvious victim of kidnapping. Hands tied together behind his back. Duct tape stretched across his mouth. A hand gripping Washburn's hair and pulling his face up to look directly at the camera.

The second photo was also of Washburn, but no hand was required to still or lift his face for the camera. His eyes were glazed over as if they were rinsed with crème. An angry black hole dotted the center of his forehead.

Beneath the second photograph—written by someone with horrible handwriting and in desperate need of a "carry-around" spelling dictionary—was written "This what happins to squealers. Complaments of my team."

The included article's date wasn't included in the scissors' path, but Maryanne recognized the article from a couple years back. The article was about a body having been found floating in the bay. Medical examiner suggested the cause of death to be a "single, small caliber gunshot to the head." The reporter carried on a bit, too long, for Maryanne's tastes, about the growing problem of gun violence in the Tampa/St. Pete area. About how the "influx of gangs and drugs meant more guns and more bodies dumped into the bay." Maryanne, her hands trembling in fear and anger, jumped to the last line of the article, which was the rote call from the local authorities that if "anyone has any information about the murder, to please contact Detective" So and So at some ten-digit number.

It had started so innocently. A simple request to draw up legal documents regarding the sale and acquisition of a tract of land outside of Sarasota. Simple. Took her two hours. Maybe her ship had come in! Though she didn't know who Brian Hilton was, the fact he had chosen her to draw up the forms and had paid her four times her normal fee to do so, was nearly as good as her winning the lottery.

After the first legal request, there came more. Each seemingly simple and each paying her well more than any of her other clients could ever pay. After a few months, the requests for legal documents started to flow in abundance. Her workload for Hilton went from one, maybe two a week, to three or four per day. She was forced to stop taking new clients as all her time was spent drawing up legal docs for the purchase or sale of homes, land, small businesses, partnership agreements. The list went on and on.

Though she never met Hilton face to face, she was certain he was one of the wealthiest men in Florida. Certainly more wealthy than all her other clients combined.

The workload and the flow of legal fees made her sloppy. She knew it was happening, knew she was probably making some minor mistakes here and there. But Hilton had very tight deadlines. She couldn't risk missing one. *"Miss one and they all go away,"* she had thought to herself.

Then, one day, about a year and a half ago, the requests for her legal services just stopped. Like turning a faucet off: Flowing one second, then bone dry the next. She thought about contacting Hilton, apologizing for any mistake or omission she may have made. But she didn't need to make any attempt at contact.

While she stood in the privacy of her own bedroom, staring in horror at the grainy photograph of a very dead, and very murdered, Craig Washburn, her phone rang.

Hilton's voice was much friendlier than she expected. He started off by apologizing for sending her so much "boring work" over the last few months. Said he was in a period of rapid expansion, thus the workflow and stiff time frames for completion. He went on and on about how happy he was to have found her. About how happy he and his partners were that she was so willing to take on the "boring" work, get it done quickly, and charge so little.

Then, that friendly voice changed so suddenly, so completely, it set her back on her heels. Hilton told her she really should be more diligent in her work. That she should analyze any requests she receives.

"I can only imagine that, in your excited haste to please me in order to keep the gravy train flowing, you neglected to even read the last two document packages I sent for you to file. Did you read even a word of them, Miss Jenkins?"

"If I made a mistake, I'm sorry. I'll certainly refund every penny of my fees…"

"You and I are not on the same page," he said, back to using his friendly voice. "As far as I'm concerned, you didn't make any mistakes at all. But, I have a feeling you might think otherwise. No matter. I'll be sending a dossier to your home later this evening. Your normal fee for such a service will be included in cash along with the dossier. I don't expect any challenges or arguments from you. And should you need any motivation to do what I am paying you to do without hesitation, I suggest you review the details of the last two legal documents you filed with the court."

It only took Maryanne thirty minutes spent reading to realize the last two legal filings she made for Brian Hilton, if ever brought under investigation, would not only find her without her ability to practice law in Florida, hell, probably in any state, but might also find herself in need of hiring her own legal representative.

He didn't mention the envelope she was still holding in her shaking hand. Didn't make one mention of how he and his partners would respond to her refusal.

She was stuck. No way out except by taking the path set before her by Craig Washburn.

•   •   •   •   •

"I'm taking you to your house. Yes, the house you said you never want to step foot in again. Not my choice. The judge made that call. You are remanded to the confines of your property for twenty hours per day. Can't even get an exception to attend your husband's funeral in Texas next week. Oh, didn't you hear? Sam's brother was given legal guardianship of your husband's remains. He should be loaded on a plane any minute now."

"You cold, heartless bitch," Jessica said softly but quite clearly. "I should have turned you and Brian in to the police when I found out what you were doing." She paused. Shook her head back and forth quickly. "Derek Cole was right. He told me that while I didn't pull the trigger, I still killed Sam. I killed him when I knew what you and Brian were doing and didn't say anything, I just kept spreading my legs for that bastard and you just kept on running his legal games for him. I killed Sam. I know that now. But I didn't put a bullet into his head and, goddamnit, you are going to make damn sure I never spend another second inside a jail cell. I don't care how you do it, just do it."

A thought flashed across Jessica's face. It took her by surprise.

"Why am I out of jail? How did you get me out?"

"Someone confessed to killing Brian."

"Who? Who confessed?"

"Man named Matthew Steel."

Chapter 30

Nikkie had just dropped Derek off at the Tampa airport then received a text message invite from Rachel Gonzales.

Iced Tea at the Overlook? One hour?

When Nikkie arrived at the only area restaurant she knew by name, Rachel was already sitting in a booth in the far corner. Rachel had filled her in on how Matthew Steel confessed to everything.

"He walked right in, told the desk sergeant he needed to make a confession. Sat down with the lead investigator in Manatee County and told him everything. Said he found Hilton passed out drunk. Put a pipe bomb under his seat, then sat around, hoping Hilton would at least come to. Said he was ready to die right alongside Hilton so he could make sure he went straight to hell. He ended up setting a timer for five minutes and then simply walked to where he had parked his car and waited for the bomb to go off."

"Jesus," Nikkie said. "How does a guy like that know how to build a freaking pipe bomb? Some terrorist website or something?"

"His business in building demolitions. International business. He's hired all over the world as an expert in demolitions. Guess if he can bring down a skyscraper he can build a simple pipe bomb."

Nikkie knitted her eyebrows. Screwed up her face a tad.

"Why in the world would Brian Hilton be interested in buying an international demolitions business? I thought he was focused on medical supplies?"

"I've asked myself that same question," Rachel answered.

"Did you come up with an answer?"

"I've been doing some investigating on the side. You know, on the Gracers' case. Seems every partner in the FJ DeNuzzio group specializes in specific industries, but each has also acquired property or businesses that don't fit with their specialty. Like Hilton going after Matt Steel's business. Makes no sense."

"Any other strange ones?"

"Plenty. Each partner has made purchases that don't fit into their area of specialty, but each odd acquisition seems to fit together when you look at all the partners' business dealings. The way I see it, Hilton was buying Steel's business to compliment the building rights Sam Gracers acquired in Chile two months ago. Turns out, and the details are very sketchy, the area where Sam purchased building rights is occupied by an old office building. That building was cleared to be demolished next January. Guess whose company won the contract for the demolition?"

"Matt Steel's."

"Exactly. I don't know what it all means or how it all ties together, but that's just one example."

"This FJ DeNuzzio is getting more and more interesting every time I hear his name mentioned."

Rachel said, "Have you or Derek approached him yet? Do any digging into his story?"

"Haven't had the time," Nikkie answered. "This case has us running in twelve different directions. Every time we think we're on to something, bam! something else, or *someone* else blows up in our faces."

"Listen, I have to get going. Still working on the Doctor Timothy O'Connell case. But I wanted to tell you the prints on the murder weapon only belong to Jessica Gracers. If Brian Hilton, or anyone else touched the gun, they didn't leave prints. Have you heard from Derek, by the way?"

"Not yet. He probably just boarded the plane to Alabama. Knowing him, I don't expect to hear anything till he's done doing whatever the heck it is he's planning on doing."

As Rachel stood to leave, Nikkie's phone rang. It was Jessica pleading with Nikkie to come by her house.

"I just can't be alone here," she told Nikkie. "But I can only leave for errands, and then for only four hours a day. Please, just come over and stay with me. You said Derek's away doing some casework. Just stay with me till he gets back. Please?"

Nikkie wasn't happy about seeing Jessica alone; Derek had made her promise she wouldn't follow his lead and go "freelancing" by herself. But now she stood just outside Jessica Gracers' home. Alone and not really sure if Jessica was the murderer she and Derek had been searching for.

The front door was partially open. More than a crack but not enough to slide inside without pushing the door. Nikkie stood, half inside, half out, her long, black hair falling like tiny arrows pointing to the floor. She wasn't one to believe in hauntings, restless spirits or that a house or location could hold captive the energy spilled out from a tragic event. Still, the air inside the house seemed too cool. Like it was cut with a frigid pain. She steeled herself, stepped inside Jessica Gracers' home, but kept the open door against her back.

She leaned to her right, giving herself a view through the opulently decorated living room and into what she knew to be the kitchen. The tile was still stained crimson, though she could see that someone had worked a brush soaked with detergent over the area. The smell of Ajax cut with bleach whispered at her nose.

"Jessica?" she called out in a weak, tentative voice. "It's Nikkie Armani. You here?"

"Jessica?" she called again. Louder. More confidently.

"I'm upstairs. Second room on the right." Jessica's voice was unmistakable, but more sullen than Nikkie imagined it could be. Desperate, almost resigned.

"Are you alone up there?" Nikkie called.

"Until you join me, I am," came the response.

Nikkie shook her arms, pushing the hopefully unwarranted fears from her body and climbed the stairs.

She found Jessica where she expected to; in a sitting room, second on the right off the landing. Jessica was sitting, facing the window, in a high-backed chair. Deep brown. Leather. The type of chair that spins around as silently as a broken promise. Looked like it cost more than Nikkie's first car.

"You probably think I'm crazy," Jessica said, not standing, not turning the chair around to face her visitor. "Not wanting to be alone in my own house. Crazy. I know."

"You've been through an awful lot lately," Nikkie offered, as her eyes darted around the room. She was ignoring the works of art hanging on the walls, and was looking instead for anything she could use as a weapon in case Jessica spun the leather chair around and had a gun in her hands. Casting aside her worries about having to defend herself, Nikkie took a few steps closer to Jessica. "Considering what you've been through, I would say you're holding up better than most."

"Five days, today," Jessica said. "This nightmare has been going on for five whole days. Each day seems to get worse than the one before. Now Brian's dead. Everyone I cared for is gone." Jessica's right arm fell to the side of the chair.

"Good sign," Nikkie thought. *"Either she's not holding a gun or is doing so with one hand."*

"Tomorrow is another day," Nikkie said.

"Day six," was all Jessica came back with. "I wonder what will happen on day six."

. . . . .

There weren't many airline options for Derek to choose from. Dothan Regional Airport was, after all, a very small airport. Delta partners with an express carrier which, fortunately for Derek, had two scheduled flights to and from Tampa each weekday. At first he thought of making the eight-hour drive but time was slipping behind him too quickly. Flying would save hours and he had begun feeling the crushing weight of time leaning against him. The slippage of time had already allowed Brian Hilton to destroy any possible evidence which may have exonerated Jessica Gracers. The passage of time had provided someone, the Trainer brothers he believed, the opportunity to silence Doctor Timothy O'Connell. And it was the steady, relentless march of time that gave someone the opening to permanently silence Brian Hilton. If each second was not fully utilized, Derek feared what other opportunities time would afford the players surrounding his case.

The flight from Tampa to Dothan was short; less than forty minutes. Derek landed in Dothan at three in the afternoon, was through the rental car line by three-fifteen and sitting behind the wheel and driving towards the western suburbs of Dothan by three twenty-six.

Though Derek liked to believe he had a superb sense of direction, the truth was revealed by him getting lost four times as he struggled to find the dirt road which lead to the Trainer's ramshackle home, run to riot yard and pole barn—which probably protected a half million dollars worth of cars. It was nearly five-thirty before he had parked his car a quarter mile past the dirt road leading to his objective.

"Treat it like it's a rental," he said after seeing how deeply he had parked the car into the low-growth shrubs off the side of the road.

He hiked back through the woods till he saw the telltale clearing which marked the dirt road. Staying in the woods, he walked the distance till the pole barn, house and the remains of a bonfire were in view. He scanned the area; saw nothing suggesting he wasn't alone. He stood still as a slight breeze, not enough to push the oppressive heat away, rustled through the leaves, listening to only an occasional car drive past the dirt road's entrance, past where he had hidden his rental and onto wherever the hell it was the road led.

He was alone.

Though certain he was alone, Derek used caution as he approached the pole barn; trying not to press his back against the burning hot steel as he wormed his way from the back, to the sides and around to the front. He pulled out the key he had taken during his last visit to the pole barn, and sent up a quick plea to his dead wife.

"Lucy, if you're up there and can hear me, please let this key work."

It did.

Inside, the lights were off. Without any windows designed into the pole barn, it was dark as night. Derek pulled out his iPhone and fumbled his thumbs through a few screens till he found his flashlight app. With the app running, Derek saw exactly what he expected to see: The cars had been moved.

The floor of the barn was poured concrete, canted slightly to his left. As he walked towards the first covered car, he shone his flashlight around the barn, looking for anything else one wouldn't expect to find in a pole barn situated on an unkempt tract of land, near a house, which hadn't seen a paintbrush or the hands of a handyman in at least a decade. But besides the five cars, each still protected from dust or the occasional trapped-inside bird droppings, the barn was filled with nothing Derek might have stored in his pole barn, if he had one, that is.

Across the length of the barn, Derek's light illuminated the double-wide garage doors, apparently through which the cars and any other large objects were brought in and out of the place. He began his inspection by pulling the cover off the car closest to the garage door.

The first car was a 2003 Surfchaser Mustang Cobra Convertible. Yellow with a wide, white stripe running down the middle of the body. Beautiful car in pristine condition, but its trunk was hardly large enough to store an ice chest, a couple pair of flip-flops and a roll of towels. No way Doctor Timothy O'Connell had spent any time in the trunk. Derek pulled the cover back over the Ford.

He passed by the next two cars, seeing from their shape and size alone they were much too small to have been used for transporting O'Connell to Tampa. He wasn't an expert, but he had been to his share of car shows and assumed the two cars he passed by were Porsche's, 911, probably.

"Three down, one to go," he thought as he stepped close to the final car.

He paused, considering the car beneath the cover. Estimated it had the right size, certainly a sedan and the trunk, from what he could tell by the shape, looked a hell of a lot more spacious than the other three. Derek found himself reluctant to pull back the car's cover. He was banking on his theory the Trainer brothers were O'Connell's killers and had used a car—this car, to be exact—for their travels and transportation needs. If he was wrong, he would have to admit to himself, Rachel and Nikkie, that he was as confused and lost as they were. It wasn't a matter of pride, but rather a matter of competence. Of feeling he was good at his job. The best, perhaps. And while the Jessica Gracers case had evolved into a much more twisted maze of a case than he had expected, a good private investigator would eventually find some piece of evidence which either proved or disproved their client's claim. A great one, however, would do a hell of a lot more than prove or disprove Jessica's claim. A great freelance detective would see how all the pieces fit together, solve each of the mysteries and bring justice to those wronged.

But, as he stood before the final car, still hidden beneath a custom fit cover, he accepted that if he was wrong about the Trainer brothers, he was utterly lost with the case. It was both fear and anger welling inside him. Fear, if when he pulled back the cover, he saw a car incapable of realistically being used to transport a dead Timothy O'Connell, that his skills as an investigator were a distant cry from what he believed they were. And anger at himself for not having already put together the pieces to the admittedly complex case.

There's a distinct difference a .12 gauge sound makes when it's racked empty compared to when a slug is slammed into place. When the shotgun is empty, the sound is thinner. Hollow. Like an empty promise. But the sound Derek heard as he extended his hand towards the rear of the car and just as his fingers clutched a solid grip onto the car cover was anything but empty. It was a deeper thudding sound. Filled with an angry promise.

The overhead lights, all three rows, flooded the pole barn, just as the sound of the fully loaded .12 gauge shotgun stopped its echo.

"I figured you'd show up here eventually. Been waiting here for at least four hours. Started thinking you'd be a no show. See, I noticed one of my keys was missing the night of our little bonfire. To be honest with you, Derek Cole, I wracked my brain about that missing key. Hell, I almost had myself convinced me or Bobby took it off the ring and misplaced it. Wouldn't have been the first time that happened. But no, it just didn't feel right."

Jackson Trainer walked confidently towards Derek. The dark barrel of his shotgun aimed directly at Derek's chest. Derek hadn't heard the door open nor saw any light spilling in from the door being opened, which meant Jackson Trainer was inside the pole barn the entire time Derek had been there.

"Mind if I see what kind of car is beneath this cover?" Derek asked. "Always been a car enthusiast."

Jackson, who was now less than fifteen feet from Derek, smiled and shook his head. Didn't take his eyes off Derek.

"That there car is one of my favorites. A 1963, model 220 Benz. Rides like you're floating on a cloud."

"Must have a hell of a trunk, a sedan as long as this."

"Hell yeah," Jackson said. "You'd be amazed how much I can fit into that trunk."

Derek raised his hands. Stepped backwards until he was up against what he thought was a Porsche.

"I know you're not going to fire that shell at me. Not with me standing in front of one of your prized possessions. So why don't we just have a conversation, man to man, without any guns pointed at each other?"

Jackson was ten feet away. Angry barrel still fixed on Derek's chest.

"That's a bold statement, coming from the guy without a gun. But, hate to tell you this, Derek Cole, that car you're leaning up 'gainst is my brother Bobby's. Now, don't get me wrong, I certainly would rather not damage his car and risk damaging the cars behind it, but, they are replaceable. You're not replaceable, are you Derek? Ain't no one going to step into your place, pick up where you left off and aim to cause troubles for me and Bobby? Ain't that right?"

Derek took a long, steady stare at the shotgun. Like he was inspecting it. Memorizing each and every inch.

"People know I'm here," Derek said, in a much more casual, calm voice than he expected. "Plenty of people. Six that I can think of."

Jackson knitted his eyebrows and titled his head a bit to his right.

"Six, you say? Let's see. There's your assistant, that black bitch with the nice ass. What's her name again? Oh, I recall. Nikkie something or other. You got that two-bit lawyer, Jenkins. Detective Gonzales. Probably your client, the murdering bitch Jessica Gracers. I can't seem to make your count of six right in my head. You wouldn't be trying to scare me into putting my gun down, are you, Cole?"

"Maybe I miscounted," Derek said through a small smile. "Three or six, doesn't matter I guess."

"Nope. Don't matter in the least. Not going to take more than one to gather all your pieces together when I'm done with you, anyhow. One is all it will take."

CHAPTER 31

With Jackson Trainer walking behind him, shotgun pressed hard against his back, Derek was led out through the single door of the pole barn.

"Head on over to where Bobby and I had our little fire the other night," Jackson said as he pressed the barrel harder into Derek's back. "Don't want to have to clean up after you."

"You plan on dropping me onto the ash pile, do you?"

"That's exactly what I'm planning on."

Derek stopped dead in his tracks. Dropped his arms to his side. Jackson rammed the barrel deeper into Derek's kidney, causing a ripping, deep pain to course up Derek's back.

"You some type of idiot?" Jackson asked.

"Maybe," Derek said. "Just don't want to make things easy for you. If you're going to kill me, why the hell would I want to be killed in an ash pile as opposed to right here where I'm standing?"

"You thinking I'm reluctant to have to get on my hands and knees to gather up your guts? Hell, boy, I'll just start another little fire right where you're standing. Kind of a fan of fires. Need to do something about this grass, anyway."

"If that's the case, I'll make a deal with you."

"You are some type of an idiot, aren't you? You think you're in the position to make deals?"

"Man to man deal. Two guys, one about to get killed, the other about to do the killing. Just looking to see if what I've been thinking is accurate." Derek nodded his head towards the ash pile. "I judge the distance between where I'm standing and where you want to kill me to be about forty feet. That's about twenty steps for me. I have five questions. I'll take four steps, stop, ask you a question. You answer it, and I'll take the next four. Keep repeating till I'm standing where you want me to be."

Derek heard a small chuckle behind him.

"You got balls," Jackson said. "I will give you that. Balls the size of cannon balls. Okay, Derek Cole, you take your four steps, ask your question, and seeing as how I can understand your desire to know why you're 'bout to be dead, I'll answer your questions. Best I can, that is."

Derek took four steps. Stopped, then asked, "Brian Hilton hired you and your brother to kill Doctor Timothy O'Connell before he could say anything about the scam he and Hilton were running, right?"

"Hilton did hire us and, yes, we did kill that doctor. But we don't ask questions 'bout why we were hired. So, I don't know 'bout the reasons Hilton had for wanting that doctor dead. Killed him in his backyard. He ain't got no wife so we didn't have to worry 'bout anyone getting in our way. Poor old doctor was all alone. Died without no one to grieve for him. Dumped his body in the bay down in Tampa. Take four more steps, now."

Derek took four steps.

"Hilton hired you to replace all the furniture in his lodge outside of Tallahassee, too. That much is pretty obvious. My question is when did he tell you to burn it all?"

"While you and your posse was sitting watch outside our home. I called Hilton, gave him the situation. He offered us fifty grand to burn it all before y'all found a way to do whatever the hell it was y'all wanted to do with the furniture. Fifty grand is a lot of money just to start a fire. And, like I already told you, I do like fires. Another four steps, if you don't mind."

Four more steps. Shotgun pressing deep into his back.

"You must have heard Hilton was killed yesterday. Explosion in his house. He was sitting right on a bomb. Blew his ass all over the walls of his living room." Derek chuckled a bit. "Sounds wrong calling it a living room. More appropriate to call it his dying room, wouldn't you think?

"Is that your question?"

"No. My question is actually two-fold. Two for the price of one. I know you didn't have anything to do with Hilton's death. Time frame doesn't work and I can't see why you'd want to kill someone who pays you a lot of money to do jobs for him. So, my questions are if you knew Hilton was killed and if you know who killed him?"

"Yes and no. I heard he was killed but don't know who did it. I'd like to find out, though. I'd sure like to kill that son of a bitch. Hilton being dead means my brother and I are out of jobs. Four steps."

Derek was close enough to the ash pile to smell its musty dampness. Must have rained overnight, giving the charred remains a sickly smoky odor. Slight wind picked up and scattered some of the ashes, which had dried out under the relentless Florida sun.

Four steps closer to the pile.

"Makes sense to me. Question four: You have another person you do jobs for? Like the jobs you did for Hilton?"

"I wish we did, Cole. Hooking up with Hilton was a godsend. One in a million. Very fortunate for us. Unless your final question is how Hilton found us and why he hired us, which, I'll tell you now for no charge that I do not know, it's time for you to get up nice and tight to the pile."

Derek took four more steps. His toes were eight inches away from a charred leg of a bed frame.

"Guess this is it. My last question."

"Sure is." Jackson paused a beat. Let out a small laugh. "Gotta say, I enjoyed this little man to man agreement you thought up. If me and Bobby find a new employer, why, I may just add it to our process. Last question, Derek Cole. Then, it's lights out for you. If your three people come looking for you and get to nosing around, I'll make sure they join you wherever it is you'll be."

"Which one of you was raped by your daddy? You or your brother?"

"What the fuck did you say?" Jackson's voice was cut with bitter hatred. A deep, growing anger.

"That's my last question. Was it you or Bobby your dad raped? I heard about what you did to O'Connell's dick. Made me think one of you had some serious issues with father figures. O'Connell was in his fifties. Probably a little younger than your dad, but I'd say he was about the same age. Close enough, anyway. Maybe your dad raped both you and Bobby. Is that it? Your daddy screwed you both in the ass? Both have issues?"

Derek felt the shotgun's barrel slide up his back and press hard against his head.

That was exactly what he hoped would happen.

When Jackson had walked close to Derek in the pole barn, Derek noticed a fluorescent sticker affixed to the stock. It was a yellow sticker with a capital "R" in the middle. Black ink made the "R" stand out against the yellow sticker. That told Derek the shotgun had been modified with a release trigger. Meaning the gun wouldn't fire until the trigger was pulled all the way back then released. Kind of like pulling a rubber band back then releasing it. Some people call it a "dead man's trigger." Guy has a gun with a release trigger pulled all the way back, gets shot, and his gun fires even though the guy could be dead before he hits the ground. Lots of terrorists use a "dead man's trigger" with their bombs. One way or another, bomb is going to explode.

Having a release trigger meant two things: One, if the person holding the shotgun had the trigger already pulled back, all the person would need to do to fire off a round was to release his or her finger. Made for a quick shot. Lots of fowl hunters used release triggers. Saved a split second and, sometimes, a split second made the difference between taking down a bird in flight and missing it.

Two, if the person holding the gun hadn't already pulled the trigger all the way back, he or she would need to do so, then release the trigger before the round was fired. That would take up a split second. And Derek needed a split second. Now more than ever.

He spun around; right arm extended and smashed the back of his fist right into Jackson's temple. The shotgun exploded, sending the racked shell into the pile of ashes. Big puff of ash and debris kicked up.

Apparently, Jackson hadn't depressed the trigger and made it ready for release. Split second made all the difference.

Derek continued his spin and landed a crushing left cross square on Jackson's nose. Ropes of blood squirted out diagonally from his face. Jackson was going down. Half due to the pain in his face and half due to being almost knocked out. Derek grabbed the shotgun's barrel with his right hand. Gave it a strong pull sending Jackson towards him in an off balance stumble. Derek raised his knee and connected to Jackson's groin.

Lights out.

CHAPTER 32

His entire body was trembling. Adrenaline was pumping through his veins as his parasympathetic nervous system did its best to counteract the fight or flight reaction caused by having a gun pressed into his back. Jackson was out cold. Would be for another ten, fifteen minutes, Derek figured. That gave him enough time to calm himself down, take care of a few things and contact local authorities.

He stood straight, took a long, deep breath, held it, then blew it out aggressively. Shook his arms then his legs, one at a time. He looked around, found a length of discarded rope on the ground near the ash pile and used it to tie Jackson up, hog style.

He ran over to the pole barn, flipped the lights on, double-timed it over to the Mercedes 220 sedan. He ripped off the cover then walked over to the driver's side door. He opened the door, found the keys sitting on the seat. Walked to the back of the car, used the key to open the trunk and took a good, long look at the dirt, clumps of sod and a deep, dark maroon stain on the gray carpet.

He left the trunk open, just in case he decided to leave before the cops showed up. He wanted to make things as easy as possible for them. Next, he pulled his cell phone from his pocket and dialed Nikkie's cell.

He gave her the *Reader's Digest* version of what happened, ending with a request for Nikkie to get in touch with Detective Rachel Gonzales.

"Do that first," Derek said. "Have her get in touch with the Dothan PD. They need to send a car over to pick up Bobby Trainer wherever he may be and one here to take Jackson into custody."

"I have a feeling you're not telling me everything that happened up there. You sure you're okay?" Nikkie pressed.

"Right as rain. Hand is a little sore but I don't think anything is broken. I'm going to call the airport next, see if I can get on the next flight back to Tampa. Let Rachel know to tell the Dothan cops I may not be here when they show up. Don't want to miss my flight."

"Your flight can wait, Derek," she snapped back. "You need to stay right where you are till the cops get there."

"Too much going on to sit around up here overnight. Only one flight back to Tampa today. Leaves at nine fifteen. Can't afford not to be on that flight."

"Stay there. Do not leave till the Dothan PD tells you it's okay for you to leave. I'm going over to speak with Jessica about Maryanne Jenkins. Really need to find out why she hired her over all her other choices of lawyers."

"Hard to believe Jessica is out on bail again. Damn hard to believe."

"Even more reason for me to do a little freelance work, Cole style."

Derek stopped dead in his tracks. The bad feeling he felt when first starting the case returned triumphantly, sending his stomach into summersaults.

"What are you planning to do, Nikkie?"

"I told you about Maryanne and how she told me she has ALS, remember?"

"Yeah, sure, but…"

"What I didn't tell you is that that day she told me, she couldn't even stand up, walk to her office door and let me in. She and I argued for a few minutes; her sitting behind her desk, me standing outside her front door. She told me where she hides a second office door key. I never put it back."

"Nikkie, remember whose initials you circled in the hotel? The person your gut was telling you was behind Sam Gracers' murder?"

"That's why I'm going to do what I'm going to do. To find out for sure if my gut is right." Nikkie paused, let Derek run through whatever thoughts he had to process. "I'll be careful and I'll be quick. I need to see if she has any files linking her to Hilton or FJ DeNuzzio. She could be the key to this whole mess of a case."

"I'll be back tonight," Derek said. "One way or another, I'll be in Tampa tonight. I'll call you before I take off and when I land. If you can't answer, you text me back right away. Agreed?"

"Listen to you," Nikkie said in a playful voice. "Getting all worried about me doing what you'd do in a heartbeat. Listen, I just met with Rachel Gonzales. Had iced tea together. While I was leaving, Jessica called me. Wants me to come over and sit with her at her house."

"I don't like the sound of that. Don't like the sound of that at all."

"She's our client," Nikkie said.

"You carrying your gun on you?"

"No permit in Florida, believe it or not. It's back in the hotel room."

"Make a stop on your way to Jessica's. Get your gun. Don't worry about not having a damn permit to carry."

"We'll see. Gotta run."

"Promise me you'll be careful and will either answer every time I call or will text me back if you can't talk. Promise me."

"I promise. Nothing is going to happen. I promise."

By the time he got back to where Jackson had tried to blow a hole in his head, Derek had convinced himself Nikkie was going to be fine.

"She's better at this investigation stuff than you are," he said to himself. *"She'll be fine."*

Derek's estimation of how long Jackson would be unconscious was a bit off. He was struggling against the rope Derek had used to tie his hands together behind his back, then to both ankles.

"If you get yourself out of that knot," Derek said, announcing his return to Jackson, "I may even give you a five minute head start before I chase you down and beat you to a bloody pulp."

Jackson stopped struggling. Dropped his forehead to the hard-packed dirt ground.

"Listen," he said in a voice more suited to a private conversation, "you let me go, and I'll give you fifty grand. Fifty thousand dollars, cash! And, I promise that me and my brother will never even so much as get within a hundred miles of you. What do ya say?"

"I say I beat the crap out of you till you tell me where the cash is, take it and testify in court against you. What do ya say to that option?"

"I can tell you more about that case you were hired for. I know a lot more than what I told you."

"I find it hard to believe Hilton would have shared any information with a scumbag like you. I'm not falling for it. Not going to let you free. You already lied to me once. Don't trust people who tell me lies."

Jackson twisted his face around so he was looking up at Derek.

"I ain't told you no lies."

"Sure you did. You lied when you told me you had no idea how Hilton found you and your brother. I figured that out after driving up here from the lodge."

Jackson gave Derek his best confused look.

"Your brother Bobby is gay. So was Hilton. Hilton told me so himself and the way you mangled O'Connell's dick told me that either you or Bobby was gay. Figured it was you doing the slashing and stabbing. I bet you did all that right in front of Bobby. Kind of a psychopathic way to be passive-aggressive. The way I figure it, Bobby met Hilton at the truck stop just over the border. He probably goes there every week or so. He meets Hilton, they get to talking and next thing you know, you got some rich guy hiring you for some small jobs. Nothing big at first. Nothing too outside the legal boundaries. But you and Bobby prove yourselves and soon Hilton is dishing out thousands of dollars for you two to handle things he can't handle himself. If I were a betting man, which I'm not, parenthetically, I'd say Doctor O'Connell was a gay man, too. Wouldn't be surprised at all to find out Hilton met him at that same truck stop. Maybe you didn't want to admit it to yourself that your brother is gay, but you knew it all along. Knew him being gay is how he met up with Hilton. So, you see, you lied to me. And I don't trust liars."

"You didn't ask me if me and Bobby had anything to do with that murder down outside Tampa," Jackson said without pausing to acknowledge or deny what Derek had said. "The one you was hired for to solve."

"That's right, I didn't. Want to know why I didn't ask you that?"

"Cuz you think I don't know nothing 'bout that murder, but you're wrong. I know all about it. See, Bobby ain't what people would call a genius, but he's one of them servants when it comes to technology. Knows how to tap into cell phones. Listening in to conversations when nobody knows someone else is listening."

"You mean 'savant,' not servant." Derek sat down hard on Jackson's back. Pinning his already twisted arms against his back. "I don't think anyone would consider you or your brother geniuses."

"Goddam man, you're breaking my arms. Get off me."

"Not going to break your arms. It's your shoulders you should be worried about. Tell you what, you tell me what you think I should know about Sam Gracers' murder and, if I find it valuable, I'll stand up. If not, I may just sit here till the cops show up."

"Like I said," Jackson said, his strained voice a clear indication of the pain he was in, "Hilton used to call us when he needed a job done. Met with the guy six or seven times. One time, Bobby grabbed hold of his cell phone, took some pictures of some of his screens. Next thing I know, we was listening to phone calls Hilton was making."

"Go on."

"He made a few calls about Sam Gracers."

"To whom did Hilton make calls?"

"Bobby couldn't figure that out, but we know what he said about Gracers. How 'bout you get off me and I'll tell you 'bout one of them calls? What do ya say?"

"I say I'm actually more comfortable sitting here than I thought I'd be. Let's stick to my original deal. Tell me something I find interesting and I'll stand up."

"Hilton was talking to some guy. He said Gracers won't be able to tell no one 'bout the doctor scam he was running. I figured Gracers found out about what Hilton was using O'Connell for and was going to blow him in."

"Go on," Derek said.

"Said they was all off the hook with Gracers taking a lead in the head. Like it weren't just Hilton playing the doctor scam. This other guy Hilton was talking with, he was in the scam with him."

"Already figured that out myself." Derek leaned back a little, putting a bit more of his weight on Jackson's arms and back. "Is that all you have for me?"

"Damn, Cole, you're ripping my arm right out the socket."

"And if I lean back another inch, that's exactly what will happen."

Derek could hear the distant sounds of sirens screaming their demands. He placed the cop cars three miles away.

"You gotta let me go," Jackson pleaded. "Bobby, he ain't cut out for being in jail. Fifty grand, man. Come on."

Derek stood up, relieving the pressure from Jackson's shoulders.

"Not going to happen. But I'll tell you what. Police will be here in two minutes. I'll point them to the Mercedes, let them know whose DNA they'll find in the trunk. I'll fill them in on everything I know about you and your brother. But I won't tell them about you putting that shotgun to my back. I'll tell them you and I were talking about O'Connell and that I accused you of the murder. I'll tell them you copped to the crime then you and I got into a little scrap."

"What the hell will that do for me? Damn, Cole. That ain't doing shit for me."

"Won't get charged for assault with a deadly weapon. That could add five years to your sentence."

"Damn, Cole. You are a real son of a bitch. You know that? You're a real son of a bitch."

"I've been called worse."

Jackson rolled over onto his back. Did an awkward sit-up. Spit out some blood that had pooled in the back of his throat.

"You was right about me telling you a lie," he said. "But you was wrong about that lie."

"You still trying to convince me to let you go before the cops show up?" Derek shot back. "If so, I give them two minutes before they arrive."

"I told you two lies." Jackson smiled as if his dual-lies were some sort of victory. "My brother ain't gay. Least, not as far as I know 'bout. He didn't meet Hilton at that gay place down south. We met Hilton through the guy he was talking to when me and Bobby heard 'em talking 'bout that murder case you're working on."

"You recognized the voice?"

"I ain't never gonna forget that voice. Ain't no way to forget it. Got a rasp to it. Like one of those old, black jazz singers, 'cept this guy ain't no singer. Little high pitched but not in a bad way. Bobby said the guy sounded like someone who mixed sand in with his beer. Scratched his throat all up."

"Who's the guy?" Derek said.

"He hired us a few years back to take care of some guy who needed taken care of."

"You shot him in the head with a .380 and dumped his body in the bay, right?"

"I see you know our work."

"And you and Bobby heard Hilton talking to this 'sandpaper' voiced guy about Sam Gracers? About the man whose murder I am trying to solve?"

"Yup."

"You gonna tell me this guy's name or do I have to twist your arm right out of your shoulder?"

"FJ," Jackson said. "FJ is his name."

Chapter 33

Nikkie nursed her glass of wine while Jessica plowed through three glasses of her own. Mostly, Jessica spoke, telling Nikkie everything she knew about Maryanne Jenkins. She told her what Sam had accused Maryanne of and about how she had found and read a bundle of papers Sam had left, perhaps intentionally, on the desk in his home office downstairs.

"What I read wasn't enough to prove Maryanne knew that what she was doing for Brian was illegal, but it definitely suggested she was involved in Brian's horrible activities."

"How did Sam get those papers?"

"I have no idea. Looked to me like a report from a private investigator. If I still had them, I'd show them to you. You'd be able to tell if they were written by a fellow private eye or not."

"And these papers, they suggested that everything Sam told you about, everything he suspected Brian Hilton was doing, was really happening? That he was working with doctors and having them tell patients they had cancer all so Brian had a better case why they should sell their businesses to them?"

"That and a whole lot more."

"What else?" Nikkie was sitting on the edge of her seat. She felt she was closer now to understanding how things were all tied together. "What else did the papers suggest?"

Jessica drained the last swallow of wine, reached to the table, grabbed the second bottle of wine and poured it into her glass.

"The rest of it didn't mean anything to me. It was about other things about Maryanne, Brian and, of course, FJ DeNuzzio. He's involved in what Brian was doing. I just know he was. I really can't remember anything more than the parts confirming what Sam told me about Brian. I was already involved with Brian at the time. I didn't want to believe any of it, so I think I pushed it from my memory."

"Yet, despite what your husband told you and in spite of what that report suggested, you continued your affair with Brian?"

Jessica grinned at Nikkie. Let out the smallest of laughs.

"I can't explain the way I felt for him. In a way, since I had been sleeping with him for almost a year before Sam told me what he told me, I guess I felt I was no better than Brian, no matter what horrible things he may be doing in his business. And Brian was so different outside of his business world. I wanted to hate him when I read those papers, I really and truly did. But, two minutes after I was with him again, all that wished for hatred just vanished like water vapor from the sea."

Nikkie leaned back in her chair. Took another sip from her glass. She wasn't going to get much more information out of Jessica. Four glasses of wine was clouding her brain, making her words mushy and her train of thought scattered. Nikkie decided to ask a couple more questions, then manufacture a reason she needed to leave. She still wanted to get into Maryanne's office, take a quick look into her file cabinets and maybe dig around her computer for a bit.

"The gun used to kill your husband," Nikkie began, expecting Jessica to dismiss the conversation her intended questions would lead to, "it only had your prints on it. No one else left any prints behind. Your alibi about being with Brian at his lodge, all but eradicated with his denial and now his death. You hiring Maryanne Jenkins because you believed she would be hyper motivated to get your case dismissed since you had leverage over her, is also now pretty useless since Brian is dead, meaning your leverage is gone. Yet you haven't hired a different lawyer. One a little more suited for a murder case. Why?"

Jessica fixed a long stare at Nikkie. For the first time since meeting her, Nikkie saw a darkness in Jessica's stare. A coldness behind her eyes.

Some people babble when they're asked a question they can't or don't want to answer. Some, who are more skilled, are able to rattle off an answer more dismissive than informative. And some just stare back at the questioner. They look like a deer caught in a car's headlights; paralyzed with fear. Lost as to which direction to take.

Jessica was staring back at Nikkie, but there was not a hint of being lost in her eyes. No suggestion of wondering whether to stand still, to run, to wait until the question asker breaks the silence.

Jessica dropped her eyes to her empty glass. Blinked hard a few times, then lifted her face to Nikkie. Her face had changed when it was lifted. The face of a woman lost in a grief few could imagine replaced that calculated look Nikkie saw, or imagined. It was the face of someone crippled with fear, with confusion.

"It's all about time," she said at last. "I've always believed time to be on my side. Yes, I hired her because of what I knew about her. About what she had done with Brian's business. I felt she would waste no time in getting me out of the terrible mess I was in. Like a fool, I believed this whole mess would be over in five days." She shrugged her shoulders. Shook her head a bit. "Five days. I figured I could get through five days of this torture. After five days, I could give Sam the funeral he deserved. I could start to grieve for him. To somehow make up for the affair I had with Brian. Now, Sam's body is in Texas, Brian is dead and I am feeling for the first time in my life that I am running out of time. See Nikkie, I don't think I have any time *left* to hire a new lawyer. Tomorrow is day six. Six days since my life has been turned upside down, and I'm still living a walking nightmare. I'm out of time."

CHAPTER 34

Derek was finishing his second cup of coffee when Captain Duane Chambers tossed his pen onto his desk.

"I know you have to get to the airport, catch that flight of yours. I think we are all set here."

Chambers spoke with a heavy southern drawl. Slow. Drawn out. Almost intentionally slow. He was a serious man. Had the type of face seen on men who lived a hard life. Probably had seen the moral decay of humanity up close and personal. Chambers stood up, extended his hand to Derek.

"On behalf of the fine citizens of Dothan and the State of Alabama, I want to thank you for your work. These Trainer boys, especially Jackson, have been a thorn in my side for too many years. Never thought they were capable of murder, but it don't surprise me in the least. Not in the least."

Chambers hitched up his pants—which looked to Derek at least four inches too big in the waist—and gestured towards the door. Chambers noticed the quizzical look on Derek's face. Saw him looking at the extra holes punched in his belt.

"Round about seven months ago," Chambers said, "I made the God awful mistake of telling Mrs. Chambers about my doctor appointment. Doc said I needed to lose fifty pounds, cut back on salt, greasy food and beer. She took that as some sort of womanly mandate. Put me on a diet that's just as sure to kill me as would a rack of ribs."

"Guess she wants to keep you around a bit longer."

Chambers let out a deep belly laugh that, had his wife not restricted his diet, would have certainly caused Chamber's belly to rumble and roll.

"I'll make sure I get a message to you, about how things turn out for the Trainer brothers. Right now, Jackson is stepping up and taking all the blame. Said he'll admit to everything so long as the judge goes easy on his brother."

"Glad to see he's taking responsibility," Derek said.

"May be some good in that boy. I do doubt there's much, but may be a little."

"Think you'll have any problems getting a conviction?"

"He gave us a full and detailed confession, right down to where we can find the shell casing of the bullet he used to kill that doctor." Chambers paused a bit. Gave Derek a sideways glance. "He was going on about how he knew things about the case you're down here working on. Said he'd trade info for some time off his sentence."

"He told me he and Bobby tapped Hilton's cell phone. Overheard Hilton talking about Sam Gracers—the murder case I was hired to investigate. Didn't know who Hilton was talking with, though. But I have a pretty good idea who it was." Derek didn't want to share that Jackson fingered FJ as the person behind Sam Gracers murder. Doing so would delay things Derek needed to take care of.

"Well, based on the way you fingered the Trainer boys for the doctor murder, I'm likely to believe you do know who Hilton was speaking with."

The two reached the front door of the small police station. Chambers opened the door, patted Derek on the back.

"Again, I thank you on behalf of…well, thanks."

"Don't mention it."

Derek checked the time on his iPhone, then hurried down the three steps to the sidewalk.

Chambers called out to him, "Hey, just in case the district attorney is interested in hearing more of Jackson's story, do you have any idea who the 'sick bitch' is that Jackson mentioned?"

Derek's face fell. Mouth hung open. Body went tense then slack, then tense again.

"What are you talking about?" Derek asked.

"Jackson said he heard Hilton say to whoever he was speaking to, that the sick bitch did them both a favor by taking care of Gracers. I take it he didn't share that bit of information with you?"

"Nikkie," Derek said, more to himself.

"That the 'sick bitch' Jackson was talking about? Woman named Nikkie?"

"No," Derek said. "Son of a bitch. I have to go."

•   •   •

Derek dialed Nikkie's cell phone, listened to it ring right through till her voicemail picked up seven times on his drive to the airport. He called her twice more when sitting in the terminal as the plane taxied up to the gate. Called her a final time while sitting on the plane. Would have called her a hundred more times if the flight attendant hadn't insisted he turn the phone off.

"You can put it in airplane mode if you'd like. But the plane cannot take off as long as any passenger has a phone on."

"You have WiFi on this plane?" Derek asked, hoping he could at least contact Nikkie through text messages.

"No sir. I'm sorry. This is just a thirty-nine minute flight. I'm sure whatever you have to say to whomever you are trying to contact can wait thirty-nine minutes."

"I hope you're right. God, I hope you're right."

CHAPTER 35

Nikkie stayed a while longer with Jessica, eventually bringing the empty bottles of wine and wine glasses to the kitchen while Jessica prepared for, what she was certain to be, a sleepless night. Once Nikkie was ready to leave, Jessica continued to talk, though understanding what she was saying had become increasingly difficult. Five glasses of wine, it seemed to Nikkie, was Jessica's point of no return.

"You still think I had something to do with my Sam's dying, don't you?" she slurred as she fell onto her bed.

"There's not a whole lot of evidence pointing at anyone else," Nikkie said. "But evidence isn't everything."

Jessica rolled her body to face Nikkie, who was standing in the bedroom doorway.

"Are you going to look for more evidence?"

"That's what you're paying us to do."

Jessica tried to laugh. Came out more like a wet cough.

"That's not an answer." She propped herself upright against her headboard. "Either you are going to look for more evidence about who really killed Sam or you're not going to." Jessica's eyes were almost closed. Her face was falling slack. Arms lay splayed to her sides, motionless. "I know where you can find more."

Nikkie took a small step closer to the soon-to-be-unconscious Jessica Gracers.

"More evidence?" Nikkie prodded. "What evidence are you talking about?"

Jessica's eyes were closed, but a palsy-like smile crossed her face. She clumsily raised an extended index finger to her pursed lips, blew out a damp *"Shhhhhhh."*

"I told you," Jessica said, eyes closed, lips showing the immediate report of how firmly she had pressed her *"shh-ing"* finger against them. "There was more stuff in Sam's report about Maryanne."

"You never told me what that other *stuff* was."

Jessica's voice rose to a drunken yell. "I told you I couldn't remember. But that report is gone now and I bet I know where it is."

"You think Maryanne killed your husband, don't you? You want me to investigate her, right? Is that the real reason you hired her? So that we'd be close to Maryanne?"

Jessica offered no response.

"If that's how you feel, why the hell are you waiting till now to suggest Maryanne may have had something to do with your husband's murder?"

Jessica pried open her eyes. Licked her lips with a thick tongue. Shot a crooked smile towards Nikkie.

"Wazz that they say?" Jessica slurred. "Keep your friends close and your enemies closer?" The wine made the word come out like "emimies" but Nikkie understood the phrase.

Jessica's eyes slid closed, weighed down by exhaustion and almost two bottles of wine.

"Just so happens," Nikkie said softly as she turned off Jessica's bedroom light, backed into the hallway and pulled the door closed, "I'm about to do a little freelancing work to find out what Maryanne Jenkins is hiding."

"Her neighbor works late," Jessica said in a much clearer, less clouded voice.

Nikkie, whose hand was still holding the door handle, pushed the door open a crack. Stuck her head inside the dark room.

"Her neighbor?"

"If you're going to look in her office files. Her neighbor is nosey. Stays late most days."

"I take it you've been to her office after hours?" Nikkie asked.

"Never admit to anything. They say that, too. Don't they? Never admit to anything."

•   •   •   •   •

Nikkie thought about calling Derek to give him an update of her visit with Jessica, but thought calling him would only either disturb whatever freelancing he was doing or would make him worry about what she was planning. Instead of calling Derek, Nikkie turned her phone's sound off and tucked the phone into her clutch purse. She'd call Derek when her work was done.

She did take his previous advice and swung over to her hotel to grab her gun. She left her hotel room with her .40 caliber, Smith and Wesson M&P tucked out of sight in her inner-waistband holster. Her decision to pick up her gun was more out of her desire to kill some time than any worry or concern she had for her safety. While Maryanne's office wasn't in the best part of Largo, it was far from the worst. In fact, compared to many places Nikkie had worked a case, Largo and all of Pinellas County seemed to be vacant of any "bad parts." Carrying a gun in her line of work, however, was just a smart thing to do.

She drove into Largo. Parked her car on the street a hundred yards north of The Law Offices of Maryanne Jenkins, Esq.

• • • • • • •

Jessica had been right; it was close to eleven-thirty before the lights in the office adjacent to Maryanne Jenkins's office were switched off. Nikkie watched from a distance as a middle-aged woman walked out of the newly darkened office, crossed the street, got into her car and headed south.

"Time for some freelancing," Nikkie whispered.

She held the key to the front door so tightly in her hand that when she loosed her grip, the key's teeth had left angry gouges in her fingers. Nikkie slipped into the alcove, put the key into the deadbolt, slid the bolt free, opened the door, and then prayed Jenkins didn't have an alarm system. She hadn't noticed one during her visit a few days ago, but she was more concerned about the health of Maryanne than looking for a flashing keypad on the wall.

She slipped inside and was greeted by wonderful silence.

After closing the door behind her, Nikkie leaned against it. Took several long breaths, waiting for her eyes to adjust to the darkness inside the office. Several seconds later, she pulled out a penlight, flashed it low around the office, then moved quickly to a bank of metal file cabinets to the right of Maryanne's desk.

Nikkie shook her head in disbelief when she pulled the top drawer open.

"Doesn't even lock her file cabinets in an office without an alarm? Remind myself to never tell Jenkins anything personal."

She bit the penlight, aimed its light with small nods and shakes of her head, as she thumbed through the well-organized first drawer. Finding nothing of interest, she pulled open the second drawer, closed the first, and repeated her method of search.

The file she was looking for, the file she hoped to find but honestly didn't expect to, was in the third drawer. She pulled the folder, which was marked "HILTON" in thick, red ink, and walked it over to Maryanne's desk. She sat, then shot back up after remembering the urine-soaked condition she had found Maryanne in when she visited this office earlier in the week.

If she had been sitting and not standing, slightly bent over the desk, the bullet, which tore into the side of her chest, may have slammed into her shoulder instead. She certainly would have been dazed, wounded but she may have been able to recover quickly enough to grab her gun from her holster. May have been able to fire back a round or two.

But she was standing, giving the shooter—standing in the dark hallway that lead to the rear exit—a larger target.

The bullet penetrated through her fifth and sixth rib. It ripped its way through her left lung, tore a two-inch wide gap into her right lung, before coming to a bone-shattering stop against her rib cage on her left side.

The first bullet may not have been a fatal introduction, if Nikkie received quick medical attention. But the only person who knew Nikkie was in mortal need of immediate medical attention, was the shooter.

The second bullet, however, was certainly, unmistakably and unrepentantly fatal.

Nikkie had fallen to the floor, grasping her side, hoping to somehow capture and hold the pain which had erupted. When the second bullet blasted through the left side of her chest, her pain suddenly lost its bite. It fell silent as if frightened away from the sound of the firing gun. Her arm dropped to her side. Lifeless.

"Find something interesting?" her shooter asked.

Nikkie looked up at the woman standing above her. The darkness prevented her from seeing any more than her shooter's outline framed against the street lamp's light leaking in through the office's distant window. She tried to answer back, to say anything. To plead for help. And if help was denied, then at least for a reason.

The shooter raised the gun, pointed it at Nikkie's chest and pulled the trigger.

As she felt the great sleep approaching, Nikkie began to cry tears no one would wipe away.

She turned to her side, dipped her index finger in the pool of her blood spilling out from her chest and side.

And scrawled two letters.

CHAPTER 36

Sunday
August 24
4:02 AM

He hadn't slept but was charged with an energy no amount of rest could ever produce. Derek walked out of the stale, musty air inside the Pinellas County Sheriff's Department and into the humid, stale air outside. It was early, too early to be as warm and as promising of approaching oppressiveness as it was, but he didn't notice. He didn't care.

He had parked his car on the street across from Maryanne Jenkins office last night. Had ridden in the back of the ambulance to the hospital with Nikkie; holding her then lifeless hand, offering silent promises to her. Nikkie was dead when the sheriff's arrived. Too far gone for the paramedics—who came in tow and entered the office after given the all-clear sign by a deputy—to even try to bring her back.

The sheriff's deputy who had first entered Jenkins's office, found Derek cradling the still body of Nikkie Armani to the left of the office desk. Gun drawn, eyes wide with trained preparedness, the deputy only said one word to Derek.

"Shooter?"

"Gone before I arrived," came Derek's answer. His voice was calm, despite the burning rage engulfing him. He knew he needed to control his emotions. Knew that if he allowed his bitter anger, his crushing pain to surface, he would tell anyone who listened about the initials written in her own blood Nikkie left behind. Those initials were not clues. They were not a suggestion from Nikkie of where Derek, or anyone else who might see the jagged letters, should begin the investigation into her death.

They were simple accusations.

Two letters. Five inches tall. Better than any GPS or map for Derek. He knew exactly what he needed to do. What he wanted to do. What he was going to do.

Derek was five minutes into the fifteen-minute walk from the department to his car when the sound of approaching footfalls behind him grew louder. He didn't turn in startled surprise. Didn't quicken his pace or position his body to launch an attack should the approaching person launch an offensive. He knew who it was. Only one person it could have been.

"Hello Rachel," he said before she drew up to his side. "Wondered when you'd get here."

She grabbed his arm, pulled him to a stop. Looked deep into his eyes: His clear and dry, hers damp with building tears.

"Derek," she said. "I am so sorry. I can't believe…What happened?"

"Ten minutes. I have ten minutes before I reach my car. When I get to my car, you're going to turn around and walk back and I'm going to do what I need to do. I need some information from you. I know you've been doing some work on the Gracers murder case, even though it isn't your case, so I need to ask you some questions. Don't ask me why I'm asking the questions I'm going to ask or where I'm going. Don't try to convince me of anything."

Derek turned away from Rachel. Started walking in the direction of his car. She caught back up to him, quietly walked next to him for a minute or two.

"I have to tell you, as an officer of the law…"

"I already know what you have to say. Consider it said and understood."

Rachel nodded.

"What questions do you have for me?"

Derek asked four questions as they walked. Rachel answered each one, as best she could.

When they arrived at his car—a second rental car booked from the Tampa airport—Rachel again grabbed Derek by the arm. Stopped him from slipping into the driver's seat.

"You already know who killed Nikkie, don't you?"

"I do," he said.

"Same person who killed Sam Gracers?"

"That's right."

"Why don't you tell me? Let us, let my department handle this. You could end up like Nikkie, do you know that?" There were more tears in the Detective's eyes. Tears caused more by fear than of sorrow.

"Because time is up."

CHAPTER 37

He arrived on Anna Maria Island shortly before five. The dashboard of his car pegged the temperature at seventy-three degrees. Weatherman on the radio he was only half-listening to promised severe storms arriving by mid-morning. Noon at the latest. Derek parked his rental on North Bay Boulevard, right in front of another tiny library where people loaned and borrowed books.

"Must be an island thing," he said as the climbed out of his car.

He walked the quarter of a mile till the road ended and a well-traveled path began. Took the sinuous path till it reached a wooden bridge with a steep incline. When he reached the summit of the bridge, the view should have been breathtaking. Should have stopped him in his tracks, made him look around at the incredible vista the modest height awarded.

Straight ahead of him, spread out like a ruffled bed cover, was the bay of Tampa and the Gulf of Mexico. They were both still and quiet but filled with promising potential. To his right, was The Sunshine Skyway Bridge, faint in the distance but unmistakable as it stretched from Terr Ceia to St. Petersburg. The bay beneath and around the bridge was calm and deeply blue. To his left, Derek saw the stretch of the seashell-strewn beach, carving an end to the sea and marking the start of the land.

He walked down the slope of the walk-bridge, through the narrow path cut through the tall grass framing the sandy beach. Turned to his left and began walking towards the western most part of Ann Maria Island.

Derek stuck close to the American dune grass, finding walking close to where the sand gave way to more solid ground easier. Faster. On his left were million dollar homes with multi-million dollar views.

He couldn't care less about any of those homes. He was only interested in one.

Derek walked a few hundred yards until the beach seemed to flatten out. Beneath his feet—on nearly every step—were hundreds of spent shells. Signs of death and decay reported their final screams of death beneath each of his footfalls. A crushing, grinding sound. The shells were all bleached white by the relentless Florida sun and the heavily salted water. Derek had walked on beaches like this before. Side-by-side with Lucy, hand-in-hand. He remembered his growing admiration of her, coupled with frustration as their walking progress was continually interrupted as Lucy would stop in her tracks, bend at her waist and inspect a fetch of gathered shells.

"We're never going to get to wherever we're going if you keep stopping to look for shells," he said, half amused with his wife's childlike enthusiasm and half annoyed by their lack of progress.

"And where," she had said, still bent over, still scanning the cornucopia of shells spread out around her feet, "are you in such a hurry to get to?"

"Don't know," he said with a shrug of his shoulders. "Nowhere, really. Just thought we were going for a beach walk. Not a 'take ten steps, stop, look for shells, take another ten steps, and repeat' type of walk."

"Sometimes," she said after having picked up a sand dollar in near perfect condition, "a journey is filled with destinations." She held the bleached-white sand dollar up for his inspection. "See? We're even making money on our little walk."

It was her smile that always set him back. Always her smile. He missed that smile, more than he would miss breathing when his final day arrived. For each breath he took was a silent reminder that he still lived and would never again see that smile.

He had never taken such a walk with Nikkie. Had never felt his soul imprisoned by her smile, her laugh or the sound of her voice. But still she had commanded a part of him. A part he was determined to never be owned by another. And with her death, the balance of what was left of his soul began to tip. To slide towards a point of impossible return.

He walked on towards the point where the beach extended a small stretch into the sea, marking the very point where the Gulf of Mexico stopped and the Bay began.

Towards the first of his day's destinations.

He dropped the cast of his eyes to the beach in front of him. Noticing thousands upon thousands of shells of all shapes and sizes. When a sand dollar, broken in two, one half partially buried in the sand, the other lost to time and the elements, came into his view, he stopped. He thought about bending to retrieve the broken and spent remains of a once-lived life, but paused, his arms only a few inches into a reach.

"I miss you, Lucy," he whispered to the deathly reminder caught in his gaze. "I'm sorry for what I'm about to do."

His first destination was fifty yards away.

• • •

Maryanne heard the knocking, the repeated chimes of her doorbell, yet she could not make the noise stop. Feeling Iron Lou's approach the night before, she had placed her cell and home phones on the bed beside her; not in expectation of being called but just in case. She had also, rather begrudgingly, slipped on an adult diaper. She hated the idea of needing one almost as much as she hated her actual and eventual need for their use. It was bulky and foreign to her as she crawled into bed, and now, lying in bed, wishing she could answer the door and stop the constant knocking calls from outside her front door, the foreign bulk beneath her sleep clothes was a damp, growing bulk. The odor, trapped for the most part in the diaper's design, was spilling forth. She had heard odors elicit the most powerful memories. But this odor, this almost palpable stink surrounding her, did not elicit memories but instead offered her promises of things to come. *"Someday,"* she thought, *"this same smell will remind me of this day. The day Iron Lou made his intentions clear."*

Her house phone rang. With weak, shaky hands, she reached the phone, answered the call and propped the phone between her ear and a pillow.

"Maryanne Jenkins, this is the Pinellas County Sheriff's Department. We have two deputies at your home right now. Are you inside the home?"

"I am," she said in a voice Derek would mistake for one from some Caribbean Island.

"Is there a reason you are not answering your front door? Is someone in the home with you, preventing you from answering the door?"

Maryanne sighed heavily. Felt tears welling in her eyes.

"I can't answer the door. I can't move."

The truth was she wasn't sure if she could span the distance between her bed and the front door. She knew she could move. Probably could stand and take a few steps. Iron Lou hadn't won that battle, yet. But she had no confidence the steps she could manage would be enough to reach her front door. She imagined herself falling, cracking her head on an end table, the hard-tiled floor or against any number of hard, bone cracking surfaces.

"Is someone in the house with you? Just say 'Yes' or 'No'."

"There's no one in my house but me," she replied, her voice echoing the resigning emotions clouding her mind. "I'm sick. They need to break the door down."

. . . . .

Jessica Gracers walked back down her staircase. She paused for a moment, looking back up the stairs as if she had either forgotten something in her room or was waiting for someone to follow her down. She smiled, then walked through her living room and into the kitchen. She glanced down at the tiles still stained with a pinkish glow. She passed the spot where her husband had died, making a mental reminder to have the stained tiles pulled up and replaced.

"Not going to sell this house with blood-stained tiles," she said as she flipped the coffee maker on.

She leaned against the marble countertop, taking a mental inventory of her day's to-do list. It was Thursday, a day she had usually spent sleeping late as she lay beside her husband. Early in their marriage, Jessica had accepted that Sam needed to work seven days a week. While for most, weekends meant days to relax at home, they only meant less traffic during Sam's drives to his office, to client meetings or to meet with business partners. He agreed—for the sake of his marriage—to devote one morning each week to doing nothing more, or less, than to spend it with Jessica.

On most Thursdays, she and Sam would go for a long walk. Probably stop at the Starbucks a couple miles from their home, drink a Grande sized coffee. Maybe share a muffin.

Those Thursdays would never be repeated. Never again would she spend a Thursday morning strolling through her neighborhood, sharing comments about how dreadful a particular neighbor's landscaping looked or sharing the most recent bit of "town gossip" with Sam. She knew Sam didn't care about gossip or how anyone decided to prune their palm trees or which color mulch someone decided to use. He couldn't care less, but he always listened to his wife's admonitions of other's tastes or practices. But still he listened, occasionally voiced his agreement with his wife's assessment, but always he would listen.

As the coffee maker began to filter water through the freshly ground beans, Jessica Gracers realized there was no one left in the world who would listen to her as Sam had. No one would just let her talk; let her say whatever she wanted about whatever was pressing in her mind. No one left to go for walks on Thursday mornings with, to share overpriced coffee and an overly sugared muffin with. She had friends, but they were friends only because of her being married to a successful businessman. The type of friends who decide who their friends will be based not on character but on the level of influence they wielded.

She had no real friends, as evidenced by no one having called her, stopped to visit her or even sent off an email, since Sam was murdered. She couldn't blame them. After all, she was arrested for his murder. Accused of the horrible crime. No wonder everyone was giving her a wide berth. The widest possible, it seemed.

The coffee maker squealed and groaned behind her, marking its completion. She pulled a mug from the cupboard, filled it with strong, black coffee, then made her way into the living room. She sat in a soft cushioned lounge chair. Tucked her feet underneath her body. Took a few small sips of the still too hot coffee, then waited for her phone to ring.

Chapter 38

A guy like FJ DeNuzzio doesn't do much alone. Based on what Rachel had told him earlier that same day, based on the off the records mini-investigation she had done and from what Jessica mentioned about him, Derek figured FJ probably was seldom completely alone. And though he had never met FJ DeNuzzio and knew very little about him, he knew others like him. Worked cases for people like FJ. Investigated guys like him, too. He had a good idea the type of guy someone like FJ would hire. Probably a guy with a serious resumé of martial arts training in his past. Maybe ex-military. Maybe even an ex-MP like Cole. Having seen more than his fair share of bodyguards, Derek knew what to look for. A guy, probably around six feet tall, muscular build but not overly bulky. Not dressed for the weather or the location. The morning was steamy, and the location was the beach. He'd be trying hard to blend in. Easy to spot, once you knew what to look for.

What made spotting the hired thug even easier was how vacant the beach area was at six-twenty in the morning. Derek counted maybe eight people scattered about the long stretch of beach. He figured the vacation season wouldn't start for another month or two, meaning the eight or so people sharing the beach with him this morning probably knew, or at least had familiarity with, everyone they might pass on their morning walk. This guy, FJ's guy, wouldn't be milling about on the beach. Wouldn't be tossing pebbles into the ocean, acting like he was waiting around for someone to join him for a morning stroll.

He spotted his mark twenty seconds after he began looking for him.

The area where the beach flattened out, the Gulf of Mexico on one side, the bay on the other, ran out a couple hundred yards from the dunes. Though there were houses spread out with only a hundred feet between them along the whole stretch of the beach, there was only the tall grass of the dunes across the point of the beach, which protruded out like a finger pointing west. Derek spotted him sitting in the dune grass. Braced up by both arms, gaze fixed to his right. To the guy's right is the direction FJ would soon be approaching.

Short dark hair, sunglasses, long-sleeved grey shirt. Probably wearing tactical-style pants but Derek could only see the top of the guy's knees sticking up above the grass. Height of his knees compared to the height of the grass put the hired gun at around six-three. Bigger than Derek thought he'd be. Bigger than Derek. Certainly better trained and with more recent experience as well. That was for damn sure.

Derek didn't try to conceal his approach. Didn't try to walk past the guy, circle back around one of the oceanside homes, sneak up from behind and do what he needed to do. He walked a direct path to the guy. Got within twenty feet before the guy stood up. Took his sunglasses off and gave Derek a long, thousand yard stare.

"Looking for something?" the guy said.

Derek kept walking right towards him.

"This isn't a shortcut to the road. Gotta walk back the way you came. Take the trail through the woods. This is private property."

"You the owner?" Derek asked, now knee deep in the dune grass.

"Maybe I am, maybe I'm not."

"If you're not, then what the hell do you care if I cut through?"

"Maybe I'm paid to keep assholes like you from cutting through."

"Maybe you are, maybe you're not."

Derek wasn't what anyone would call a gun-freak. He saw guns as necessary tools of his trade. He owned two semi-automatic guns. One was the one he used when he put a bullet through the left side of his face. That one was a Glock 19 model. 9 MM. Tried a true. The second gun he owned was a Smith and Wesson M&P Shield, chambered for .40 caliber. That was the one he was carrying in his concealed holster.

When he was in the Army, Derek was expected to fire at least one hundred rounds every two weeks. Twenty-five rounds from one hundred yards. Twenty-five from fifty. Twenty-five from twenty-five and twenty-five from ten to fifteen feet. The last distance, ten to fifteen feet, were really the only ones that mattered. Ninety percent of handgun battles are fought from within that "up close and personal" distance. So while he was expected to fire twenty-five from ten to fifteen feet from a target, Derek regularly fired three times that number. Kept the same discipline when he joined the Columbus Police Department, too. Was still firing off seventy-five to one hundred rounds from ten to fifteen feet from his target at least once a month.

But as good as Derek Cole was firing a gun and drilling the center of his target from ten feet away, his aim was nothing as impressive as was his speed to draw. Most amateurs take four-seconds to pull their gun out of an inner-waistband holster, line up the shot and pull the trigger. Well-trained shooters look to get their time from pull to fire around two seconds. Derek could draw and fire off two to three rounds in those same two seconds. Important when split seconds mattered.

Before FJ's hired gun could get his pistol free from his holster, Derek had his pointed dead-aim to his chest.

"Hands up, fingers clasped behind your head."

The guy, clearly impressed as well as pissed off, did as he was told. Even went down to his knees, assuming that would be the next order from the quick-drawing son of a bitch standing in front of him.

"You work for DeNuzzio?" Derek asked.

"You're in the business," the man said, smiling a little. "You know the rules."

"Not in the business, but I know the rules. Don't offer any information about the guy who signs your paycheck. Right?"

"You know the rules."

"Close your eyes," Derek growled.

The man squinted his eyes, gave Derek a quizzical look.

"You gonna shoot me? Here? You know the attention that would bring you?"

"Not planning on shooting you," Derek said. "But may have to if you don't close your eyes. I'll deal with whatever attention I attract."

"You don't know who you're messing with, buddy."

"Neither does your boss."

The thug closed his eyes. Derek figured he'd snap them open the second he heard Derek move an inch. So, to test his theory, Derek shuffled his feet an inch or two in the grass. Sure enough, the hired gun's eyes flew open.

"Keep them closed. You'll live to tell your buddies about what a shitty day you had today. Open them again, and they'll all be wondering who got the jump on you as they sit in the back of the funeral home at your wake. Close your eyes."

"My name is Arnold," the man said as he closed his eyes.

"Goodnight, Arnold."

Like Arnold, Derek wasn't dressed for a hike on the beach. It wasn't his long pants that didn't fit the weather or the location; it was his black, steel-toed boots that served as his fashion faux pas. They would have been fine if he had been walking on a rocky trail someplace, or in an area where poisonous snakes were known to have a taste for human ankles. But the boots weren't right for a walk on the beaches of Anna Maria Island.

But his boots were damn good for kicking someone in the head and sending that person into an unconscious state. Damn good for that.

• • • • • •

"Are you absolutely positive on the ID? Nikkie Armani? Are you sure?"

Maryanne, after refusing the detective's offer to call an ambulance for her, had, with the help of those same detectives, made her way out of her bedroom and into her kitchen. She was sitting at her small, ovular dining table, drinking a tall glass of water.

"Hundred percent, Miss Jenkins. Her partner found her in your office. Armani was dead when we arrived. Not sure if he arrived before she died or not, but, he confirmed her identity."

"Oh my God," Maryanne said.

"What we want to know, is…"

"…Is why Nikkie Armani was in my office that time of night. Why was she there, what was she looking for and who else was there with her. Am I right?"

"Spot on."

Maryanne dropped her head. She had enough strength in her arms to raise the glass of water to her lips. Took a short sip then placed the glass back on the table.

"I can tell you why I believe she was there, and I can tell you what she was probably looking for," she said in a shaky voice. "But, you need to get the person who killed her before it's too late."

"You have anything to do with Nikkie Armani's death, Miss Jenkins? You have to know we're here to find that out."

"Look at me," Maryanne said. "You think I could have killed anyone in my condition? Look at me."

"We see you now. Didn't see how you were last night."

"Last night, I was putting on a goddamn diaper because I knew I wouldn't be able to get my ass out of bed when nature called. You're wasting time. I'll tell you whatever you want to know. I'll tell you everything, just get someone to go arrest Nikkie's murderer. Same damn person who killed Sam Gracers, too. I'll guarantee that."

The detectives gave each other a long look. One nodded his head. Sat down next to Maryanne, and said, "Okay, you answer our questions, and we'll get a squad car rolling to wherever this person you think murdered Armani and

Gracers is."

"Good enough," Maryanne said.

"Who should I tell them to pick up, Miss Jenkins?"

· · · · ·

Jessica checked the time on her watch. Took a long draw of her coffee. Placed the empty mug in the sink, rinsed it out, dried her hands, then checked the time again.

"If they only give me four hours of time outside this godforsaken house, I'd better get moving."

She grabbed her purse off the breakfast table and headed towards the garage. She paused, hand on the doorknob of the garage entry door. Thought about running back upstairs, going into her master bathroom and retrieving something from her medicine cabinet. She pulled the door open, then paused again when an idea struck her. A small smile played across her lips as the thought spawned an idea. She dropped her purse to the floor, turned and trotted through her house, up the stairs and into the en suite off her master bedroom. She retrieved a tall bottle of medicine from the cabinet, took out one pill and slid it into her front pocket. She glanced at her watch again, then hurried back to the garage.

She pulled the door open, reached her hand up to the right side of the door jam and pressed the button to open the garage door. She checked her watch one more time before starting up her car.

"Plenty of time," she thought as she backed her car out of the garage.

CHAPTER 39

Julia Steinberg was never a fan of early mornings. For her, reasonable people woke at a reasonable hour and started their workdays a reasonable couple of hours after rolling out of bed. When Julia was first offered an associate's position from a law firm in Orlando, Florida, her workday began no later than eight in the morning, every day. To her, eight was foolish. What was more foolish were the looks she had received and the whispered comments she overheard the first day with the firm. She strolled in a few clock ticks before eight, only to find the other thirteen associates, five partners and an unidentifiable number of office workers, already two cups of coffee deep into their day. Seven o'clock, it seemed, was the actual expected start time. Six if you had any hopes, or chance, of moving from associate to partner.

Julia worked with that firm for nine months before accepting a position with another Orlando-based firm. Though her career path wasn't as optimistic with the new firm, she was hired to provide legal services to west coast based clients who conducted business in the eastern part of the United States. Seeing no need to arrive at her office before her clients had even punched in the security codes to their offices, Julia started her workdays no earlier than nine in the morning.

It was the classic nine-to-five most white-collar professionals crave.

But she went above and beyond, often staying till seven in the evening. She didn't have anyone to go home to; no kids, no husband, no significant other, so putting in a few extra hours meant nothing to her.

But they meant an awful lot to the firm's partners.

Julia was offered full-partner status three years after she had joined the firm and was soon after asked to run the Tampa-based office. Her main task in the Tampa office was building relationships with local authorities, high-powered business owners and local politicians. Five years (and zero work days which began earlier than nine-thirty) later, Julia ran for and was elected to the District Attorney's office.

Perfect. Late mornings, early evenings and a slew of aggressive assistant

DA's, all desperate to make a name for themselves.

As DA, Julia worked a total of forty-three cases over her five-year term and spent more time forming important relationships with important people than sitting behind her desk, shuffling papers and staring at the clock. She was fine knowing she was better at politicking than providing legal council and was more excited about expanding her political career than her legal career.

But when her phone rang at five-twenty that morning, and after hearing the voice of Walter Wiggins welcoming her to a very early start of a brand new and exciting day, Julia wondered how many more early morning calls she'd be receiving after she stepped away from the quiet life of a DA and into the hectic life of a US Congresswoman.

"Hope I didn't wake you," Wiggins said, sarcasm dripping from his words. "I have a call with DeNuzzio today at nine and need to give him an update on a few matters. Your head clear enough to fill in a few blanks for me?"

Julia pushed herself upright, swung her legs off the bed, rubbed her eyes vigorously before responding.

"Absolutely. Of course. Anything you and Mr. DeNuzzio need. I hope you both know that by now."

Truth was, she couldn't care less what FJ DeNuzzio and Congressman Wiggins wanted. All she cared about was Wiggins' endorsement and DeNuzzio to come through on his promise to fund her campaign and to uncover, or create, enough dirt about her opponent as the public could swallow.

"That's our girl," Wiggins said. "First things first, we need to understand your logic behind letting Jessica Gracers out on bail again. You understand the timeline of things, don't ya?"

"Too much exposure keeping her locked up," Julia answered, cautiously. When it came to legal matters, she knew she was on unfamiliar ground. This in spite of her law degree from FSU and her years of experience. "Thought we had her ambulance-chaser of a lawyer under control, but she filed a damn compelling writ in support of getting her client released. Couldn't ignore it."

"You could have delayed it, though. Should have ignored it for another day or two. Timeline, Miss Steinberg. Remember the timeline?"

Julia shook the remaining cobwebs from her mind.

"I...I know. I can retract the bail. Pretty sure I can have one of the DA assistants..."

"Too late for that, Julia. Talk about exposure! No, this call is not intended to provide instructions, but rather to remind you of your obligations to Mr. DeNuzzio. To me as well, come to think about it."

"What would you have me do?" Julia asked, more fearful of the answer she might receive than in whatever task she might be asked to complete.

"There was a murder last night, or so I've learned. That pesky private investigator Jessica Gracers hired. His assistant. I believe you met with her in your office earlier this week. Nikkie Armani. Name ring a bell?"

"Yes. I didn't say hardly five words to her."

"And no one is suggesting you did. However, she is dead. Murdered in Maryanne Jenkins' horrible little office. Jenkins, you may recall, does possess a certain amount of information. Information, should it be leaked, which would severely damage reputations, along with any hope you are certainly holding for a position on Capitol Hill."

"Did Jenkins kill Armani?"

"You did," Wiggins said, his voice frigid. "At least, that's what will be floated around the area in the form of rumors should Jenkins be allowed to speak." Wiggins paused several beats. He wanted Julia to fully absorb the severity of the situation. "Authorities have already been dispatched to Jenkins' home and have certainly begun questioning her. Those questions must cease immediately, but me making a call to whoever is in charge of the police department would not serve our purpose."

"You need me to make sure Jenkins isn't questioned about the murder in her office? You need me to make sure she doesn't start spilling her secrets?"

"I'm sure you can see the ramifications of her doing so. Imagine, an ill, past-her-prime attorney, seeing what she must consider to be a horrible injustice having been committed, might be willing to share with interested ears. That cannot be allowed to happen. Make the call, interrupt any investigation, immediately."

"I'll make the call right away."

Wiggins laughed a bit, and said, "Do take a moment or two and pray Jenkins hasn't said a word. Pray fiercely Miss Steinberg."

CHAPTER 40

Derek spotted him right away. Small framed man, mid to late fifties. Short, grey hair, dark-rimmed glasses. Walked swiftly and without any demonstrated effort. Slight smile revealing either contentment or the birth of a plan.

FJ was walking towards the point of the beach where the bay ended and the Gulf of Mexico began. He was wearing a brilliantly white shirt, pressed shorts, white and grey sneakers. No socks. Had an expensive looking watch on his right wrist.

As FJ drew closer, Derek, who was sitting just in front of the tall dune grass, walked directly towards him. Derek noticed the moment FJ recognized his approach. Saw him lift his head an almost imperceptible inch. Watched FJ's eyes glance quickly to the dune grass.

"He's not in any position to help you, FJ. Won't be for a while."

FJ kept walking. Didn't increase his pace, nor slow down. Even when Derek pulled his hand out from his pocket enough to show his gun's grip, FJ walked on. Either FJ had another hired thug keeping watch or truly was a man who lived without fear.

"You think you can get away with whatever you want, don't you?"

"Apparently," FJ said, his voice higher than Derek expected and as gravely as Detective Gonzales suggested it would be, "since I have no interest in being anywhere near you, yet, here you are, then it's apparent I can't get away with anything I want. Do you plan on using that gun in your hand or just trying to intimidate me?"

"That all depends," Derek said as he now kept pace with FJ DeNuzzio.

"Depends on what?"

"On how this conversation turns out. On whether you're an asshole or not."

FJ sounded a laugh that lived less than one second.

"I'm pretty sure I'll be an asshole." FJ pointed a thumb towards the dune grass. "I pay that man a lot of money to keep people like you away from me. A lot of money. The research I did on him suggested he was one of the best. How did you get the drop on him?"

"Walked right up to him. Kicked him right between the eyes. Tied him up with his bootlaces. Took less than ten seconds."

"Impressive," FJ said. "If you don't kill me, we should talk about you working for me. I could use someone like you."

"How much of Sam Gracers' money are you expecting to steal?"

"Steal?" FJ said. "Last thing I stole was a bag of licorice when I was eight years old. My father caught me. Made me return the licorice and pay the shopkeeper twice what the bag would have cost me had I paid for it. Had to volunteer to sweep the store's floors everyday for three weeks after dinner. Had to walk from home to the shop every damn evening. Three miles, each way. That's the last time I ever stole anything in my life. You planning on telling me who the hell you are?"

"You already know who I am," Derek replied. "Knew who I was and all about me four days ago when I arrived in town. Knew about my partner, too."

"You are suggesting we dispense of the guessing game. Correct? Than if so, follow your own suggestion."

"So, how much? How much will you, as Sam Gracers' alternate power of attorney walk away with?"

"You know anything about life insurance, Derek? Mind if I call you Derek?"

"I know it pays when people die, and I don't give a shit what you call me."

"How about key person insurance, Derek? Know anything about it?"

"Probably could figure it out. The name says it all, right?"

"I take out a key person policy on every one of my partners. They all do the same as well. I'm sure you know by now there are eight people in my corporation. Each of us eight takes out a key person policy on the other seven partners. Tough as hell at first to get through underwriting, but, the policies are in place. If a partner dies, the key person policy pays out to each surviving partner. Sort of to make up for the inevitable loss in revenues and profit. Every one of us is a key person in my company, Derek. Every one of us."

"You must be doing all right with two key persons dying in a week. Must be doing damn well."

"Not at all. You think a ten million dollar life policy can even come close to making up for what the partnership has and will lose after Sam's and Brian's deaths?"

"So you and the other partners all get an easy ten million because Sam and Brian were murdered? Sounds like I'd be watching my back if I were you."

FJ stopped, dead in his tracks. Looked Derek straight in the eye.

"You're not me, Derek. Not even close."

•   •   •   •   •

By the time Maryanne Jenkins had finished, the two detectives were hustling out through her front door. Both had their cell phones pressed to their ears, barking out orders or filling in their superior officers. One of the detectives paused, turned around to face Maryanne. He motioned to his partner, the other detective in Maryanne's house, to hold up a minute.

"That was my captain who just called me," he said directly to Maryanne. "Told me to stop questioning you. He told me you've already been cleared of the crime and should not, in any way, be considered a suspect in this murder." The detective gave a long, hard glance at Maryanne. "My captain asked me if you told us anything yet. Asked if you had said anything about people you believe may have been behind the murder."

"And what did you tell your captain?" Maryanne asked.

"I told him you hadn't said a damn thing. And that's exactly what I'm going to tell my partner in a second. I'm going to tell my partner to not investigate anything you suggested we should investigate," he said directly to his partner who was staring at him, his face screwed with confusion. "But I'm not going to tell him to forget what you told us. And I won't forget a word you said, either."

"So, what are you planning on doing?"

"Don't know, yet, honestly. But we're keeping a deputy stationed right outside your front door. Don't even think of trying to leave."

Maryanne looked down at her legs, knowing they were still attached to her body, but terrified over her inability to stop the icy chills racing through them.

"Where in the world could I go?"

"You need us to call someone for you?" the detective asked.

"I'll make my own calls, thank you. You need to get your ass in gear, detective."

He turned, closed the door behind him, and left Maryanne alone with Iron Lou.

"What a way to go," she thought. *"What a damn shame way to go."*

•   •   •   •   •

Jessica Gracers kept a close eye on her car's dashboard clock. She knew she only had four hours to get everything she needed to do accomplished. Not that a deputy would be knocking at her front door exactly four hours and one-second after she had left her home, but still, four hours was four hours. For Jessica, that arbitrary time became a personal challenge to her.

"Earn one hundred and eighty-five million dollars in less than four hours."

She had everything in place to meet the challenge. In fact, she really didn't need to do anything at all. Just spend four hours outside her home, make two phone calls, spend ten minutes on the Internet and fulfill the last promise she had made to someone she hardly knew at all. And if a deputy did knock on her door four hours and one-second after she started this trip, no one would be there to answer.

Her decision to race back up the stairs and grab what she needed from the medicine cabinet was the only thing she could possibly imagine wanting from the house which saw her husband murdered. And that one item was tucked safely into her pocket.

CHAPTER 41

"Ten million in life insurance probably doesn't hold a candle to what you're expecting to get out of Sam's accounts. Have to believe his wife is the primary power of attorney, meaning after five days, she gets first crack at the funds."

"Unless my calendar is inaccurate, today would be that sixth day," FJ responded with a smile.

The two walked a bit over two miles, according to Derek's internal gauge of distance, when FJ stopped, turned around as would a marching serviceman in a military parade, then began walking back in the opposite direction.

"Today is the sixth day. You're right about that."

"And," FJ said through a widening smile, "has your investigation arrived at any conclusions?"

"Several," Derek said.

"Care to share them with me? After all, you have interrupted my walk. Though I can't say I haven't enjoyed your company. I'm not suggesting you owe me anything, mind you. I'm just curious about why you decided to pay me a visit."

"Don't mind sharing at all," Derek said. "You first, though."

"Pardon me?"

"You had one goon near the start of your walk. Close to your home. Figured a guy like you would have another hired thug near your turn-around point. Call in sick or on another assignment?"

"Reassigned for a more urgent need. At least, I thought it was more urgent. Didn't expect to be joined on my walk by an investigator carrying a gun in his pocket."

"Makes sense. Taking matters into your own hands. That's what I would have done, too. District Attorney can't pin Gracers' murder on my client, meaning Jessica is out and about. You needed to intervene. Make sure she doesn't get what you're after."

"Making sure she doesn't get what she does not deserve, Derek. She doesn't deserve a thin dime of her husband's capital."

"And you do?"

"Better me than her," FJ said as he lifted his face to catch the first warming rays of the rising sun.

"Fair enough."

"Your turn," FJ said. "I shared, now you share. What did your investigation uncover? What brilliant conclusions have you reached?"

"Craig Washburn was probably costing you more money than he was bringing in. He was worth more dead to you than alive. Didn't put that together till you told me about your 'key person' policies. Makes sense, though."

"What are you suggesting?"

"You had him killed. Had the Trainer brothers dump his body in the bay. You walked away clean as a whistle and with an extra ten million in your pocket."

"Improvable," FJ replied.

"Glad to hear you're not denying it."

"No reason to. Deny and you're certain to believe me to be a liar. Confess that I had Craig murdered, and you'll run to the police. I'll just listen to what your investigation uncovered, but I have no interest in debating your conclusions."

"Your turn."

"And your question would be?"

"How the hell did a guy like you ever cross paths with a scumbag like Jackson Trainer?"

"I own or have owned properties all over the southern United States. Had an apartment building in Alabama, which needed some repair work completed."

"One thing led to another."

FJ simply nodded.

"What else? What else with regards to your investigation?"

"I know you had nothing to do with Sam Gracers' murder. Nothing to do with Brian Hilton's, either." Derek paused, took a long, staggered breath through his nose. Pushed back the tears he expected to make an entrance. "And you didn't kill my partner. That's the only reason you're still alive. If I even suspected you had anything to do with Nikkie's death, your brains would be washing up on shore."

"You've reached the appropriate conclusion on all three unfortunate events. Most unfortunate about your partner."

"Your turn. What time does the financial institution open?"

FJ stopped again. Knitted his eyebrows, squinted his eyes.

"What are you talking about? Which financial institution?"

"The one holding Sam Gracers' private accounts. The ones you have power of attorney over. Or at least you will once Jessica is out of the picture. Your goon isn't going to find her. Not at her home. Not at the bank or brokerage house or wherever the hell Sam's money is. But you knew that already. Sending one of your thugs was a long shot at best. Figured you could manage your beach walk in safety with just one thug keeping watch. But you knew your other goon wouldn't find Jessica curled up in bed. Knew he wouldn't put a bullet between her eyes the second before she logged on to the bank's website, entered the proper credentials and transferred every last cent into some offshore account of hers. You just sent him over in case he got lucky. The real work was going to be done by you. Sitting in front of a computer, sipping some damn protein shake or smoothie, clicking away till Sam's money was moved from one place to another."

"What are you suggesting?"

Derek could see a hint of panic behind FJ's eyes. A trace of worry, blended in with a pressing fear.

"Want to know why I came all the way down here to see you? Why I took out your thug? Because I'm not going to let you near a computer, phone, tablet or anything capable of accessing Sam's money."

"You'd rather Jessica have it all? You know she murdered Sam. She murdered your partner? You know that, don't you? Yet, you'd see her walk away with nearly two hundred million dollars?"

"Had to make a choice," Derek said. "Either confront Jessica or keep you from getting Sam's money. I had no evidence to prove Jessica killed Sam and no evidence she killed Nikkie. None. Only thing I would have done was to kill her myself. Would have ended up in jail for the next fifteen to twenty. You'd not only get whatever funds were in Sam's private accounts but probably a whole lot more. Couldn't let that happen. Won't let that happen."

"You're seriously going to let Jessica Gracers get away with two murders and close to two hundred million dollars? She killed your partner."

"Only thing that makes sense."

"You could have called the police. Told them what your thoughts were."

"Did that. Had a chat with a detective this morning. Told her everything I suspected. Everything I knew. Told her exactly what I was going to do and why. Jessica isn't in jail and she can leave her home for up to four hours a day. She's probably gone already. May have even let the police know she was leaving and would be back before the four hours were up. Nothing they could do."

"They could have questioned her about your accusations. Could have brought in for questioning. Damn Cole, you let a murderer free to roam the damn world."

"I'll catch up with her. That's for damn sure."

FJ glanced at his watch. Started to move when Derek grabbed his arm.

"You can't be serious, Derek? Are you actually planning on holding me so I can't return to my home?"

"Not exactly," Derek said. "You and I are going to keep walking. Going to keep talking. I'm going to make you an offer and you are going to accept my offer. Figure you'll be back in your house a little after nine."

"You do realize we are not the only people on this beach? All I need to do is call out for help and someone would certainly assist." FJ turned his head, looked at the two sets of footprints which led to where he and Derek were now standing. "I appreciate your situation, Derek. I do. But I have business to attend to. Feel free to join me, but I'm going back to my home."

Derek released his hold of FJ's shoulders. Let him start walking back the way they had come.

"Jackson Trainer tapped Hilton's cell phone," Derek called to FJ who was twenty feet away. "Actually, his brother Bobby did the tapping. Only, I'm not sure it's called tapping when you listen in to a conversation on a cell phone. Probably call it some fancy term, but 'tapping' gets the message across."

FJ continued walking, didn't slow down or turn around.

"Whatever was heard is inadmissible in court. No judge in the country would allow a hacked conversation to ever see time in court."

Derek started after FJ. Gripped his pistol, hard. Drew it up an inch or two.

"They overheard you talking about Sam Gracers being killed by the 'sick bitch.' You said she probably did you a favor. Sam knew about the cancer scam you and Hilton were running. Taking advantage of people like Matt Steel."

"Inadmissible," was all FJ said. He kept walking. Same pace, same stride. Same carefree glide to his steps.

"Jackson recognized your voice. Said he worked with you in the past. Said you hired him to kill Craig Washburn. Didn't hear the whole story, but the officer up in Dothan told me Jackson was angling for a plea bargain agreement. The way I figure it, the DA up in that county will be calling Julia Steinberg this morning. She'll be asking a whole lot of questions."

"Call came in last night," FJ said as he waved his right hand dismissively in the air. "Nothing to be concerned about on my end."

"Kind of figured that," Derek, who had closed to within five feet of FJ, said.

"I was told Steinberg is the odds on favorite to replace Congressman Wiggins when he announces his retirement. Figured Steinberg would need to have someone like you backing her bid for Congress. She probably called you the second after she got off the phone with the Dothan area DA."

"I don't get involved in politics, Derek. Haven't the stomach for it."

"Don't blame you. Not at all. Only problem is, if Julia runs for Congress and gets elected, there'll be a new DA in town. Julia won't be calling the shots about who they investigate and who they don't."

"I'm sure a replacement has already been handpicked. Like I said, nothing to be concerned about on my end."

"You're probably right," Derek said, now walking stride for stride next to FJ. "Still, there is that other doctor in Tampa you need to be concerned about. With the Trainer brothers behind bars, I'm curious about what that doctor will say when the cops show up at his door this morning." Derek pulled his iPhone from his left pocket. Checked the time. Looked at three text messages he was expecting, then slid the phone back. "Probably getting a knock on his door any minute now."

"This walk has taught me something, Derek. I don't think I need to have two of my associates watching my back while I'm walking. One should be enough. That is, of course, as long as you won't be planning on subduing my one remaining associate during any of my future walks."

Derek fell silent. Started thinking about FJ's other goon. The one who would usually be posted at FJ's turnaround point. He assumed FJ would have reassigned the second thug to either pay Jessica Gracers a visit or to call on Mark Ruggerio. FJ probably had more than two hired guns working for him. No reason to believe FJ couldn't have sent one to Jessica's and one to make sure the doctor was taken care of. For all he knew, Jessica could be lying dead; bullet between her eyes and the doctor could already be shoved into the back of some nondescript sedan, headed for a deserted stretch of ocean coast.

During his walk with Detective Rachel Gonzales earlier that day, Derek told her what he believed happened to Sam and Nikkie. Told her what FJ would probably be planning. Had her work with the Tampa City Police to watch over Mark Ruggerio's house. Also asked her to have an unmarked sheriff's cruiser outside Jessica's home. The text messages he received were from Rachel, telling him the surveillance was in place in both locations.

Rachel had written in the first text message:

All quiet on both fronts.

The second text, sent thirty-minutes after the first, read:

Gracers leaving house. Got a tail on her. Will let U know what happens. Stay safe and remember what I told U."

Chapter 42

"I am seriously beginning to grow curious about how exactly you plan to prevent me from doing the work I need to do." FJ had resumed walking back to his home. Same pace as before. Same half-grin playing across his lips. "I'm wondering if you plan on tackling me and holding me down for a couple of hours, or knocking me out, tying me up with my own shoe laces and tossing me beside my associate in the dune grass. I know you won't use your gun, so you may as well tuck it back into your pocket."

"Don't worry about me," Derek said. "You'll find out soon enough."

FJ shot Derek a sideways glance. Shook his head a little. Started to pick up his pace.

"You know, people like me, we have access to plenty of resources."

Derek said, "Not here you don't. Not on this beach. No one here but you and me. The few others walking around, don't give two shits about you or me."

"How terribly shortsighted of you, Derek. You need to learn to look beyond the present. Learn to make calculated assumptions about the approaching future. Doing so effectively is key to success."

Derek offered no response.

The two continued walking in silence, with both taking occasional glances at the time.

When they reached the point where the bay began, FJ made no attempt to hide his interest in looking for movement in the dune grass. When, after ten long seconds of staring, his eyes fixed for any movement, he saw nothing, he turned to Derek, and said, "Just how hard did you kick my associate?"

"Hard enough," Derek said as he too turned to scan the grassy area. "He'll be fine. Probably."

"Your attack on him will be enough to land you in jail," FJ said.

"Never will happen."

Derek began scanning the beach behind and in front of him. Waiting for the right time.

"Preparing for something, are you?" FJ asked. Though his voice wasn't revealing it, fear was building in FJ. Derek was still a complete unknown. While FJ knew some basics about him—having been briefed by his security team about Derek and Nikkie when it was reported the two were visiting Jessica in jail—he had no knowledge of Derek's history to make an educated assumption of just how far this freelance detective was willing to go to keep him from completing his work. FJ looked at his watch again, saw the second hand drawing close to 7:30. H knew that if Jessica Gracers was still alive, that she'd be preparing to access the brokerage house's online portal. She'd probably have her finger hovering over the "Transfer Funds" button on the accounts page, just waiting for eight o'clock to arrive.

Derek's left hand was plowed into his pocket. That was a relief for FJ, for the gun was in Derek's right pocket. Only thing he'd seen Derek pull out of his left pocket, was an early model iPhone.

"It's amazing what things you can learn if you just listen closely to what people tell you," Derek said after a long stretch between FJ's question. "Most things you hear are useless. Idle banter, trivial crap. Completely useless. The mistake most people make is treating too much of what they've heard as useless. Take for example what Jessica Gracers told Nikkie and me when she was telling us her alibi." He paused, waited several beats. "She was telling us about one of your new partner announcement dinners. In fact, it was the dinner she claimed to have had sex with Brian Hilton for the first time. Upstairs at the country club."

FJ dropped his head, starting shaking it. Put a broad smile on his face.

"You were played, Derek. Sorry to have to be so blunt, but Jessica played you. That country club Jessica told you about? The one she claims to have had sex with Brian? It doesn't have an upstairs. Single story club house. Pro shop set back from the first tee. A few smaller structures, used for maintenance and offices. None have a second story. Unless she and Brian had sex on the roof, she lied to you."

"I figured that out already," Derek returned, a smile filling his face as well. "Hilton told me he was gay. Don't know much about being gay, but I don't think a gay man would risk much of anything just to have sex with the wife of one of his business partners. Wouldn't make sense. Never believed the story from the get-go. But, she did mention something else I found interesting. Didn't know it would be useful at the time, but I stuffed in the back of my mind. You know, just in case."

"And what, if I may ask, lie from the lips of Jessica Gracers did you tuck away for future use?"

FJ heard a cracking sound. Sounded like it was coming from Derek's left pocket. Derek's hand was still plunged into the pocket and as he looked down, FJ saw Derek was making a fist with his left hand. Angry looking knuckles causing sharp looking points in the cloth of Derek's shorts.

"Cracking your knuckles?" FJ asked. "Going to knock me out? Here, right on the beach? Go ahead and try." FJ stopped in his tracks. Puffed out his chest a bit. Clenched his own fists. "You're going to be surprised to find I'm far more difficult an opponent than was my associate."

"Not planning on kicking your ass, FJ," Derek said. "Just wondering if you're interested in a little snack. Long walks always build my appetite. How about you?"

Derek shot his hand from his pocket, pressed his open palm into FJ's face. Rubbed the crushed peanuts, along with plenty of the peanut dust, into FJ's face. Then he pulled his hand back, blew the remaining peanut dust from his hands directly into FJ's face.

"I hear you have quite a reaction to peanuts."

FJ stumbled backwards, his hands furiously brushing the peanut dust and debris from his face. He kept stumbling backwards until he was knee deep in the salt water of the bay. He plunged his face into the water. His hands working beneath the water to scrub away the dust. When he raised his face from the water, Derek could see how immediate FJ's body was reacting to the peanuts. His eyes were already showing signs of the approaching swelling. His face was reddened, not by the furious wiping of his hands, but from the coursing histamine being flooded into FJ's blood stream.

FJ buried his face in the water again. Dropped his entire body beneath the water. Stayed like that for several seconds. Looked to Derek like he wasn't going to emerge on his own.

Derek pulled out his cell phone, dialed 911. Told the dispatcher there was a man having what looked like a heart attack on the beach. Gave the specific location. Offered his name, said he was walking next to this guy, offered him some peanuts and "The guy just freaked out. Said he was allergic to peanuts. Started to get all red and puffy in the face. Jumped in the damn ocean. Better get someone down here, quick."

Derek slid his phone back into his pocket, and then walked over to the still body of FJ DeNuzzio. He grabbed him by the back of his shirt. Dragged him onto shore. Turned him around so his mouth wasn't buried in sand.

"Damn," Derek said. "That's one hell of a reaction to peanuts. You really should be more careful about what your morning walk partners carry around in their pockets for snacks."

Derek heard someone calling to him from down the beach. He looked up; saw an elderly man jogging towards him.

"Heart attack?" the jogging man said.

"Don't know for sure," Derek said, as he kneeled beside FJ. "Wondering if he has some peanut allergy. I pulled some out from my pocket. Guess the wind blew some of the peanut dust in his face. He got all red in the face. Jumped in the water to wash off the dust. Went all still."

"You call 911?" the man, who was now checking FJ's neck for a pulse, asked.

"Sure did. You a doctor or something?"

"Dentist, but, don't worry, I've had extensive emergency medical training."

"Good thing. I was starting to think I killed this poor guy."

CHAPTER 43

Rachel joined Derek in the hotel's bar. He was sitting at the far end, working on a double scotch when she walked up, sat down, gestured to the bartender towards Derek's drink.

"Same as he's having. And bring him another."

"Some people think I have a problem, you know? A problem with booze."

"You don't seem the type to care what others think about you," Rachel said, her eyes still yet to meet his. "You think you have a problem? Then stop. If not, let's have a few drinks together before you leave."

Derek picked up his glass, rocked the brown liquid back and forth with small turns of his hand.

"Peanuts? You shoved peanuts in FJ's face?"

"How was I to know he was allergic? Just thought it would be friendly to share."

"He's going to press charges, you know?"

"For what? Sharing a snack? Not worried. Not worried at all."

Rachel laughed. Flashed a smile at Derek.

"So, where did she go?" Derek asked.

The bartender placed Rachel's drink in front of her. Put Derek's "on deck" drink off to his left.

"Doesn't matter where she *went,* what matters is where she's *going.* And, before you ask, I have no idea. My department put out bulletin to every police force and agency between here and Alaska."

"Woman like her won't make a mistake. Won't get caught on camera at some ATM machine or using a credit card at a Wal-Mart. She started planning this a long time ago. Probably had every step worked out down to the finest detail. Smart woman."

"When did you know it was Jessica?" Rachel took a small sip of her drink, then winced as the brown liquor assaulted her throat. "How the hell do you drink this crap?"

"One sip at a time."

Rachel forced a small laugh, then turned in her chair to face Derek.

"Seriously, when did you figure out Jessica was behind everything?"

"I wrote down four initials in my notebook the other night. FJ, JG, BH and MJ. Figured they were the only four who could have killed Sam Gracers. Handed the notebook to Nikkie, asked her to circle the initials of who her gut was telling her was the killer."

"And she circled Jessica's initials?"

"Not at first," Derek answered. "She circled FJ at first, but when you called and told me Hilton was killed, she grabbed the notebook, crossed out FJ's initials and drew a big circle around JG. I wasn't sure until I heard what Jackson Trainer told the cops up in Dothan about what he heard when he and Bobby were listening in to Hilton and FJ's phone conversation."

"What did he hear them say?"

"One of them, either FJ or Hilton said the 'sick bitch' did them a favor by killing Sam. That they didn't need to worry about Sam going to the authorities about their cancer scams. I spoke with Nikkie right after I subdued Jackson. She told me Jessica had called her, asked her to visit with her at her house. Nikkie also told me she was going to use Maryanne's spare key to get inside her office to search for any files on Hilton." Derek shook his head slowly. Took another draw off his drink. "I knew she was in trouble the second the Dothan cop told me what Jackson said."

Rachel rubbed Derek's shoulder. Gave it a little squeeze.

"But, I still don't understand how you figured it was Jessica. Maryanne's the sick one. ALS, right?"

"When I met with Hilton at his home on Snead, he mentioned both he and Sam suspected Jessica had some mental illness issues. I asked Sam's lawyer about it as well. All he could tell me was the main reason Sam was about to file for divorce was something about was Sam believed Jessica was declining mentally."

"He was filing for divorce because he believed Jessica was sick, mentally."

"Firmed up everything I was thinking. The details of Jessica's alibi were my first clue. Either she was telling the truth or she was pretty sick in her head."

"Or," Rachel offered, "she really had everything planned down to the smallest detail."

"Yup," Derek agreed. "Thought about that, too. Wasn't certain until I was holding Nikkie as she died." Derek looked off in some imaginary distance. Saw himself holding Nikkie's body as she died. Like he was watching the whole scene as a third person. "Nikkie didn't die right away. She waited for Jessica to leave the office, then wrote the initials 'JG' in her own blood."

"Oh my God," Rachel offered. "Derek, I'm so sorry."

"Jessica did plan everything down to the last detail, including how she could get Nikkie to start taking a hard look at Maryanne. Don't know for sure, but I'd bet my life Nikkie told Jessica she was already planning on breaking into Jenkins' office. She told Jessica exactly where she'd be. Don't know how Jessica ambushed her. Nikkie was too good for someone like Jessica to get the upper hand on her. Someone like Jessica Gracers doesn't think like an assassin. Doesn't know how to outsmart someone as skilled as Nikkie was."

"Unless…"

"Unless their minds are all twisted up. I guess whatever Jessica is suffering from gives her the mind of a psychopath. A murderous one, at that."

Rachel realized her hand was still rubbing Derek's shoulder. She pulled it back. Rested it on the bar.

"This whole case, we were trying to work out time frames, but we missed the most important one of all."

Rachel said, "Which time frame are you talking about?"

"Jessica had to wait five days before she could access her husband's accounts. Sam's lawyer told us that. Sam set up some legal hold on his 'private accounts' that prevented any funds being withdrawn for five days if he died in a suspicious manner. Jessica found that out from Sam's lawyer. She was sleeping with that scumbag."

"What?" Rachel snapped. "How the hell do you know that?"

"A comment the lawyer made when Nikkie and I were watching him eat a hundred dollar steak dinner. He said something about just because Jessica was great in the sack must have not been enough for Sam to want to stay married to her. Guys don't tell their lawyers about how their wives are in bed. He had first hand information. Jessica was sleeping with Peter Maxim, not because she had feelings for the guy, but to get intel on what Sam was planning. Was probably sleeping with the guy for a while."

"That could cost him his license to practice law," Rachel said.

"For what? Sleeping with a client's wife? No way. Plus, Jessica's gone. She won't be around to spill the beans on Peter Maxim."

Rachel looked confused. She was trying to tie everything together. Trying to work out what Derek had already worked out.

"Sorry," she said. "Still don't get where you're going with the five days thing."

"She waited a full day after killing Sam to give us her alibi. She knew we'd spent at least a day investigating Hilton. She also accused FJ DeNuzzio of murdering Craig Washburn. Figured we'd spend a day looking into his past. She hired Maryanne as her lawyer. She knew we wouldn't understand why she would hire a lawyer like Maryanne instead of some high-powered law firm. Knew we'd spend some time digging into Maryanne's past as well. Everything she did was to cause delays before we could take a deep look at her.

"She knew Hilton and FJ were dirty. Knew we'd find enough to keep us interested in them as the suspects. And she knew Maryanne was wrapped up with Hilton and FJ with the bullshit scams they were running. I guarantee she hired Maryanne as a fallback plan. Just in case Nikkie and I didn't find enough about Hilton or FJ to warrant spending too much time on them. Maryanne was her ace in the hole. She had dirt on Maryanne. Plenty of it. Knew the right time to show Nikkie that dirt. Add the days and time all up and you arrive at five days from the time of the murder to the day before yesterday. Jessica went on the wind on day six."

Derek looked away, off into a place where regrets and sorrow dominated the scenery.

"So, after five days, Jessica had access to Sam's accounts. Probably transferred the money from his accounts to some offshore account she had set up. I thought about going to her house. Confronting her, but I figured I had nothing to prove she was guilty. Guarantee you and your department would have found enough evidence given enough time, but all she needed were those five days. I know if I went to Jessica's instead of going to see FJ, I would have killed her. Be in jail right about now. Only thing I could think of is making sure FJ didn't beat her to the punch and get all the money from Sam's private accounts."

"What do you think will happen with FJ?"

"Nothing," Derek said in a flat, unemotional tone. "Jackson Trainer will try to work a deal with the cops over the O'Connell murder. Will tell them he has information on FJ DeNuzzio. Problem is, again, the time frame."

"I don't follow."

"Jackson won't tell the DA up in Dothan anything about FJ till he gets a deal. Probably the deal will be about his brother, Bobby. Jackson will tell the DA everything he knows about FJ, about being hired by FJ to kill Washburn, about hearing the conversation between FJ and Hilton and will tell the DA he's ready to testify in a court of law against FJ. But not until his brother is given a reduced sentence. Deals like that take time. FJ will find out about Jackson talking about him. Guys like FJ always find out when someone is talking about them. He'll have plenty of time to make sure the Trainer brothers are taken care of."

"You think he'll have them killed? In jail?"

"Happens all the time. Jackson and Bobby Trainer are dead men walking. That's for damn sure."

"I'll call up to Dothan right now. Have them put a guard on both Trainer brothers. No way anyone will be able to get close to them."

Derek gave a sideways grin to Rachel. Lifted his glass, took another long sip.

"Worth a try, I guess. Won't do much, though. Guy like FJ DeNuzzio has friends in high places and in low places. One way or another, he'll walk away clean as a whistle. He'll recruit replacements for Gracers and Hilton and be back running at full steam within three months. I won't be around to see it, so I'm hoping you let me know if I'm right."

"How about the doctor in Tampa? The one you asked to have a Tampa Police car watching over? Think he'll talk?"

"Probably, but there's no way in the world he's ever heard of FJ DeNuzzio. No way. May have known Hilton was behind everything but I'd be willing to bet O'Connell recruited Ruggerio and swore on his life to Hilton that he wouldn't ever mention names. With O'Connell dead, Ruggerio won't have any information you can use to pin FJ to the cancer scam."

"But you thought FJ might have sent one of his hired guns to take out Ruggerio, right?"

"Insurance. The fact the Tampa Police Department told you no one showed up or even looked suspicious around Ruggerio's house tells me FJ knew the doctor didn't know about his involvement."

"Ruggerio has an awful lot of explaining to do. Hope they string him by his balls."

Derek shrugged his shoulders.

"He'll get some heat, no doubt about that. But I don't think he'll see the inside of a prison cell. I'm sure his lawyers will have a parade of happy and very much alive patients willing to testify what a wonderful doc Ruggerio is. They'll build some defense about the medical industry is so bogged down with process and regulations, that the only thing Ruggerio is guilty of is not running his own tests on the patients sent to him by O'Connell. He'll lose his license, maybe, but he won't be convicted."

There wasn't much else for the two to discuss. For the most part, nothing Derek was saying was all that surprising to Rachel. None of his conclusions were asking for an argument. All in all, Rachel felt the entire case was an utter disaster; an embarrassment to the sheriff's department. If Derek was right,

Jessica Gracers had gotten away with two murders and close to two hundred million dollars. FJ DeNuzzio would replace Hilton and Sam Gracers, and be back at earning millions of dollars in a matter of months. Doctor O'Connell was dead and wouldn't be able to tell his story about how Hilton and FJ had paid him to convince a few of his patients they were dying of cancer and wouldn't be able to explain how Doctor Ruggerio was involved. Everyone who could have possibly shared information which would have put FJ and Jessica behind bars was dead. Including Nikkie. All dead. All terminally quiet.

Rachel put her hand back on Derek's shoulder. Dragged her hand back and forth in a small arch.

"Kinda nice area down here, don't you think? Plenty of business for a freelance detective as good as you. You could do better than okay down here."

Derek looked at the drink in his hands. Rocked the ice against the sides of the glass a couple times.

"Probably right," he said. "And thanks for the compliment. But I have unfinished business with Jessica Gracers I need to take care of."

"Derek," Rachel said, "as good as you are, finding Jessica will be impossible. You going to spend your life chasing after her?"

"Not exactly. Just can't be tied to one location. I'll keep doing what I do best and will keep looking for Jessica when I'm not working a case."

"You can do that from here just as well as you can do it from Ohio. Better weather down here. And, who knows, other opportunities may present themselves."

Derek turned to face Rachel. Almost moved in close to her, when he saw the hotel's front desk attendant walking towards him.

"Mr. Cole?" the desk attendant asked.

"Yup."

"A woman dropped off a package for you yesterday. Gave us specific instructions not to deliver it to you at this exact time today. She said it's a birthday present for you. Happy birthday," the attendant said as he handed over a box wrapped in colorful paper. The carefully wrapped present was the size, weight and feel of a book.

Derek took the box, laid in on the bar in front of him.

"What the hell is that?" Rachel asked. "It's your birthday today?"

"Nope. Not for a few more weeks."

"Then, what's this about?"

"It's from Jessica," he said. "Guarantee it. Part of her game plan."

Rachel's eyes darted back and forth to the Derek, to the package, back again. Over and over.

"You going to open the damn thing or do I have to do it?

"Figured you'd say it's evidence. Tell me not to touch it," Derek said as he drained the last bit of his scotch.

Rachel picked up the present, tore off the wrappings.

Beneath the wrapping paper was a paperback book. Lee Child. "*One Shot*. A Jack Reacher novel." Looked to be brand new. Binding free of any wrinkles or creases. This was the book Jessica said she and Hilton used to pass notes back and forth to each other. At the book's halfway mark, there was a note sticking out through the top pages.

Rachel placed the book onto the bar, flipped it open to where the note was waiting. She rubbed her hands vigorously against her thighs before pulling the notebook-sized piece of paper free from the book.

"What the hell?" Rachel said as she noticed a small, yellowish pill taped to the bottom part of the note. The pill was round, made Derek think of the aspirin his mother used to give him when he had a headache and was busy trying to convince her he was too sick to go to school.

Rachel pealed the tape off, freeing the pill.

"You read the note," she said, handing the single slip of paper to Derek. "I'm going to find out what kind of pill this is."

Before he began reading the note, Derek waved to the bartender.

"I guess I need a birthday drink," he said. "She's paying for this one," he said, nodding his head towards Rachel.

There were two double scotches, both sitting on napkins, in front of Derek and Rachel as Derek began to quietly read the note aloud.

"Derek, Just a quick note to say 'Thank You.' Actually, thank you a hundred and eighty-five million times! Very sorry about your partner but the way she was looking at me the last time we were together got me concerned. You understand. Nothing personal.

"Things didn't go exactly as I had planned but, in the end, all worked out. You gave me the five days I needed. For that, I owe you my gratitude. Your final payment can be found on Anna Maria Island. Tucked beside another copy of this book. It will be on the top shelf of that little community library. Just like the one on Snead Island. Better hurry on down there before another Lee Child fan makes off with ten grand in cash.

"You were right on the money about Tom Cruise being entirely wrong to play the part of Jack Reacher. What was it you said? Five foot seven actor playing a six-five character?

"Again, thank you and I am sorry about your partner. Had to be done.

"JG

"PS. I won't be needing my pills any longer. Not that I ever needed them even while I was taking them. Doctors? Who can trust them? But of course, I think you've learned that after this case."

• • •

Derek dropped the note on the bar. Looked at it. Started to read it again but all he could see were Nikkie's dying eyes staring up at him from the white paper.

Rachel's face was a mixture of anger, confusion and interest. Staring down at her phone's screen, thumbing her way through images of pills.

"Son of a bitch," she said. "Take a look."

She handed her phone and the yellowish pill to Derek. On one side of the pill, the numbers "347" were etched. On the flip side, a single line stretched across the middle of the pill.

"Unless there are other pills exactly like this one and with the exact same markings, Jessica was taking Clozapine. It's a drug used to treat schizophrenia."

"Sounds about right," Derek mumbled, taking the glass of scotch into his hands, raising it to his lips and taking a heavy draw.

"A hundred and eighty-five million thank you's," Rachel read from the note.

"That's how much her husband had in his private accounts. That's how much she was able to transfer to her account five days after she murdered him. FJ mentioned I was letting Jessica walk away with close to two hundred million. Hundred and eighty-five is close enough."

Rachel stood up, her face set in a determined countenance.

"We can find where she's gone. We get Gracers' lawyer to tell us where Sam's private account was set up, trace where the money was transferred to."

Derek just nodded his head a bit. Put a crooked grin on his face.

"What's the problem?" Rachel demanded. "We can trace where she went."

"All you can do is find where the money was sent. Jessica won't be anywhere close to wherever the bank or financial institution is located. She's gone. Only one way to find her now, and it's not the way you're thinking."

Rachel sat back down on the barstool. Raised her drink to her mouth and drained the contents in one long pull.

"We need to make one more trip together," she said. "To Anna Maria.

Maybe, along with whatever cash she left for you, Jessica also left another note."

"You can keep the money, if you want. I'm not interested."

"She may have left another note. Come on, I'll drive. It will take less than an hour. You're not in a hurry to get anywhere."

"There's no note," Derek said. "Just an envelope with a bunch of bills stuffed inside."

"How can you be sure? Isn't it worth a try? Damn, Cole. It's one hour away. She could have left a note with information to blow FJ's world apart."

Rachel could tell a horrible realization came to Derek. Something awful by the look in his eyes.

"You need to call whatever police department is down on Anna Maria. Tell them to clear the area around that community library. Do it now, before someone else gets killed."

"What now? What are you talking about?"

"When Jessica told me about this book," Derek said, waving the copy of *One Shot* near his head. "When she was telling us Hilton and she passed notes to each other using the book, she told me the she read the book. Said it had an explosive ending."

The look of confused interest etched across Rachel's face slowly gave way to a different look. A look of fear. Of terror. Of urgent horror.

"You think she planted a bomb in the book?"

"She didn't plant a bomb," Derek said as he stood and dropped a hundred dollar bill on the bar. "She planted information. And, you're right: We need to get down to that community library on Anna Maria before someone checks out the wrong book."

CHAPTER 44

With the blue lights mounted behind the car's grill flashing, Rachel sped south towards Anna Maria Island. She had called her department's dispatch, gave a full run down of where she was speeding off to as well as specific directions to be relayed to the Manatee County sheriff's department. Her directions were clear.

"Have them dispatch two cruisers immediately. Find the community lending library on Shore Road and make sure no one goes near it. Probably will need to canvass the area to find out if anyone checked a book out in the last few days."

After telling her dispatcher to give the Manatee Sheriff's Department her cell number, she ended the call and focused on getting to Anna Maria Island as quickly as she could.

"So you think after Jessica left Snead Island, right before Hilton was killed, she drove down to Anna Maria, put a copy of *One Shot* in the library along with ten grand in cash and a note with some explosive information? That's quite a risk, don't you think? Anyone could have checked the book out, taken the cash, before her five days were up."

"Not much of a risk, actually. Tourist season is just getting going. Most of the people on the island are residents. Probably getting their places ready to rent out. People like that are too busy to bother getting a book from the community library. But today is Friday; meaning tourists taking a long weekend will be making their way to their rental homes on the island. Most vacation homes I'm familiar with have check-in time around three. It's past three already.

"People who vacation on an island like to do two things: Lie on the beach and read a book. Jessica planned it perfectly. Planned everything perfectly."

"What could she have left there? In the book? What information do you think she left that could be explosive?"

"I bet she knew a lot about what FJ DeNuzzio was up to. Sam probably shared more with her than just what Hilton was doing. Could've told her something about FJ. Something he'd be willing to kill to keep secret."

As Derek finished talking, Rachel's cell phone sounded. She answered the call, then listened quietly for close to a minute. She ended with "Thanks for the information. I'm on my way down."

She reached under the steering wheel, flipped a switch, turning the warning lights off.

"That was a deputy with Manatee County. Said a copy of *One Shot* is in the little library but there's no envelope."

"Did they touch the book?"

"Nope, thank God. Said there's a slip of paper sticking out of the book. Maybe a bookmark?"

"Probably a note. The note we are looking for, I hope."

"Think someone made off with your payment?"

"Doesn't matter. Things get expensive when you're on vacation. Ten grand of found money is a great way to take the pain out of most vacations. The book is still there. That's all that matters."

"I'll ask the deputies to canvass the area. Found out who took the money. You earned it."

"Don't bother," Derek said. "If I found it in the library, I'd leave it for the next guy. May have even written a note on the envelope. Something like 'Courtesy of Nikkie Armani.' Something like that."

The two finished the ride to Anna Maria Island in silence. Derek was thinking about Nikkie, about Lucy and about how seashells would always mean something different to him from then on. *"Deathly reminders,"* he thought. *"They're nothing but reminders of death."*

.　　.　　.　　.　　.

There were two marked sheriff cruisers, both with their lights flashing, parked alongside the road. Right in front of the community lending library. The library was a three-shelved bookcase, about three feet wide and three feet tall. Painted white, sitting on a white painted post. Sliding glass doors afforded access to the forty or so books. A tattered, dog-eared copy of *One Shot* sat on the middle shelf, a little to the left of middle.

After speaking briefly with the two Manatee County deputies, Rachel led Derek to the library, snapping on blue latex gloves as they neared. She slid open the glass door, grabbed the copy of *One Shot*. She flipped the book opened to where the note was peeking out from the top of the pages. Held it in front of her so Derek could read along with her.

"Holy shit balls," Derek said. "Holy, holy shit balls."

"Is this what I think it is?" Rachel asked. "Are these the notes Jessica said she and Brian Hilton wrote to each other?"

"Have to do a handwriting analysis to be certain," Derek said, "but the note talks about going away to his lodge for the weekend,"

"Does this mean…that… Was Jessica telling the truth about her and Brian? Was she really gone when Sam Gracers was murdered? She was with Hilton at his lodge last weekend? Derek, what the hell does this mean?"

"Flip the note over," Derek said, not caring to attempt answering any of Rachel's questions. "Looks like there's writing on the back."

Rachel flipped the note carefully in her hands. Together, Derek and she read what Jessica had written on the backside of the slip of paper.

"You really are a great detective, Derek. That is to say, if you are reading this. I tried not to give away too much. Didn't want to make things easy for you. But, you put two and two together and figured it all out. I am impressed! I put another note in with your cash. Separate envelope. Sure hope it's still here when you arrive. The info in the other note should be more than enough to take care of FJ. One way or another - Jessica"

"Please tell me she's right and you got this whole thing figured out." Rachel was staring at Derek. The note in her hands was displaying the effects of the tremble in her hands.

Derek's only answer was a slow shake of his head.

CHAPTER 45

Donald Reagan wasn't what anyone would consider to be a gullible guy. Sure, he was taken in by Hilton and those two fucks who called themselves "doctors." Cost him his business along with some permanent damage to his nervous system as a result of all the damn chemo and radiation. Still, he wasn't what people would call a gullible guy. The man who had called him sounded pretty convincing. Convincing enough for Don to find out for himself if what the man had told him was the truth.

It wasn't a long drive from his home in Sarasota to the main post office in Bradenton. The man who called him said there would be a key taped beneath the bench outside the post office. The key could be used to open PO Box 185.

"Now listen, man, I have no idea what this is all about. All I know is I went to get a book to read out of this tiny little library and I see an envelope with cash sticking out. I figured, 'What the hell?' right. So, I stuff the envelope in my pants, walk back to the house me and wife and kids are renting, open it up and find ten grand in cash. There was a note in there, too. Said the money was free to whoever found it but it came with a simple responsibility. Said I had to call you and tell you about where to find the key and what post office box the key would open. Said there's information in the box you've been waiting to find. Good luck, man. Hope whatever is in that box is good for you."

Donald Reagan found the key exactly where the anonymous caller said it would be. And, just like the caller said, the key opened PO Box 185. Inside the tiny box, was a thick, manila envelope. Too big for the tiny PO Box. Was shoved inside, all curled up the sides of the box. Reagan took the envelope out to his car. Sat down, started the engine and blasted the air conditioning. Pulled out the stack of papers inside.

On top of the stack of papers was a handwritten note, addressed to him.

"Mr. Donald Reagan.

I am terribly sorry for what Brian Hilton and FJ DeNuzzio did to you. Tricking you into believing you were dying of cancer, just so you would sell them your business? Dreadful. Positively dreadful. Inside this packet, you will find notes, which came into the possession of my recently departed husband. The information contained in these documents should be enough for you to demand prosecution of FJ DeNuzzio. To bring him to justice, once and for all. And I don't care what form of justice you decide FJ DeNuzzio should receive.

Good luck, Mr. Reagan. And again, I am terribly sorry for all you've been through.

JG"

Chapter 46

The idea of flying home turned Derek's stomach. Though he enjoyed being above the clouds, high above the same ground that contained the spilled blood of his wife and of Nikkie, he needed time to think. Three hours in a plane wouldn't be long enough for him to see where his thoughts were leading him. Not nearly long enough.

He made no plans, no reservations for overnight stays. He just headed north, and drove.

He had barely passed the Florida state line before his cell phone rang. He wasn't surprised to hear Rachel Gonzales' voice.

"You're not one for goodbyes, are you?"

Yesterday, after Derek and Rachel had driven back to his hotel from Anna Maria Island, he simply thanked her for all she had done and told her he'd keep in touch. The next morning, the only call he made was to Hertz to extend his rental and to change the drop off location.

"Had a few too many goodbyes in my life," he replied. "And I'm pretty sure you and I will see each other again."

"Soon?"

"Who knows? I have a feeling someone is either going to bring DeNuzzio to justice or will go vigilante and try to bring the ultimate justice to him. When either of those scenarios happens, I hope you let me know. Either outcome, I'd like to be in town for either his court case or his funeral."

There was a short pause. Deep silence during which Rachel battled between telling Derek how sorry she felt for him or telling him how her growing feelings towards him were consuming her mind. In the end, Rachel's internal battle in the silence was brought to an end as Derek resumed the conversation.

"I'm going to find Jessica. One way or another, I will find her. And I'll make her tell me the truth about who killed her husband. About Nikkie. About everything."

"Then what?"

"Two possible outcomes. If she killed Nikkie, I'll kill her. If not, I'll turn her over to the local authorities wherever I find her."

"Shouldn't be telling a cop you may kill someone. Could get you in trouble."

"Not telling a cop," Derek said. "I'm telling a friend."

. . . . .

He had just finished eating dinner at a roadside BBQ joint outside of New Orleans when Rachel called him again. It had been three days and over six hundred miles since he had left Florida, and he was no closer to being home than after mile one. In fact, he was further away. He had been thinking over the last several hundred miles, about just how far away from ever being home again he really was.

"You must be home by now," Rachel began.

"Not even close," Derek replied. Made it as far north as Kentucky before turning around."

"You coming back down here?" she asked, her excitement palpable, practically pulsing its way through the cellular airwaves.

"Not unless you have something about FJ or Jessica. Not yet, anyway."

"Well not exactly about either FJ or Jessica, but something I'm sure you will find interesting."

"Go ahead. Tell me."

"Tampa police department put out a bulletin this morning. All police departments do it when they have a serious crime and no one guilty sitting in their jail. This bulletin went out to a stream of departments surrounding the Tampa area."

"And what did this bulletin say that was so interesting it inspired you to call me? Not that I mind the call, mind you. Just looking for some meat to chew on."

"They had a homicide. Guy named Marcus James."

"Name doesn't ring a bell. Should it?"

"No, and neither should the name of his wife. Shantel James."

"No bells going off with that name, either. They looking for her for the murder?"

"Not at all since she's sitting in my county's jail. She's been sitting there for six weeks now, waiting for either someone to pony up bail money or for her case to go to court. Why she's in jail isn't important. What *is* important is who her cellmate was awhile back."

"Jessica Gracers," Derek said.

"Yip. Now, Shantel isn't talking, but the guard who opened the cell door for Jessica when she was released stated Jessica and Shantel were talking to each other when she walked up to their cell. Said Jessica leaned in and whispered something to Shantel, who replied by telling Jessica her husband's name."

"Son of a bitch," Derek moaned, knowing, somehow that Jessica was behind the death of Marcus James. "I need to stop Jessica before more people get killed. Any leads on where she might be headed?"

"Nothing yet, but, there's more."

"What else?"

"I spoke with the detective on the James murder case. Said James was killed by a small caliber gunshot wound to his head. Middle of his forehead. Typical Jessica Gracers style, I suppose. He also told me something else. He told me about what was left at the scene. He didn't think anything of it, but I sure did. I sure *do*, I should say."

"And?"

"DVD case. Official looking one. The type of case big Hollywood movie studios put out for their movies. Want to take a guess which movie the case was made for?"

"*Jack Reacher*. Based off Lee Child's novel 'One Shot.' Same novel Jessica Gracers said she and Brian Hilton used to pass notes back and forth from each other."

"Yup," Rachel said, her voice a mixture of playfulness and anger. "But, the disc inside wasn't the movie. Any guess what was inside?"

"Can't even begin to guess."

"I found it strange that people as wealthy as the Gracers were didn't have a top of the line security system installed in their house. I know they had a system, but I was curious why they wouldn't have had a camera system set up as well."

"Don't tell me they had one but your department never checked the footage."

"Four cameras. One with a panoramic view of the front of the house, same set up around the back. There's one camera facing the front door and one in the garage."

"And no one from your department thought about checking the recordings? You've got to be kidding me."

"I asked Mathers—he's the lead detective on the Gracers case, in case you've forgotten. He said he did check for any recording but was told the cameras hadn't been working for over three months. When he checked the recording device at the Gracers house, he found the system unplugged."

Derek took a long breath in. Held it for a second or two.

"What was on the DVD?"

"Just Jessica Gracers walking up the walkway, then entering her house. She looks straight up at the camera, smiles and pulls out a copy of that Lee Child book. She smiles again, tucks the book into her purse then pulls out her gun. There's no sound on the recording, but you can see her calling Sam's name. She was staring right at the camera and made a point to make sure anyone seeing the video could easily read her lips. About fifteen minutes later, the recording ends."

"She pulled the plug after downloading the video. Probably deleted the memory after she burned the disc."

"She killed her husband and left this damn DVD to let you and everyone else know she got away with murder."

"Not sure if I'm impressed with how she pulled this off or scared to know she's still out there." Derek paused a beat. "I'll tell you one thing, FJ DeNuzzio had better up his personal security details."

"Think she'd go after FJ?" Rachel questioned. "Seems like it would be too much of a risk. She's got all the money she could ever possibly need and for the most part, is off the grid. Going back to the Tampa area would be a tremendous risk."

"And in her mind, it may be a risk worth taking. And considering I was able to walk right up and next to DeNuzzio that day on the beach, suggests his security would need a major upgrade."

"You neglect to admit you may have had something to do with incapacitating his bodyguard."

"All heresay," Derek quipped.

There was a brief moment of silence before Rachel continued.

"Still pretty damn confused, but maybe Brian Hilton and FJ weren't involved in killing Sam Gracers after all."

"Seems that way to me," Derek replied. "Seems to me Jessica Gracers covered all her bases, including the whole 'note passing' thing. By the way, was that note we found in the community library ever tested by your handwriting experts to see if it was Hilton's handwriting?"

"It was tested, but, you're not going to like the results," Rachel said.

"Wouldn't expect anything less."

"Inconclusive. Either it was Hilton or it was someone talented in forging his style. They use a grading system with eighteen points being a definite match.

Any score below ten is a 'highly probable forgery' and a score of fifteen and above is considered to be 'highly probable authentic.' The experts tested that note as an eighteen to match Jessica Gracers' handwriting and a fourteen point six on Hilton's."

"Unbelievable."

"I guess the only way we'll ever know for sure if Hilton was involved with Jessica is to ask her ourselves. Still," Rachel said after a brief pause, "I'm back to questioning the timeline. If Jessica was the killer and if she was with Hilton the weekend Sam was killed, how in the world did she pull it off? Time of death doesn't make sense."

"On the DVD," Derek asked, "was there a time stamp?"

"That was the second thing I asked about. And no, there was no time stamp."

"The only thing that makes sense to me," Derek said through a deep sigh, "is Jessica arrived home two hours or so earlier than she told everyone. Shot her husband, did whatever a woman who just killed her husband does for two hours, then staged the running out screaming bit."

"And neighbors being what they are in most parts of the country, just didn't notice that her car was parked in the driveway two hours or so earlier than when she said she arrived home."

"In general, people don't notice things that aren't unusual. Probably twenty people saw her car parked at her home well before she said she got home, and never gave it a second thought. Not even sure neighbors were asked what time they noticed her car in the driveway."

Rachel asked, "Another miss by my department?"

"Not really," Derek answered. "Most detectives would probably ask, knowing most people wouldn't know for sure about when they saw a familiar car parked in the driveway of a familiar house. Low chance of getting any reliable intel about something as mundane as what time they noticed a car parked in a driveway."

"Would have blown her alibi out of the water if someone had noticed it."

"As smart as Jessica was about everything," Derek finished, "I guarantee she had multiple time lines ready to be plugged in to her alibi. Multiple time lines."

•　　•　　•　　•　　•

It was two days more of driving before Derek received another call from Rachel.

"Where are you now?" she asked. "Alaska? Hawaii? France?"

"Ohio. About fifty miles from home."

"That's good, Derek," she said through a sigh. "You need to be home for a while."

"You about to tell me something that's going to make me want to drive back down to Florida?"

"Not exactly, though the invitation is a standing one. Just wanted to tell you Don Reagan was killed early this morning. He took a shot at FJ DeNuzzio with a high-powered rifle while FJ was out for his morning walk. Shot missed completely. One of FJ's bodyguards found Reagan's hiding spot and shot him four times. Killed him instantly." Rachel paused, waiting for Derek to reply.

He said nothing.

"Well," she said, "unless someone else has any information linking FJ to crimes, looks like he's going to walk away a free man. So much for justice huh?"

Still, Derek said nothing.

"I suppose whatever information Jessica had sent to Reagan could have been sent to other sources. Could be FJ wronged a whole bunch of people and one of them may be seeking revenge as we speak. Hell, I was even wondering if Maryanne Jenkins would tell her story to the authorities, but, it doesn't look that that's going to happen."

"Why not?" Derek finally said.

"I guess I shouldn't say she *won't* do anything to bring FJ to justice," Rachel said so quickly her words seemed to blend together, forming one, long word. "It's just that she has her own set of legal issues to deal with. From what I've heard, she's assuming full responsibility for her actions, which is good, I suppose. Shows me she has character. Integrity. But, again from what I've heard, she's not mentioning anyone else beside Brian Hilton as being involved in what she did."

"Wouldn't think drawing up paperwork for the sale of a business would be illegal?" Derek stated. "Despite the motivation behind the sale. It's not like she was the one convincing the doctors to get involved in duping those business owners into believing they were dying of cancer."

"No," Rachel answered, "but the DA had enough evidence to prove Maryanne knew the business owners were selling under false pretenses. That may not put her behind bars but she'll certainly lose her license. Not that it matters, I suppose. I hear she's quite ill."

"Julia Steinberg," Derek said after a long period of silence. "She still running for the open Congressional district seat?"

"Sure is. Based on what I've read in the papers, she's practically got the election in the bag. A day after her opponent was announced, a huge news story broke linking Steinberg's opponent to a child pornography ring. He's denying it of course, but damage done."

"She'll win, despite Jessica Gracers making her look bad."

Rachel searched her imagination for something else to talk about. Something that would lead to more conversation, which might open up the door to the two of them making plans to get together some time soon. When she heard Derek clear his throat, she knew the conversation was about to end.

"Listen, Derek," she shot out, "I know you just went through hell with everything that happened with Nikkie, but..."

"The U-P," Derek interrupted. "That's where Jessica went to. Maybe still there. It's beautiful up there this time of year."

"Not following you," Rachel said, her voice sounding resigned.

"First time I met her, in the jail, when we were talking about bail. She said she shouldn't be seen as a flight risk. Made a joke about her running away to Canada via Neebish Island. I never heard of Neebish Island before, so I didn't think anything of it. The name came to me last night while I was busy not sleeping. I searched for Neebish Island on my phone. It borders Michigan's Upper Peninsula and Canada. That's where she either crossed or is planning on crossing."

"And so that's where you're headed, I assume?"

Derek drew a long breath. Held it for several seconds.

"You're right, Rachel. You're right I need to be home for a while. Maybe take a month or two off from chasing bad people, Gracers included."

"Or maybe a vacation?" Rachel suggested.

"Can't imagine where I'd want to go."

"I know a place."

About the Author

One thing about writing Derek Cole thrillers I've found is there's always another story begging to be written. This book, Deathly Reminders, was written in my head while I was driving home from a family vacation on Anna Maria Island. The drive was split into two days, twelve hours each day. And before I pulled in to my driveway at home, another story had began clawing at my mind.

The next Derek Cole book—the title of which has yet to come to me—is all about coming home. About coming full circle, completing journeys.

I've included the first chapter for your "very early" sneak peek and would love to hear your ideas about it. In fact, I'd love to hear your thoughts, comments and suggestions on any of my novels. Because hearing from people who read what I write is like coming home for me. Reviews complete the circle for an author.

Thanks for reading!

T Patrick Phelps
November 3, 2016

Connect with T Patrick Phelps

Contact through his email tpatrickphelps@gmail.com and receive a free eBook, formatted to whichever eReader you use.

Facebook Fan?
https://www.facebook.com/authortpp/

OTHER BOOKS BY T. PATRICK PHELPS

The Derek Cole Series

Heartless
Those of the Margin
The Observer
The Devil's Snare
Still, Heartless

Stand Alone Titles

The Demon Senders

Connect with T Patrick Phelps
Sign up for his newsletter and receive a free ebook!
www.tpatrickphelps.com

Facebook Fan?
https://www.facebook.com/authortpp/

FULL CIRCLE

He drove for nine days. Sixteen hours each day. Sometimes heading towards his home in Ohio, sometimes headed towards California. Three and a half thousand plus miles after leaving the Tampa area, Derek Cole was no closer to being home than when he shut the car door and pulled out of the hotel's parking lot.

And he didn't care.

Didn't care if he was back home in one more day or in twenty more days. Didn't matter.

He was waiting.

Waiting for Rachel to call. To let him know Jessica Gracers was spotted in Kentucky, or Texas, or Arizona or Costa Rica or that someone had found proof that she did cross into Canada from Neebish Island. Didn't matter where she was spotted. Wherever it was, that's where he would head. Waiting to hear if someone had taken matters into their own hands and brought FJ DeNuzzio to a whole different level of justice. He took breaks every four or five hours to use a bathroom, fill up his gas tank, grab something to eat and to scour the Tampa Bay area news websites for any news related to Jessica Gracers or FJ DeNuzzio.

He found nothing about either.

It was close to eleven at night before he pulled into a roadside motel. Dropped a wrinkled hundred dollar bill on the grimy counter, grabbed the room key and walked into his rented room. Hadn't even closed the door behind him before his iPhone sounded.

It wasn't Rachel calling. It was his old partner from the Columbus Police Department.

"Where the hell have you been? I've been to your office around twenty times in the past week looking for you."

"You stalking me, Terry?"

Terry Manner was a fifteen-year veteran with the Columbus Police Department. He and Derek were assigned to be partners in his fourth year on the force. The two remained partners until the day Derek turned in his badge and started his own private detective agency.

"Just want to make sure you heard it from me and not from some damn news source. You haven't heard anything, have you?"

"About what?"

"You haven't heard, have you? Seriously, where are you?"

"Not sure where I am. Somewhere between Florida and Oregon. What the hell are you talking about? What haven't I heard that you're so concerned about?"

"It's about Lucy, Derek. About her death."

Some wounds never heal. Not fully, at least. Some lose their ripping sting, lose their bite, but not their penchant to deliver immediate, all encompassing pain. Hearing Lucy's name from most people usually made Derek smile at his memory of her. Talking about her took more of his pain away. Made him focus on what he loved about her, not about how she died.

But when someone who knew her, knew how she died, was standing beside Derek, watching her die, mentioned her name, the pain erupted as if time hadn't weakened it in the least.

Derek choked back tears. Took a short breath to steady his voice.

"What about Lucy?"

"Listen, brother. I'd really rather sit down face to face with you. Rather tell you in person," Terry said, his voice low, controlled, pregnant with worry.

"That's not going to happen," Derek said. "Tell me."

"Derek," Terry stammered, "I don't know exactly how to say this and, trust me dude, I don't know all the details yet but I'm working on them, but, the asshole who killed Lucy? He wasn't working alone."

View other Black Rose Writing titles at www.blackrosewriting.com/books and use promo code **PRINT** to receive a **20% discount** when purchasing.

BLACK ROSE writing™